Joanne Graham is the winner of the 2012 Luke Bitmead Bursary. Born in Wolverhampton in 1970, she is the youngest of five children. *Lacey's House* was inspired by her maternal grandmother, who was lobotomised in the 1960s as a result of the depression she suffered. Joanne lives near Exeter, Devon.

You can discover more about the author at www.joanne-graham.weebly.com

LACEY'S HOUSE

Lacey Carmichael leads a solitary life. To her neighbours she is the mad old woman who lives at the end of the lane, crazy but harmless — until she is arrested on suspicion of murder . . . When Rachel Moore arrives in the village, escaping her own demons, the two women form an unlikely bond. Unravelling to each other tales of loss and heartache, they become friends. Rachel sees beyond the rumours, believing in Lacey's innocence; but as details of the older woman's life are revealed — some of them monstrous, from a past filled with the ignorance and cruelty of others — Rachel is left questioning where the truth really lies.

JOANNE GRAHAM

LACEY'S HOUSE

Complete and Unabridged

CHARNWOOD
Leicester

First published in Great Britain in 2013 by
Legend Press Ltd
London

First Charnwood Edition
published 2015
by arrangement with
Legend Press Ltd
London

A catalogue record for this book is available
from the British Library.

ISBN 978–1–4448–2594–7

Published by
F. A. Thorpe (Publishing)
Anstey, Leicestershire

Set by Words & Graphics Ltd.
Anstey, Leicestershire
Printed and bound in Great Britain by
T. J. International Ltd., Padstow, Cornwall

This book is printed on acid-free paper

This book is dedicated to my Grandmother, Hilda, who put the flesh on Lacey's bones.

And to my children, Kiera and Sam. I love you all the atoms in the universe.

Acknowledgements

There are so many people I have to thank for the creation of this book. First on the list is my maternal Grandmother who this book is dedicated to and whose barbaric experiences will, thankfully, never be repeated in our society. I must also thank my incredible family for putting up with me through the writing process and for giving me unfailing support and encouragement. I would especially like to say a huge thank you to my brother, Dave, who always said I could, my mother Val for believing in me, and of course, to my children for putting up with my grumpy tiredness.

Thanks also go to Wendy Bowen, who read the first draft of the book and asked me why, to my niece Sarah for her words of support, and to Eve Jones and the women of the Halberton Book Club for reading the original story and giving me invaluable feedback. I would also like to thank my incredible Rhiannon sisters for supporting me through a year of growth and transition, and making me believe I could do this.

Special thanks also go to the Tiverton Community Police team and Heavitree Police Station for answering my many questions, to the Royal Albert Memorial Museum in Exeter for having a 'Gerald' to visit as well as many other wonderful things, and to Aerosaurus Balloons

Ltd for letting me know the laws around hot air ballooning, and what you can and can't do! I am also grateful to the creators of the website www.exetermemories.co.uk, which proved invaluable during my research into how the war affected Exeter.

My thanks also go to Ariella Feiner, Tom Chalmers and the Legend Press team, as well as the incredible Elaine Hanson, Luke Bitmead's mother, who works tirelessly in his memory. And finally no end of appreciation goes to my friends Julie, Sacha, Sam and Chen for keeping me sane, you are all marvellous.

Anything contained in these pages that is inaccurate is entirely my fault and please forgive me if I have forgotten to mention you, it wasn't deliberate.

Prologue

Lacey

She hadn't spoken to her father in years. The silence had expanded to fill every room in the house until it was a tangible, solid thing that they had to push past whenever they moved. A plate of food would be placed in front of him as he sat at the dinner table, his laundry gathered unrequested, his boots tidied away into the hallway, his medical bag prepared. But not once did she open her mouth to speak, not once did she so much as look at him.

Sometimes he would open his mouth and a faltering sound would emerge, not quite a word but far from the common silence. And before the syllables were formed, before his lips closed to shape it into something recognisable, she would be gone and the word would fall into nothing.

She would feel his eyes on her at times; sense the questions in that look with the heavy brow and the pinched mouth. His frustration beat against her like waves in winter, but she kept her balance and maintained her vow.

How many years had it been? She couldn't remember and when she tried to, it ached in her head until she frowned and rubbed her eyes. It had been a long, long time. So much had happened that she should hold on to, but the memories skittered away like cockroaches when

1

the light was turned on. They moved too fast and couldn't be grasped.

Some things were remembered, as if through a haze, but at least they were remembered. Her mother, already slight, had grown stick thin and begun to fade until finally she had lain in a darkened room in a pale ball of agony and failed to breathe in. Stood beside him in the graveyard, drizzly rain seeping into black clothing, she had looked at the coffin and heard her mother's voice calling from inside.

People had come to the house for the wake and she had prepared food and looked at the carpet as she handed plates around. They looked her way with curious eyes, waiting for her to behave with something far removed from normality. Some had exchanged greetings, asked her questions, and they had been answered with a soft, faltering voice that became quieter as her eyes were pulled towards the window and beyond to the distant hills.

Her father had sat in his chair, rigid and dour, shaking hands with the local men, nodding politely to their wives and daughters and not looking at the pretty, silent woman that hung like a weight around his neck.

Now though, as she lay on the bed and watched the ceiling lights pass, her eyes tried to find him. There was a flash of dark fabric behind the others tucked tightly around the bed and she craned her head to see beyond them until a hand curled across her forehead and pulled her head flat against the mattress. Several attempts wielded the same results and she felt the panic rise in her chest. The sharp stink of disinfectant filled her nostrils kicking up a vague memory. She had been here before but couldn't remember enough to know why her heart raced and fear spread through her limbs.

The movement stopped and it seemed that everyone spoke at once. She raised her head again and this time nobody stopped her. Someone moved away and there he was, his coat in dark contrast to the white of the others. He stared at her dispassionately before his eyes moved to look at something she could not see.

'Please, father, please stop them!' She felt the vow of silence shatter around her but the words were propelled by fear. In that moment all that mattered was getting out of there. He remained rigid and unmoved. She looked at the walls and felt the hands on her again. White room, white coats, hands on her ankles, hands holding her wrists. Her eyes moved to the faces suspended above, their weight pressing her further into the bed. Mouths moved in masks of concentration but the words blurred together, grew hazy around the edges until they became white noise hanging over where she cowered and urinated in fear.

But then she saw it: a flash of colour beyond the crushing bodies. The big red shiny ball held by little hands that bounced it against the hard floor tiles before catching it again. Bounce . . . slap. Bounce . . . slap. She looked to the space above those perfect, dimpled hands and met the eyes of her young son, crinkled at the edges as he smiled at her and bounced his ball.

She knew then that she had to stay calm, more afraid now that she might scare him; she looked into his eyes and started to sing,

'Hush little baby, don't say a word, Mamma's gonna buy you a mocking bird.' Her voice faltered and stumbled over the syllables, shaking while she was manipulated by the hands of the doctors, but she carried on and was rewarded with a bigger smile that she managed to return. She saw the doctors turn and follow her gaze before looking at each other, but she forced herself to concentrate on the red of that ball, the width of his smile.

Bounce . . . slap. Even as they turned her and tied the straps across her forehead, she could still hear the ball, and she still sang. As she felt the leather around her limbs and heard the metal buckles grate as they were pulled tighter and tighter, her voice shook but was still there.

Fingers reached from somewhere above her and pulled her eyelids up and up until her vision blurred and she could barely see the craggy face of the man that moved close and stared into her eyes. He moved back again and the face was replaced by hands. Those hands would haunt her years later, when screams would echo down a tunnel that was decades long. She would see those hands with their half bitten nails and the specks of dirt in the comers that told her the owner cared nothing for hygiene. She was tainted by them.

She saw the point through teary eyes and it hovered like a star above her, moving closer, growing bigger and bigger until it filled her

4

vision. She heard the hammer blow before she felt the pain, a cricket ball hit for six on a distant village green. A metallic echoing sound that she was still contemplating as the pain exploded behind her eyes and pushed the song from her mouth with a scream. She was burning, burning in her head as sound became a whine in her ears and the room began to drift.

1

Rachel

It began with an ending. In the darkest part of the night when the moon had long passed the window and all I could see were shadows within shadows. When I awoke to pain that should not be there and felt the fear of it carve through me. When I felt the cloying wetness of her absence and shied away from it. It began with a chill that painted goose flesh across my skin. It began with a bloom of red on white sheets.

That long night gave way to a bitterly cold January day, the kind that paints diamonds on the pavements. The slump from Christmas had cast shadows in the eyes of passers-by, their shoulders heavy enough to rest on their hips as they walked. I looked at them and did not want to carry the weight of them, the misery of them. I looked up the street and wanted to keep on going, to keep on walking and never look back. I wanted to walk right out of my life and leave it behind. But I didn't, not then.

Instead, I sat in the shabby waiting room with its worn chairs and peeling paint, feeling like the invisible woman as people bustled around me. I had sat and waited and prayed that everything would be alright. But sitting before the doctor as he looked at his computer screen and then right through me, I felt that hope wither away.

'We'll send you up to the hospital for a scan just to make sure.'

'To make sure? You mean there's a chance the baby is still alive?' I felt the jump in my chest, a flicker of possibility that I wanted to cling on to. His head shook slightly, a movement small enough that I could pretend I hadn't seen it if I wanted to go on fooling myself for a little longer.

'There is a very small chance but I think it is highly unlikely. The scan will verify the situation.'

Cold and clinical, the words were a dagger in my belly and I fought against a rush of tears. He saw my face crumple and had the grace to look contrite.

'I am sorry, it's just one of . . . '

I held up my hand, a visual full stop sweeping the words from the doctor's mouth and catching them in my palm; I curled my fingers tight around the empty phrase that meant nothing to me and even less to him. He reached forwards to pat the back of my hand, still clenched around his words, still damp with the tears and snot that I had wiped there a few minutes before in the waiting room. His concern seemed to be no more than a reflex response from someone who has seen it all before, said these words before and had long ago stopped caring. Perhaps for him a lost baby was frequent enough to become commonplace, but not for me. His sympathy touched lightly upon his face and stayed there, penetrating no deeper beneath the surface, not touching his heart or mind. Did he practice that look in the mirror? Too easily I could imagine him making small adjustments, getting the right

7

element of frown and downturned mouth, the perfect, subtle nuances in his cheeks that reflected an ideal study of empathy and compassion. A mask he could wear over his usual, everyday smile as the need arose.

I wanted to scream at him, 'Not to me, never to me!' To tear myself apart in front of him, pulling skin from flesh and flesh from bone so that he could examine every fibre of my being and see the loss reflected there; see how empty and barren I was without my child to fill the empty spaces. I wanted to shock his actor's face into something other than meaningless pseudo-sympathy. I wanted to show him that I wasn't going to take all the hopes and dreams I had created around my tiny baby, bundle them up into a little dusty package and tidy it away. She wasn't just 'one of those things' to me. Those things were birds shitting on my head, a broken heel or spilled coffee. Surely those words couldn't apply to my broken baby who had curled up inside me and died beneath my heartbeat. She wasn't one of those things, she had been so much more.

I opened my mouth to tell him, to send barbed words into his skin so he could hurt as I hurt, but they travelled as far as my throat and stalled, stumbling over the unshed tears lodged there. I felt powerless, frozen in that silent moment. I got to my feet and saw the brief spasm of relief on his face before he covered it by turning around to his desk and busying himself with his keyboard. He had got over the difficult bit. The patient wasn't going to melt into a boneless puddle on the floor that he would have to mop up before the next one came in. He had done his job well and everything was going to be fine.

I stumbled home, pausing only long enough to make the appointment that would tell me that my baby was dead and everything was different now. I fought the urge to keep on walking past my flat, to just keep on going until exhaustion forced me to stop. I slid my key into the lock, waiting for familiarity to settle about me, seeking the comfort of my own space. I saw my paintings on the wall, my rugs, my furniture and they looked two dimensional, flat and colourless as though the life pouring out of me had stolen the life from everywhere else. I stretched out on the floor, deeply tired but unable to bear the thought of going into the bedroom and facing blood stained sheets.

At some point the clouds had rolled in. Fat, pregnant raindrops splattered onto the skylight above and I watched as they exploded into smaller droplets and trickled slowly down the glass, meandering along until they joined up with others and became larger, running faster until they faded at the edges of the frame.

The wooden floor lay uncomfortably against my shoulder blades as I watched these raindrop races, the foreground to a lowering, oppressive sky that pushed me further back into the floor and pinned me down. Slowly I began to move my arms and legs, no snow to leave an angel in, just the unyielding polished wood that smelled of lemons and age. I wondered whether what I did now would leave any impression on those that would come afterwards. Would they sense somehow that I had lain here? Would their shadows dip a miniscule amount as they spilled over this section of the floor, a subtle change they could sense somewhere deep within them?

I would never know for sure whether the baby had been a little girl, but somewhere deep down I was certain of it and I felt her absence fill the space around me. I realised that I couldn't stay here, where a blue line on a plastic wand had become wet, red linen; where for too short a time I had imagined a different reality from the one I faced now. Everything felt strange, alien, and I no longer belonged in the place where I had lost her. I needed to find somewhere else, anywhere else.

But as I made the plans that tried to keep my mind focused away from grief, I saw the swift flash of bird wings as it passed the glass and I thought, why stop there? What was there for me here in Birmingham? The relationship with my baby's father had been over before I had even discovered the pregnancy; a short-lived romance that neither of us had wanted to take any further. I hadn't had the chance to tell him about the baby and now there was nothing to tell. There were few ties left in the city and those that existed would stretch or be easy enough to sever.

I had my work, but as a freelance artist I could do that practically anywhere. I could move away and start over. I grasped the idea as if it were a lifeline; a fresh start somewhere completely new. The more I thought about it, the more appealing the idea became until it seemed that there were no other options. I told myself that this was what I needed, that this was the best thing to do, that I wasn't running away.

I let my mind drift along with thoughts of what I could do the following day to set everything in motion, and I tried not to think about the force behind these decisions. I tried to ignore the cramps and aches, and willed myself to push aside my longing. I tried to forget that as she left, she took with her the fulfilment of a dream I had carried since childhood.

2

Rachel

I listened to the wet slap of feet on the glistening grey pavement, the gritty tyres scouring the roads, and I thought about the plywood sign. Whenever I looked back at the child I had been, the sign was the first thing I would see hanging in front of me, compelling me to turn away. It had been hastily made, roughly broken from a larger sheet so that the edges were sharp, splintered. Harsh enough to draw blood as it poked through my clothes. I can still feel the friction burn on the back of my neck from the twine; I still recognise the sharp sting of my humiliation.

The children's home I grew up in stood near the crest of a small hill on the outskirts of Downham Market in the wild Norfolk countryside. I had no memories of a time before it. I would screw my eyes shut tightly as I tried to force a memory — anything — but there were only empty spaces that would eventually be filled by other people's tales of a life I didn't recognise as belonging to me.

I couldn't even remember my arrival. I had been barely eighteen months old the first time I set foot in the old house. I often wonder what my first impressions of it were. Was I intimidated by the size of it? Did I take a step across the doorway on tiny, nervous feet that teetered and stumbled? Or did I enter in the arms of someone appointed to care for me? Did I turn my face away and bury it in a stranger's shoulder?

All I really know is that my earliest memories are of that house and the children that lived within it. Despite its size, it didn't look bleak and dark and cold, though it should have. The house was built of warm brown stone, with windows in the eaves and a big porch. If you looked closely enough, the signs of age and lack of care were visible beneath that first impression. I saw it in the paint that I flaked off with my fingernails and in the crumbling wood beneath it. But despite its flaws the house looked majestic and beautiful. I wonder if that would have given me hope when I had first arrived with nothing but a name and a cloak of neglect.

How long was it before I couldn't see its beauty at all? Behind the front door a different story emerged. Cracked and worn lino on the floors and a smell of disinfectant. Inside it felt as though it was no-one's home, just a collection of walls to hold the unwanted children whose identities were left firmly at the door.

It was all I knew until I was eight years old. Like all the other kids I existed only as a problem to overcome; a frequent thorn in the sides of those paid to make sure I made it through another day without getting hurt. Sticking plasters were given out for gashed knees and grazed elbows but emotional wounds were left to fester untended and ignored.

There were good care workers and bad. Some

of them just wanted to get through the day, others tried to make it better for us, dishing out sweets and cuddles, holding our hands when we were upset. But they couldn't take away what we were; the foundlings, the kids in care, lost boys and girls. We were charity cases, all of us. Our donated clothes were frayed and worn. I had someone else's name tag in my school uniform as if I wasn't a person in my own right. Everyone at school knew what we were, and walking the corridors became another source of torment. Sly pokes in the ribs and chinese burns from children who forgot all about me and the hatred in my eyes as their parents tucked them up snug and warm at night.

I would sit on my bed, up in the eaves watching the room around me grow darker as the natural light faded. The streetlamp beyond the window would come on and behind it the sky was vast and gloomy. A huge dome of clouds, bleak and heavy with rain hung above the flat wasteland of the Norfolk countryside. How I hated that oppressive sky; the weight of it made me feel as small and insignificant as an ant beneath someone's shoe.

I was small for my age, an easy target for the displaced angry children that lived in the home. I rarely spoke and spent a lot of time on my own. I made no attempt to fit in with them, to do things their way and so I stood out, I was different.

I had a bedroom of my own because I wet the bed and screamed out in my sleep, waking the other children and the carers posted to watch over us. Sometimes I would get the slipper for disturbing the house, other times the scorn and laughter would pour over me from the mouths of others. I preferred the slipper.

The room was no larger than one of the store cupboards but it had the window, through which I watched the world outside and for a few hours I was free. Those hours of silence painted dark shadows beneath my eyes, as I yawned my way through the following day. My solitude was more than recompense for the exhaustion that made my heels drag, bringing sharp words from the teachers as I failed, once again, to pay attention.

I watched the changing seasons pass slowly. Autumn was my favourite time as the leaves turned the colour of fire and began to fall, turning the dull grey of the drive into a soft, patterned carpet. Immersed in the beauty of their colours I would weave dreams from nothing, creating a life I had never known.

I sat in my room feeling like Rapunzel as I waited for my mother to come and rescue me. I designed a mother who was alien and strange but whom I was sure existed somewhere. I had no knowledge of her but I had seen other families on their way to school and envied their easy laughter and warm glances. She was woven from strands of hope and longing until the image took on a deeper resonance and became almost real in my mind. If someone had asked me what she looked like, I could have told them in detail, right down to the curve of her smile and the glint in her eyes as she looked at me with pride.

I was sure that my mother had lost me

somehow, through no fault of her own. I wondered if we had been on a trip to the park or the shops and I had been accidentally left behind. I knew that she would be desperate to find me and I waited and waited for her to turn up and take me back home, wherever home was. I simply couldn't accept that I was stuck in that soulless house forever.

How long was it before that hope faded? Before I finally realised that she wouldn't come? How long before waiting and watching from my window became a chore, something I felt I should do but had no patience for? The sense of identity I had created around my mother faded over time and left a space behind. I no longer recognised the person I was in the mirror and I drifted through the house wondering if I was solid, whole.

My room was a sanctuary for me, somewhere I could sit at my dressing table and look at my reflection. I stared at the darkness of my eyes, the shape of my nose, my lips, my smile. I committed every tiny detail to memory and wondered if I would one day recognise my features on the face of a stranger in the street. And as I sat there one day, the door burst open and my reflection disappeared into a crowd of grasping hands.

I was pulled roughly from the room, my feet sliding out from underneath me as I fought for balance. They dragged me down the first flight of stairs into the corridor below where there was more space to gather round and join in the fun. 'Call me stupid' the sign read, black poster paint daubed on with a childish hand. And they did, over and over again. Chanting it until the words blurred together. They pushed me between them, hands moving faster and faster until I became disorientated. Their sly kicks aimed at my shins as the board slapped against my ribs.

I didn't fight back. By then I had already learned that fighting back only prolonged the torment. I hung my head so that a curtain of dark hair fell across my eyes, hiding my face from theirs so that they couldn't see my shame, so that I couldn't see their sneers and cruelty.

I lost my balance, tripping over an out-stretched foot and sprawling onto the sandpaper floor. I heard the jeering laughter, but it died as quickly as it started. When I looked up one of the wardens was there, her tight face slightly flushed and pinched with irritation and I knew that, for the moment, it was over.

★　★　★

As I walked back to my flat from the hospital it was these thoughts of childhood that filled me, that prevented me from thinking too closely about the moment that surrounded me. As I looked at buildings reflected in grey puddles, I tried not to think about the poignancy of lying on a bed as a sonographer gazed into an empty womb.

I knew that other people who lost children felt their absence as keenly as I did. I had seen it in the eyes of another woman in the waiting room, as we sat isolated amid the excited chatter of women who would soon see their unborn children for the first time. I saw loss in

17

her eyes mingled with a tiny thread of hope that, for me at least, would soon be cut. She turned away and her gaze remained fixed on the worn floor tiles. I understood her confusion, her discomfort, knowing that she had seen what I saw. Her own grief mirrored in the eyes of a stranger; it was the insidious thing that bound us together. A fraction of time that would sit tightly in my memory. I would always remember that moment.

Was the loss particularly bitter in my mouth because I had never known my own family? Was that why as I walked home I was regurgitating memories of a childhood I frequently tried not to think about? The devastation I had seen on the face of the other woman in the waiting room ran equally as deep as my own, yet I knew that I not only grieved for my child, but for that connection. For something sensed only briefly before it was gone.

I saw movement out of the corner of my eye, a flash of colour vivid against the grey and turned to it, watching as a robin hopped among the bare branches of a huge tree. I stood beneath it and felt tiny, insignificant and remembered that not so long ago a tornado had hit Moseley and wrapped itself around trees just like these. I had watched as it bent and broke the vast trunks, snapping them like matchsticks. I remember the agonised sound they made as the wood splintered and tore apart. Small though I was, insignificant as I felt, I had survived the tempest that had felled these magnificent giants. Perhaps I could do the same again.

3

Lacey

The house stood at the end of the rough track. It was past all of the other village houses, beyond the tentative reach of the orange streetlights that ended where the lane began. Surrounded by trees and high hedges, the house was easy to overlook by any that passed. Few people ventured through the old wooden gate and up its path to the front door. Even the postman stopped on the other side of the hedge, leaving rare deliveries in the half hidden box nailed to the gatepost.

Tonight was Halloween and after darkness had fallen, the children would come. Spurred on by taunts of cowardice, their hands would tremble as they opened the gate and crept up the path. It had been like this for years now, becoming as much a village tradition as the autumn festival at the church, the day after which the vicar would be seen walking up this very path to deliver offerings to the occupant.

This was where the mad woman lived. They had grown up with tales of her whispered over tables in the school canteen, or from within sleeping bags on sleepovers. The tales grew with the children, passed from the older ones to the youngest. Each year the stories would be further embellished, entering the realms of the worst kind of horror. She was a witch who ate from the carcasses of dead animals. She plundered flesh from new graves in the graveyard to make spells with. She ate dead babies in mad rituals. The tales became more shocking, more unbelievable, but the children soaked them up and felt the fear coil through them when they were alone in bed at night.

The latest tale was more exciting because they had evidence. They had seen the ambulance and the police pulling up the lane, they had been witnesses to the hunched shape with wild hair sitting in the back of the car with her face turned away. They had heard the murmurings from the adults when they thought there were no small ears to hear them. No longer was it just a whisper, a tale told in darkness. Now there was a body and the mad old woman had a new title: Murderer!

Because of this, more children than ever were seeking to take the dare, to creep into the shrouded garden and launch eggs at the old house. The fear was greater than ever before and what had seemed a good idea in daylight was fast becoming the stuff of nightmares now darkness had fallen. For the first time there was a real chance that they could be hurt, even killed. Few would back out though, somehow the fear of public humiliation was worse. They had stated their intentions, received the admiring looks from those too sensible or too afraid to try and they knew that their reputations would be greater because of it.

And so they went. Sneaking into the garden

and launching their missiles, some of the braver ones began to chant 'witch, witch' and the others joined in, until their voices rolled into one and poured over the house like a flood. The smooth shells exploded against the whitewashed walls, the window sills and the path, painting everything yellow and sticky in the light from the full moon. Peals of laughter flew behind the children like balloons as they ran, jubilant, back towards the village centre, congratulating themselves and each other, amazed at their bravery.

By midnight all was quiet. The garden was still and the adventurers were long since tucked up in bed, some still awake and terrified that they had brought a curse down upon their heads. Slowly the front door opened and a round face peeped out. The door opened wider and a small, vague shadow stepped through carrying a bucket and broom. For a time the only sound was the swishing of the brush as it erased the yellow patches within reach, accompanied by sniffing and an occasional sigh.

The shadow stepped away from the house towards the centre of the garden where the moonlight painted detail onto the dark figure, giving her soft edges and a downturned mouth. The old lady stood statue still and looked north, as she often did, searching for the orange glow that had faded to embers so many years before. She raised her face to the clear sky and sniffed at the frigid air, tilting her head to one side, a puzzled look on her face. The chill filtered into her lungs and stalled the breath there. Her eyes took in the bright circle of the moon, the scant light of the stars and then glanced deeper into the darkness near the horizon.

The old woman closed her eyes and let out her breath in a deep, keening sigh that clouded around her. She nodded in deference to the chill of the approaching winter before turning back to the house. Collecting her bucket she stepped back through the door, pausing for a moment to check the silence, to make sure she was definitely alone. Her gaze briefly fell on the shotgun that rested against the wall just behind the door. Picking it up she could still feel the warmth in the wood from where she had held it so tightly. Taking the gun to the larder, she tucked it away on a shelf beneath an old sack before she closed and locked the door. Slowly, she headed back upstairs to bed.

4

Rachel

And so I mourned for that little extension of myself. For the tiny creature whose blood was familiar, whose eyes might have looked like mine. I felt foolish, as if I grieved over shadows, something intangible. But even as I felt lost within that void, I pushed onwards, forwards. I drew a map around my feet and saw a road leading to somewhere else, somewhere better.

I immersed myself in planning and preparing and didn't once pick up the phone and feed words down the line that spoke of loss and heartbreak. It was intimate, secret; it was mine and mine alone. My grief became hard and impenetrable. It sat in my abdomen like a stone, occupying the space where my baby used to be.

I was so impatient to find somewhere new and yet I was unsure how to go about creating a new life for myself. I didn't know how to paint a new scene over the top of an old, familiar one. How to choose where to go? I almost took the clichéd route of stabbing a pin into a map. I went so far as to get the sewing kit out. I held the metal in my hand, felt the sharp point of it before putting it away again. I was too afraid of the randomness and self-aware enough to know that I would filter the results anyway. Shying away from the totally unfamiliar.

At this time of year, anywhere north of Birmingham seemed too cold although I did think about Cumbria for a few hours. The striking dominance of the mountains and the poetry of words like ghyll and tarn appealed to my artist's nature. I was pulled away from it by the threat of the summer season, when the roads would become clogged with tourists and the scenery would become multicoloured with walkers and climbers.

I had been there once before at the height of summer and had spent all my time trying to cross traffic logged roads, a sea of people threatening to sweep me away. Searching for a secluded place in which to set up my easel had been futile and eventually I gave up and stamped my way back to the hotel. Seclusion evaded me. It seemed that everyone else was searching for the same thing and had got there first. I had painted the scene from the hotel window, the constant ebb and flow of rainbow raincoats and cars splashing through puddles. The picture was a reminder to only ever visit Cumbria when the tourist season was over.

For a brief moment Norfolk, too, seemed a possibility. I thought of it merely as a known entity, a place where the names were familiar if nothing else. I turned from that idea so quickly I felt dizzy. The county was never a real contender but I had lived there for so long that the name popped into my head and threw itself into the hat along with all the other possibilities. Norfolk, where the skies were too big and the memories were too harsh. It was a painful, lonely place.

Whenever I thought about Norfolk it always seemed to be night time. I had pushed away the beauty of the daylight, the majestic forests, the triumph of the sunsets as they bled across that huge canvas sky. I had cast aside all seasons there apart from winter, when the earth lay barren and frozen beneath a bleak, wet sky and the fog rose up to meet the low cloud until it was impossible to distinguish where one ended and the other began.

Yet sifting through the past to find the path to a possible future didn't only lead to dark places. There were the distant memories of blazing sunshine on a Devon beach. Of ice cream melting between fingers, sticking them together, a lure for flies and the tongues of the dogs that ran across the beach. There were brief flashes of easy laughter that bubbled from my chest, spilling out of my mouth like a waterfall that had been dammed for too long. Legs buried in the sand, cold and tight while the tender skin on my shoulders burned a delicate pink. Of the seaweed that brushed against ankles in the water, clinging on to my skin and turning my insides to liquid when I thought they might be crabs that would snap at my toes.

I remember the two of them standing with their backs to the sunshine so their faces couldn't be seen. Their hair had caught the sunlight and glowed like bright halos around their heads; Diane and Richard, my foster parents. The two people that I would forever think of as my family. Whenever I thought of them, the Devon beach was the first place I

25

looked. The memory pushed forwards on a rush of emotions that carried the warmth of that day.

Other memories would follow close behind, two figures diminishing through the rear window as I screamed and held my hands up. The guilt that would tear at me because of a hastily written letter that I posted and then regretted forever. The realisation that the two people I loved so much had become little more than a full stop at the end of a sentence, the last sentence of a book. But these things were pale and cold against the day at the beach and it was those sunshine memories that meant Devon reached out with bright fingers to pull me in.

When a programme came on about people house hunting in South West England, I took it as a sign and made a final decision. I didn't allow myself to think about the magnitude of such a choice being hung on something so flimsy. I pushed aside the worry and knew that I would choose to go anyway. The urge to leave surpassed the worry about what might happen and as I fixed my gaze on one spot on the horizon all I could feel was relief.

The next day I contacted letting agents and told them what I was looking for, I spent hours researching properties on the internet. I wanted to live near a city but in a rural location, in a small village or the middle of nowhere rather than a town, a house with a decent garden and at least two bedrooms, no flats, no house shares. I had made the decision not to live near the beach, worrying that the link to Diane and Richard would be too strong and then there would be nothing left for me but disappointment that they were not there to share in the experience.

After more than a dozen phone calls to various agencies I found myself growing increasingly frustrated. Perhaps I was being too fussy. The properties available were too small or in the cities; they had no garden, not enough rooms, or too many people to share with. I began to wonder if Devon was the wrong choice after all. If perhaps my lack of success in the search was some kind of divine intervention trying to point me in a different direction. The phone calls had grown ripe with repetition from both ends of the line and I had to clamp my teeth together to prevent myself from snapping at the hapless agent on the other end, who could not help this lack of choice.

Several days later I finally found what I was looking for. A little, detached cottage on the edge of a small village, surrounded by a large garden, described as 'slightly unkempt but charming in its own way.' It sounded perfect.

The cottage had been empty for six months but there had been little local interest. Perhaps foolishly I agreed to take it there and then, sight unseen. I promised that the first month's rent and bond, along with my references would be in the post the following morning. I felt that I couldn't take the risk that someone would take it from me before I had the chance to travel down to see it for myself. I felt an attachment to the house even then. Perhaps it was simply the success after days of frustration, but I carried with me a strange sense of homecoming, of rightness. I imagined the house waiting for me. Dove Cottage, Apple Tree Lane, Winscombe. Six chocolate-box words that already felt at home in my mouth.

5

Lacey

'What is your name?'

'Lacey Eleanor Carmichael.'

She sees him pause for a moment as he writes on the pad in front of him, as if he's not quite sure he has heard it correctly, as if he is uncertain about what to write.

'It's a family name, Lacey, after my Grandmother. And in my case, sadly, it is far more exotic than the person it belongs to.' She offers a smile that falters and dies as she sees beyond the young policeman's shoulder, and notices the black shiny eye that tells her she is being watched, that eyes other than his will see her sitting there, pale and afraid. He finishes writing and stabs a full stop onto the pad before turning to her with a wry smile that lifts one side of his face and leaves the other dimpled.

'Mine is just John, plain and simple. I think you got the better deal.'

There is silence for a few seconds and in the distance she hears a door slam. He remembers why she is there and thinks that perhaps it is better in this moment to be plain and simple John. His face begins to colour a little as her eyes sweep across him and he remembers reading somewhere that when people blush, their stomach lining blushes too. He wonders how they know.

'How old are you, Lacey?' His stomach must be glowing even more now. He hates having to ask, as though in doing this job he is breaking the unwritten rules of social nicety. He clears his throat and wiggles his pen back and forth and she frowns a little, like she can't quite remember. She looks up into her eyebrows and moves her eyes from side to side as though reading the answer from the air.

'I'm eighty-four.'

Sergeant John smiles, 'Are you sure?'

'Is it 2008?' she asks and he smiles some more, but this time there is more of a question in it, as if she is trying to trick him.

'Yes it is.'

'Then I'm sure.'

He writes it down, and Lacey reaches for the cup of tea that someone had brought her when she first came into this room, and looked at the pale walls that reminded her of another time when she felt equally helpless and afraid. The tea is lukewarm but at least it is in a proper cup, not a flimsy paper thing that she could squeeze too hard and spill on herself. There are even biscuits. They have jammy centres and look like they should be on a plate at a children's party, not here where people are locked behind metal doors. She wondered who it was that went out and bought them, who it was that thought they were a good idea. But she doesn't ask, she just waits to see what happens next.

She sees Sergeant John talking to the lady that

drove her here in the back of the police car. There had been no flashing lights, no sirens. There had been no hurry. She hears the policewoman justifying why she has brought Lacey in and the custody sergeant nods and writes something down, as if he is little more than a waiter taking someone's order. They talk in hushed tones and Lacey loses the words in the space between her and them. She looks at her mug and wishes it were full again.

Before she can ask if it is possible to get another, the sergeant approaches and asks her to follow him. Through a door, down a corridor, all painted the same shade of cream until she is shown into a tiny room with a cot bed and little else. A different policewoman comes in and the room shrinks even more. When the sergeant leaves she is asked to remove her clothes, all of them. Turning her back, she hunches into herself as she strips. Handing her clothes to the woman as she tries to cover her flaccid breasts with her arm, she grasps at the grey material passed back in return. The officer turns her back as Lacey dresses again, and busies herself putting the removed clothing into a clear bag.

'Someone will come for you soon.' She closes and locks the heavy door behind her and Lacey covers her face and cries into her palms beneath the black, watchful eye of a camera.

★ ★ ★

She doesn't know how much time passes before Sergeant John comes back. She has lost track in front of the pale walls that she stared at and looked for blemishes. He gestures her to follow and she does. He leads her to a new room and tells her to sit at the table attached to one wall and then he stands by the door and waits until it opens again, revealing two new faces.

Sergeant John moves towards the door. He doesn't say goodbye, merely turns and offers a half smile and she realises how awkward the moment is, in this room where the usual conversations and departing words don't matter, in this room where no-one talks as equals.

The new arrivals reach over and shake Lacey's hand. The first almost reaching all the way to the table top before she realises that she needs to raise her palm to meet his. The handshake is dry and impersonal before he passes her over to his female equivalent, as though they were dancing, the three of them. They introduce themselves but within minutes their names have disappeared from her mind. She will see their faces for days afterwards; she will wake up with her heart hammering in her chest from the dreams in which they laugh at her, but their names are gone forever and she is not sorry about that.

The man and woman opposite her could have been cut from the same cloth, both dark eyed and dark haired. The woman is slender and pretty in a way that she has tried to hide with ill-fitting clothes, heavy framed glasses and hair scraped back in a tight bun. The man is thicker set with a five o'clock shadow and a heavy brow. They look at Lacey and she feels the weight of their eyes, flinching away from them before the questions even begin.

'I understand that you have waived your right to legal representation, Ms Carmichael?'

He raises an eyebrow in a gesture that says so much. He thinks she is doing the wrong thing but he says nothing more, he doesn't tell her that she is foolish. Lacey nods in response, staring at the strip that runs past the table and around the room. She recognises it as a panic strip and wonders who it is meant for, her or them. There is a sigh but she is not sure who it comes from.

'Do you understand why you are here, Ms Carmichael?'

She frowns at the question. 'Call me Lacey, please. Ms Carmichael sounds too formal.'

His own brow creases in return. How much more formal could this situation be? He wonders about her, about whether she is altogether with it, about whether or not he should have her evaluated by the mental health team before going any further. But he decides that he will ask a few questions first and see how aware she actually is.

'I'm here because I've been arrested for murder,' she says, as her chin trembles. The policeman nods, satisfied, and begins to talk randomly, a list of instructions. She realises it is for the benefit of the tape recorder that will capture her every word and make her afraid of what she might have said later when she can no longer remember clearly.

'In your own words, Lacey, could you tell me what happened last night?'

And she does, because this she can remember,

all of it up to a point. She takes a deep breath and feels her knee begin to shake under the table, her right knee, the one with the arthritis that grips and bites at her whenever she tries to stand. She moves her hand under the table to push it into stillness. It helps a little.

Four eyes stare at her with questions behind them, but they disappear as she puts herself back into the world she lived in yesterday, a better world where Albert wasn't lying dead in his hallway, with his blood as a pillow.

6

Rachel

Dove Cottage sat empty for another five months. I pictured it there waiting for me as the grass grew longer and flowers lifted their faces towards the sun. The days became weeks, steamroller slow, as I posted yet another rent cheque and wished the time away. This chapter of my life was over and yet it clawed at me with dying fingers, desperately clinging on and refusing to let go.

It wasn't simply a case of packing up and moving. There was a painting to finish, a portrait commissioned by a local councillor, a fleshy, stern dowager who was insistent that she sit for the portrait in her drawing room, almost certainly for the prestige rather than the convenience. She had no desire to have me paint her from photographs, which was always how I preferred to work. Much though I loved my work, right at this moment I felt a twinge of angst at my chosen career. Unfortunately I had agreed to do the portrait before deciding to move and the lady was paying good money. I couldn't afford to turn her down.

As I lifted the brushes to transfer the councillor's round, ruddy face onto canvas, the frustration coiled within me like a viper, I could sense it waiting to strike at any moment. As the subject fidgeted and grumbled, I fought hard not to do the same as, with agonising slowness, the portrait was completed.

The finished piece turned out better than I had expected under the circumstances and drew glowing praise from the pinched mouth now immortalised in acrylics. The councillor gave me a bonus and promises of recommendations to wealthy friends. I replied that my days in Moseley were finished, that I would still happily take commissions to work from photographs and I passed over my agent's business card. The lady smiled as she showed me to the door, lifting her soft, doughy hand to touch lightly upon my tense shoulders, and in that moment showing more life and warmth in her face than she had during the entire time she had sat for her portrait.

I filled the moments in between work commitments planning everything about the move in detail. I made lists upon lists of all that needed doing, all I had done, all that I would do once the move was complete. Everything was planned with military precision, in total contrast to how I would normally accomplish anything.

Two weeks after finishing the portrait I found myself drifting through each of the rooms in my attic flat. It looked bigger and my footsteps echoed back at me. Light filtered through the skylights in the room I had used as the studio, perfect rectangles of sunshine on the bare floorboards that I stood in for a moment, allowing the warmth to fill my body now that the rest of the rooms seemed so lifeless and cold.

The walls, once a kaleidoscope of colours from the many paintings resting on them, now

appeared naked. Empty picture hooks punctuated the plaster. I hoped that whoever came here
after my departure would make use of them; the
thought of bare walls reminded me too much of
institutions.

The rooms looked bleached, sterile. Nothing
was recognisable. The flat had been reduced to
little more than square walls, square floors,
square boxes. The rich fabrics and rugs which
had adorned every space, the eclectic canvasses
painted by my own hands, all of these things had
reflected so much of my personality that I felt as
though it was me who had been packed away, my
life reduced and surrounded by cardboard and
parcel tape.

Pouring wine into a plastic cup, I sank down
onto the sofa, legs curled up beneath me. I felt
out of place in the middle of the room, facing the
empty space where the TV had been. I was worn
out, exhausted yet excited too, counting down
the seconds until tomorrow when I could close
the door for the last time and drive away without
looking back.

I thought about the village I was moving to. I
had tried to research it, but found little
information. I knew that it was to the south of
Exeter, I knew that it was tiny compared to
Birmingham, as most places were, but beyond
that there was nothing. I felt anticipation run
through me at the thought of discovering
everything for myself.

'To new beginnings.' My voice was loud and
echoing against the empty walls as I raised my
cup in a toast to nobody. I knocked back what

was left of the wine before unfolding my sleeping bag and curling up on the sofa to try and get some sleep.

The next morning I pointed my car towards the noon sun, pulled back the bowstring and let myself fly. With every mile that blurred and faded beneath the tyres I felt my shoulders become lighter, my breath become easier until it felt like I floated high above the road with a bird's eye view of the horizon. I drove as fast as I could and didn't bother to stop and break my journey. I was too impatient to be on my way and as the miles disappeared I felt my anxiety fade away. I watched the hills grow bigger and greener as I passed, until I finally reached my destination.

From the broken, pitted road that wound its narrow way down the edge of the valley I saw Winscombe for the first time. The sky was a brilliant blue with no trace of cloud, light reflected from thatched roofs and white-washed walls, the whole scene dazzling in its old world perfection. Would I have felt differently about the village if the sky had been overcast and heavy with rain? If the scene had been tinged with grey? It was possible but somehow I doubted it.

Before my eyes rested on the village, I had carried with me a sense of things being as they should. Maybe it was wishful thinking but Winscombe felt like the right place to be. The warmth of the sun shining on the gentle swell of the hills added an air of energy, creating an image of such clarity and perfection that it would stay with me always.

I pulled into a lay-by at the crest of a bend where the road doubled back on itself. The village nestled below, a vague comma shape curving along the valley, with the church and the village green in the centre of the rounded section. The streets twisted and turned randomly, as if they had been built by someone who had designed the layout while chasing a butterfly. I loved how unpredictable it was, the way some houses seemed to lean drunkenly against each other with barely a hair's breadth between them, like friends staggering home after a night in the pub. I loved that no two houses were the same. Overwhelmed that after so much waiting I had finally made it, I reached up a hand to brush away the warm tears that clung to my eyelashes as I blinked in the sunshine.

Later, when I saw the village from this vantage point again, I would see the things that had been missed that first time. The more modern, box-like houses that added to the tail of the comma, the telegraph poles and wires, the cars that lined the winding streets. Yet even years later if I closed my eyes and pictured the view, it always maintained the rose-tinted perfection of that first time.

7

Lacey

When had it all began with her and Albert? She couldn't quite remember but it was long enough for their meetings to have become routine. There was nothing between them but friendship and they were both more than happy with that. Both of them had experienced what it was like to be loved, Albert in the traditional sense and Lacey for a tragically short time, but for them it was enough.

When Albert's wife had developed a headache he had thought nothing of it, she had been plagued by migraines most of her life. He had held her tight and persuaded her to have an early night, he made her hot chocolate, tucked her in, turned off the light and watched television for an hour before he joined her. Her breathing was light when he went to bed and he had kissed her soft cheek before drifting off himself. When he woke up the next morning she was cold and still beside him and from that moment, he had blamed himself. He had bumped into Lacey at the graveyard and they had found a strange kind of unity as they stood in their separate grief. His guilt about the night his wife died, and the loneliness and silence in which Lacey lived her life had bonded them together somehow.

They would meet once or twice a month,

always in Albert's house. Sometimes they would play cards and always they would eat together. It wasn't much but it filled a gap, especially for Lacey. She wondered if he knew that he was often the only person she would speak to, she wondered if he knew that it was those evenings, those brief moments that held her in the present and gave her a measure by which she noticed time passing. She wondered how she would cope now without him to hold her feet on the ground.

It had been a normal evening; they played gin rummy, which Albert had won. He had said that she seemed a little dreamy and it was true. There had been a sense of mist in her head, as though reality had taken a little step backwards and all her senses were dimmed and vague. It happened sometimes. They had laughed a little, in the sad and slightly sombre way that those who share losses do, they had drank some wine and they had sat in comfortable silence for a time.

Lacey had grown tired and felt herself drifting. Albert had smiled at her drooping eyes and told her to get herself home to bed. She stood to get her coat, she turned to say goodbye and after that her memories blur, a chalk smudge on dark paper.

She can't remember beyond that moment, she can't remember leaving Dove Cottage, she can't remember getting home.

'What about the following morning, Lacey? Can you remember what happened then?'

She startles at the voice that pulls her out of her head and back into the room with bare walls and no windows. She had forgotten they were

41

there. She shakes her head a little as though trying to dislodge a fly, a buzzing thought. The policeman thinks she is saying no, that perhaps she is in denial.

'It's okay, Lacey, take your time.'

She wants to ask him how it can be okay, how any of this can be okay, when her friend lies dead and she can't remember how it came to pass.

She can't remember if she is guilty of his murder.

8

Rachel

Tearing my gaze away from the scenery I returned to the car and continued my descent into the valley, following the road towards the largest part of the village. The letting agent had sent a map with the cottage circled on it as well as written directions. I knew from them that Apple Tree Lane was near the top end of the long curving sweep of Winscombe, leading onto the fields that lay parallel to the road I had travelled in on.

The lane proved easy enough to find, a dirt road that began between two old oak trees, forming a natural, tall arch where their upper branches whispered against each other. My little car bounced along the dry, red-tinged earth, straddling the central strip of grass as I made my way slowly towards the house.

Up ahead I saw the roof of the removal van, and my heart skipped a beat. Leaving the car on a grassy patch of ground on the opposite side of the lane, I hesitated, feeling suddenly reluctant to pass through the gate in the hedge. I didn't want the sense of relief at finally being here to fade; I felt an urge to stay this side of the hedge, to remain in ignorance of what awaited on the other side. What if the house was not what I hoped? What if the agent's description had been wrong or exaggerated? Uncertainty gripped at my ankles, stalling my steps until I found it hard to move and simply stood there in the middle of the lane, trying not to peek over the hedge as my lower lip caught between my teeth.

It seemed like hours that I stood there, trapped between my past and my future. When I finally plucked up the courage to move past the squeaky, wrought iron gate and looked at the house for the first time, the relief poured from me. The white painted walls and wooden framed windows looked like they belonged in a different time. Clematis grew over the wooden porch; an apple tree spread its branches over the lush grass that in turn had covered the edges of the curving stone path that led to a stable door. Wild flowers filled the borders with glorious colours and sporadically dotted the lawn where they had taken seed.

In the corner of the garden, a pergola nestled beneath climbing roses, so overgrown that the seat was shaded and barely visible. Everything about it seemed picture perfect and I was moved beyond thought. I stood for a moment, slowly turning as I took it all in, fatigue draining through my feet into the cool, verdant ground.

'We're all finished, love.' I turned to smile at the ruddy face of the removal man. 'Do you wanna just check everything's okay before we head off?'

'No, its fine thanks, I'm sure it's all in order.' I wanted to be alone with the house, to have no-one present when I walked through the front door for the first time and introduced myself.

The doors slammed and the engine belched into life, billowing acrid smoke that rose in a cloud. I watched as the removal van squeezed its way back down the narrow lane, high branches on both sides of the little dirt track bending as it passed.

I paused for a moment to glance again around the beautiful, wild garden that surrounded my new home, feeling the long grass moving against bare ankles as trees laden with blossom showered confetti into the breeze. It was the sort of garden that would be a haven for wildlife, a haven for me. I closed my eyes and inhaled deeply before stepping towards the front door.

I had wanted a hiding place where I could run from my grief and shut out the world for a little while. Until that moment I wasn't sure if I had actually believed I would find it, I had been wary of hoping. Hope was too often a prelude to disappointment; the hope that my mother would find me, the hope that I could stay with Diane and Richard, the hope that one day soon I would hold my baby in my arms. Hope was the first falling domino.

9

Lacey

She can hear a clock ticking. It is above her somewhere, to her left and each little tick that it makes seems to be removed from the others by far more than a second. She does not look, she has no desire to see how time has warped and twisted inside this room. She does not want to drown in the sand of the hour glass.

She rocks back and forth a little, her fingertips pressed into the skin above her eyebrows, her eyes tightly closed. She hears material shift as the people opposite her become restless against her silence. A throat clears, fingers tap and she tries to push the sounds away as she searches her mind for an answer to his question.

'Ms Carmichael, do you need anything?'

She notices the lack of concern in his voice. Perhaps he too is trying not to look at the clock, trying to avoid the passing seconds. He knows that here, in this room, time is a limited thing and that when it runs out she no longer has to speak, she no longer has to stay. She murmurs something against her wrists that he doesn't hear clearly.

'I'm sorry I didn't catch that, could you repeat it please?'

'I said, frontal lobes.' She giggles, a spontaneous sharp sound that lacks humour and bubbles away into a sob that catches in her throat. She twists her hands around, presses the ball of her palm into her eyes as though trying to push the tears back in. In that moment she doesn't see the exchange of concerned glances between the two detectives.

'I'm sorry,' she says. 'I'm a little emotional today.' She sniffs, rubbing her sleeve across her eyes and nose before clasping her hands together beneath the table.

'When I woke up this morning it was still dark and I had a headache. Too much wine maybe, or not enough sleep. I looked for my bag, to find some painkillers and realised I didn't have it. I must have left it at Albert's. So I laid back down and waited until a more reasonable time to go and get it. Albert liked his lie-ins.'

She didn't say that as she had lain there it felt like her head was splitting open. She didn't tell those two expectant faces that this kind of headache always followed one of her blackouts, or that parts of the previous night had fallen forever into a void. She didn't tell them that there was part of her that believed it possible that she had done what she was accused of. She had no way of knowing if she had or hadn't. The lost parts never came back.

'What time was it when you got up again?'

This came from the woman detective. Lacey was surprised by her voice. It was rough, husky, as though she smoked too many cigarettes. It didn't sit right with the deep eyes and the long lashes.

'It was about nine o'clock. I must have fallen

asleep again because Peachy woke me up. He's my cat. He came and sat on my chest, he always does when he's hungry.' She gives a half smile. 'It's a good job I don't need lie-ins, I'd never get away with it.'

The smile dies away quickly as though doused with a bucket of water, because she remembers and the pain is a sharp thing that steals her breath away.

'I made myself a cup of tea and decided to go and get my bag while it was cooling down. It would give me an excuse not to get stuck talking for too long, my head . . . you know?' Her voice breaks and she stops speaking. Too many thoughts crowding through her head all at once. The guilt that she was being selfish in not wanting to talk for too long, that it had been a conscious decision that she would be quick; as if friendship should be hurried, as if there were nothing there to savour. And the memory, the thing she can remember too clearly, the scene that she stumbled across. Her eyes open wider and she covers her mouth with her hand as if she cannot bring herself to say it, because if she speaks the words, lets them out, they become true, they become real and she can't take them back.

'Take your time, Ms Carmichael,' the detective says and the very words make her want to speak quicker because she knows he doesn't mean it, she can hear it in the sigh that chases his voice.

'I don't know what time it was that I finished making the tea and left the house. It was all quite normal you see and I never really pay much attention to the clock anyway.' Her eyes flick upwards and to her left as if they want to betray her, to prove her wrong. They stop short of staring at the hands. She wouldn't remember them anyway.

'I knocked a couple of times and there was no answer so I tried the door. Albert is like me, he can't get into the habit of locking it when he goes out.' She winces at the present tense. It hangs over the table, a solid thing that is out of place and uncomfortable in this room where everyone knows the end of the story.

She falls silent. There are no sounds from the corridor, no sounds from the room apart from the clock; the rest of the world has disappeared. If she opened the door now would there be nothing beyond it but mist and echoes? She fights the urge to try. She becomes still, so very still and the two people opposite her can barely see her chest rise and fall as she breathes. On some level she hears them, the metal hands she will not look at, ticking past the minutes but she is not really there anymore, she is not in this space, in the chair opposite the two people who must decide whether or not to keep her here. She is somewhere that no longer exists, she is in yesterday and she sees her hand lifting to open the door.

10

Rachel

I closed my eyes and stepped through the doorway, breathing in deeply as I went. The house was dusty, and yet beneath there was a scent of polish and care. It felt warm and comforting on my skin and I savoured it for a moment before I opened my eyes.

From where I stood I could see all the way to a second stable door at the back of the house. The stairs began near the back door, the banister unpainted wood like the floor in the hallway. The living room was small with an open fireplace that I couldn't wait to curl up in front of. When my paintings were unwrapped and hung in there it may look a little crowded, but I never had mastered the art of minimal décor so that was just fine with me. In that moment the room looked haphazard and chaotic with boxes and pieces of furniture scattered everywhere, but it was easy enough to see beyond that, to see the potential.

The dining room would be perfect for a studio and I fell instantly in love with its beautifully square shape, its windows on three walls allowing it to get the best of the day's natural light. My fingers twitched at my sides as I fought the urge to reach out for the containers from which would spill out my livelihood.

I knew from past experience that if I started now I would still be standing in front of the canvas at dawn with bleary eyes and right now I didn't have the time for that luxury. I would have to leave unpacking this room until last or the rest of the boxes would sit around gathering dust until the final stroke of acrylic was drying.

The garden to the back of the house was smaller than the front. Surrounded by hedges it contained an old shed that had seen better days and several empty flower beds covered in black plastic. I had never owned a garden before. A couple of herb plants and miniature roses on the windowsills didn't count. I couldn't believe the space and relished the thought of spending time outside where no-one could see me. The idea was in sharp contrast to memories of the many flat dwellers that filled the green spaces in Moseley.

The kitchen was something of a disappointment. After the lovely wooden floors of the hall and dining room, the cheap brown lino looked out of place. But despite its cosmetic flaws the room was large with ample space for a table to compensate for turning the dining room into a studio.

The stairs were steeper than I was used to and bowed slightly in the middle, making me feel as though I was slightly drunk as I walked up them. They were old and several of the treads creaked. In the bedrooms I glanced at the boxes piled high and decided that other than locating the one that had sheets and curtains in, I was doing nothing else upstairs today. I could take my time over it and there was something comforting in that thought. There was no rush to get things done.

After a cursory look in the bathroom — more seventies decor and a hand-held shower — I went back down to the kitchen. Finding the box marked 'emergency' I prised it open and removed the kettle, teabags, mugs and milk, which I sniffed at to make sure it hadn't gone off in the back of the hot van.

Sitting on the front doorstep with a steaming mug in my hand I breathed the clean air in deeply. I let my thoughts wander, losing myself in the petty details of all the chores to come. I wondered where I should place my scatter cushions, where my rugs would go, what curtains should go where. In the moments that I stopped thinking, I worried whether I had done the right thing. Sitting here miles from the city I knew, miles from anything familiar, I finally felt a hint of the hesitation that I had ignored for so many months. I didn't want to think about my reasons for moving or the thought that, maybe, I was simply being a coward and running away. I didn't want to consider that I might have made a mistake. So I shut it out and reached for the practical instead, hoping that for a little while I could keep my subconscious at bay.

11

Lacey

It was the smell that she noticed first. It wasn't overpowering or strong, it was barely even noticeable below the scent of the soap she had used that morning. But she knew what this space normally smelled like and it was the difference that she noticed, that sense of something slightly changed.

The house felt empty, as though it was waiting for the return of the energy that sustained it, that kept it warm. She had been alone for long enough to know what that felt like. She turned to leave, not wanting to stay where she was unobserved, uninvited. It was the shoes that stopped her. Harmless as they were, the sight of them screamed a warning, nudging the memory of a conversation they had once had.

'Why do women have so many pairs of shoes?' He had asked her, as if she was typical of her gender, as if she could speak for all women everywhere, instead of being outcast, invisible.

'I have no idea. Why do they have so many pairs of shoes?' It was like a joke, the way he had asked it. She wondered if there would be a punch line.

'I was hoping you could answer. I've always wondered about that. I have one pair, what's the point of having more? I do, after all, only have the one pair of feet!' And they had laughed a little before the conversation had moved on to other equally unimportant topics, the way it often did.

And now she stood there just inside the open door, staring down at Albert's one pair of shoes. Her skin grew cold; she wanted to turn but was equally afraid to look away. Albert would not have gone anywhere in bare feet. She stared hard at the brown brogues and took in the shine of them, the style of them, the area where they had worn around the heel. Her peripheral vision disappeared until she stared down a tunnel with those shoes at the end. The fear grew and hammered painfully against her chest. She wanted nothing more than to run and not look at things that she didn't want to.

But she thought then, what if he was hurt? What if Albert was lying up in his room, on the cold floor having fallen out of bed? What if he had tripped on his way to the bathroom? What if he was ill and couldn't call out? She knew then that there was no choice; she had to find out if he was okay.

Two steps, that was all it took; two tiny steps that changed everything. She stepped away from the door, opened her mouth to call his name and as she looked down the hallway, her voice stalled. She saw a hand, palm facing up, fingers half curled. The rest of him was hidden around the curve of the stairs and she was so afraid of him then, afraid of his brokenness, his vulnerability.

Wide, wide eyes came slowly around the banister. She saw him and for long, long minutes

54

she failed to move as her eyes absorbed every part of that image. A montage of tiny little things that would take up residence in her memory for the rest of her life, no matter how many times she tried to forget them and put something lovely in their place. The clawed hand, the twisted body so bent out of shape that one of his legs disappeared beneath him in hideous contortion; the halo of blood that painted his hair stiff and dark. And his eyes, those empty, empty eyes, blanched of their colour and so very still.

She bends to him then, her knee smarting and protesting as she touches it to the floor beside his head, careful not to press it into the blood that smells so much stronger now that she is closer.

'You lucky, lucky man,' she says and kisses him on his forehead, so hard and cold and unyielding beneath her lips. Her eyes close above his open ones and in that moment, when she can smell him above the blood, she feels his loss so keenly it steals the strength from her. She struggles to her feet, using the banister to propel her past the point at which her legs want to stop.

'Bye bye, Albert.'

She backs away from him down the hallway, holding her breath until she reaches the door. Feeling behind her for the doorframe she walks backwards all the way down the path until she gets to the gate. She turns and hurries back down the lane, through her own garden and into the kitchen where she scrambles beneath the table and rocks back and forth with her hands over her ears.

It doesn't seem that long before she hears the scream, the strange keening sound that seems to be the closest depiction of grief she has ever heard, raw and harsh. The sirens come and indistinct voices filter through the palms of her hands. Then comes the calm, the stillness, where there is nothing but the sound of the wind in the trees, though this too dies away. Until the sudden knock at her door, slightly too loud, that makes her flinch.

She moves slowly towards the sound, reaching it as the knock comes again. She rears back and claps her hands together over and over again in front of her closed eyes before the clamour from the other side propels her to open the door, shocking the policewoman on the other side into stepping backwards.

'Lacey Carmichael?'

Lacey nods and pulls her bottom lip between her teeth. To the policewoman she looks terrified, her breath coming too fast, her skin pale and clammy.

'Could I come in for a minute? I'd like to ask you a few questions.'

There is a strange movement where Lacey's nod of assent changes direction, curls around on itself, her head moving in a little, tight circle until she is shaking it and her mouth forms a single word. 'No!' She steps backwards, her hands raised in front of her towards the policewoman on her doorstep who is looking at her, perplexed.

'It will only take a few minutes Ms . . . ' The door slams in her face as Lacey kicks out at it.

Sometime later she hears a knock, followed by another and then another. Someone tries the handle; she hears movement in the downstairs rooms, footsteps on the stairs. They find her sitting on her bed, with her coat and shoes on.

'I left my handbag at Albert's house, I need to go in and get it.'

They tell her that she can't and that they are arresting her for the murder of Albert Allen. She has the right to remain silent.

12

Rachel

The sun rose steadily above the hills behind the house, pushing the night from the landscape as it came, the darkness receding into pools of shadow beneath trees and fences. I stirred as the light outside the window began to grow brighter. Dawn was my favourite time of the day. There was something magical about the way the light would seep into the land, a pastel perfection that the birds would greet with song. Overcast days were no less beautiful as dark silhouettes became recognisable in the grey light.

As I blinked away the sleepiness I had a feeling of difference, of absence, that I couldn't put my finger on. It took me a few more moments to realise I couldn't hear any traffic. There was no background hum of engines, no sound of tyres on tarmac or doors slamming, people talking, none of the familiar noises of the city coming to life. How long would it be before the stillness became just as familiar? Exhausted though I was, I had found it difficult to sleep and perhaps this was why. The silence was deafening.

I took my morning tea out into the still shaded garden, pulling a blanket around my shoulders to ward off the morning chill. There were few clouds in the sky and only a slight breeze to stir the trees. I munched on a cereal bar and decided that after dressing I would go for a wander into the village and find the grocery store that the letting agent had told me about.

It was still early when I stepped into the lane, and I had plenty of time before the store opened. I wanted to walk around the village as it was waking up and I relished the idea of being alone in the streets for a while before doors opened and people started going about their business.

The lane I lived on opened up on to a single-track road. There were no signposts and the hedges were high enough to only offer a view of the church tower. I knew that the village lay to the right and after a short time of walking between the maze-like hedgerows the road widened and the first houses began to appear. They were typical chocolate-box cottages, some thatched with walls that looked like they were bowing outwards because of the weight of all that straw; others were tiled, but all of them seemed not quite comfortable in the twenty-first century.

From the beginning of the village I could see more of the church over to my left, the tower peeking out over the rooftops and I headed towards it. I loved churches. There was something about the peace and stillness inside the ancient buildings that I cherished, the sense of hope in the air as if the very stones of the walls had absorbed the centuries of prayer offered up to whoever happened to be listening.

Stepping through the iron gate that left flakes of black paint crumbling beneath my fingers, I looked around at the headstones. Old and lichen-covered, weather had long since erased the words that identified the people beneath. Some had toppled over completely; others leaned towards each other, conspirators of secrets long since forgotten. On my left were the more recent graves, some yet to have their headstones placed. These were the graves I turned my face from, my own grief lending a depth of compassion to the recently bereaved. It was too easy to imagine strands of sadness coming from the turned soil and stretching beyond the churchyard, disappearing towards houses where families would wake with the loss etched on their faces. I averted my eyes and walked on.

Through the graveyard and out through another gate on the opposite side of the church, I determinedly pushed my thoughts away and looked at the scene before me. I had thought places like this only existed in paintings. Opposite the church lay a village green, complete with a duck pond and bench. The paths around the beautifully kept grass were cobbled and well worn. Two pubs, perpendicular to each other stood behind traditional signs that swung slightly in the breeze. Next to one of the pubs, the Rose and Crown, was the village shop, its leaded windows completely at odds with the bright green sign above the door.

Walking to the bench beside the pond I sat down. Everything was perfect. Despite the unpacking waiting for me at the cottage, I was overwhelmed with the novelty of it all, the age of it all. Here in the newness of the day, I felt like the only person in the world and I submerged myself in it. But as I watched, the sleepy little village slowly came to life around me, chasing away my solitude and leaving a slight feeling of regret in its wake. I sighed and leaned back. The wooden bench cool against my skin as I looked for familiar shapes in the wispy clouds and waited for the shop to open.

★ ★ ★

A bell rang, discordant and grating as I opened the door. A man stood behind the counter watching me with one eyebrow raised in question, laughter lines wrinkled his eyes and sparse salt and pepper hair receded back from his sunburnt forehead.

'You must be the young lady that's just moved in to Dove Cottage!' He smiled at me and I returned it, nodding and feeling my cheeks tinge pink.

'Old Albert's place, been empty a little while now.' He was laying out newspapers as he spoke and I reached out for a local one to see what I could learn about the area.

'I haven't met Albert, I rented the cottage through a letting agent.'

The shopkeeper's smile grew some more, stretching across uneven teeth. He had the kind of look I would love to paint, all lines and character, lived in and interesting.

'Only way you'd get to know old Albert now is if you's one of them mediums. He passed some time ago. His daughter Martha's got the cottage now but she lives in the newer part of the village. Guess if you've not heard about Albert, you've not met her?' I shook my head and he carried on, his strong West Country accent refreshingly different from the singsong lilt of Birmingham.

'Martha's alright, bit opinionated but harmless enough to most people.'

He smiled again and turned back to his papers. I wandered around the shop, browsing through shelves of random things from everyday food items to fuse wire and added to the basket what I needed for the next few days.

'The name's John by the way.' He belatedly offered his hand as I placed the basket on the counter and shook it lightly, calluses pressing into my palm. 'If there's ever anything specific you need, you just let me know. I've a tendency to cater for individual tastes rather than buy a load of crap that won't shift.'

'I will, thank you. I'm Rachel,' I said smiling at him as I gathered my things together before turning to leave.

Walking back through the graveyard with bags swinging from both hands, a flash of colour caught my eye. I glanced towards it and saw an elderly woman kneeling in front of one of the graves in the newer section. She was an explosion of colour against the headstones as she roughly plunged a trowel into the soil, preparing a hole for the rose bush next to her. The woman wore orange baggy trousers and a lime green sweater, with bright red wellies. She was muttering under her breath, the words swept away on the light breeze and indistinct from where I stood. Her brow was furrowed beneath a shock of pure white hair that stuck out in every direction, her cheeks full and rosy like fresh apples. Moving nearer, I stilled the swinging bags so they wouldn't disturb the kneeling woman.

She didn't look up as I passed but continued carefully pressing the rose bush into place with chubby hands as I reached the gate.

'There you go, you miserable old bastard, choke on that.'

Surprised, I turned back to look at the woman, who was getting to her feet and rubbing the dirt from her hands. Her eyes met mine and she paused, looking self-conscious, like a child caught with a forbidden sweet.

'He hated roses,' she said simply, by way of explanation. She turned quickly away and headed out through the other gate.

13

Lacey

She sits in the same room as before. Not room. Cell. She tries to get her head around that word. It is simple, small; one syllable that hangs over her head. She feels it pressing down on her. What if they think she is guilty? What if she has to stay here? What if she murdered her one and only friend?

They have told her that they are waiting for forensic evidence before they decide whether they can keep her or let her go, as if she is a bug caught in a jam jar. They tell her that they don't believe her to be a flight risk and she replies that she has no passport. They tell her that isn't what they meant and she is confused and doesn't say anything else.

This world is alien to her and it makes her afraid. She wants — needs — to be back in her home, where the walls and every mark on them are familiar, where she knows how to get through the days. Where she knows what the light looks like at dusk and she can tell which birds are visiting her garden by the song that they sing. She needs to be where Charlie is, she needs to feed Peachy and her chickens.

This place, where the corridors echo and the smell is cloying, this place is not good for her. In this place she is forgetting things, like a curtain pulled around that separates her from the time that came before, from the everyday life that she lives. She needs that; she needs her routines, her walls, her trees and garden. She needs the full picture of her life so that she does not forget it, so that she knows where she is, because she lets go of it all too easily and it falls to pieces around her.

She sits beneath the little eye of the camera and tries hard not to look at it. She tries to act normally, as if this is an everyday thing, a normal thing. She tries not to draw attention to herself. She wonders if they are watching her right at this moment and she turns slightly, so her back is to the lens, so that at least they cannot see the fear on her face, they cannot see her cry.

She lost track of time but through the little window that is high up in the wall she can see the sky and she watched as it grew dark, then saw when the darkness faded altogether. She listened to the birds tell her it was morning, but she didn't recognise their voices. Someone came and gave her food and it stayed untouched on the plate, she only drank the tea that came with it. She couldn't face eating.

She hears a door open and close in the corridor outside, she hears footsteps approach and stop outside her door, the rattle of keys. A man she hasn't seen before comes in and tells her to follow him. She tries to stand but her legs are aching from where she has been sitting for too long. He reaches out and helps her to her feet. He towers above her and she shrinks back from him as his hand curls around her elbow and he tries to guide her forwards.

He takes her back to the same room as when she first arrived and she sits wondering what next. Will she be taken to the prison now? What will happen to Peachy? She imagines him sitting by his empty bowl, his tummy rumbling, wondering where she could be. She has never been away from him. She wonders how long it would be before he realised that she wasn't coming back. And what would he do then? Would he slowly walk away, leave through the cat flap and try to find someone that could love him enough to fill his hungry stomach? Would he come back once in a while hoping she had returned? She thinks of him searching the empty rooms, desolate without her and she starts to cry; huge shaking sobs that hunch her shoulders and make her curl into herself.

A hand on her shoulder pulls her upright and she looks into kind eyes in a concerned face. It is the custody sergeant, John. He sits in a chair next to her and she feels as if she has known him for far longer than just a day.

'I'm going to explain what happens next, Lacey.'

She nods to let him know that, despite the tears on her face and the redness around her eyes, she is ready to hear what he has to say. Whatever he says, she will try to stay strong, to handle it in a dignified manner befitting a doctor's daughter.

'You are going to be released on bail . . . '

'I can go home?' she asks, interrupting him. He nods in return and she throws her arms around him and cries into the dark cloth of his uniform. After a few moments his hand reaches up and pats awkwardly at her shoulder before he moves away and she apologises.

'You will be on bail for a period of up to eight weeks. If, during that time, we decide that there is no case to answer, there will be no further action against you. If you don't hear from us then you need to come back here to the police station on your appointed date, which I'll write down for you.'

All she can think is that she can go home, she can go back to her little cottage. His voice is blurred and distant. But then she realises she has nothing with her, no money, not even her own clothes, as if this is someone else's life she is living, a life that she accidentally stepped in to.

'How do I get home?' she asks, hearing the tremor in her voice.

He smiles then, a gentle smile that is kind, reassuring. 'We'll arrange for someone to take you home.'

14

Rachel

I awoke in a room swept grey by the rising sun and tried to recall what day it was. Somewhere amongst the sea of boxes the days had begun slipping into weeks. I had spent hours among cardboard and packaging, sliding the craft knife down the tape that held the cartons closed and allowing myself to get swept away in the tide of possessions that spilled out. Photographs, books, letters, a duvet cover I spilt red wine on the first night it was used, rag rugs no longer fashionable but old and worn and loved. So many things that created an image of me as they flowed through my hands.

Several times I looked down and when I raised my eyes, day had again turned into night, so immersed was I in the business of finding unfamiliar places for familiar things.

I had asked my agent, Jane, to hold off on any commissions whilst I got organised, and the house was beginning to feel as though I belonged within its walls. It was more chaotic and cluttered but among the wealth of fabrics, ornaments, paintings and collections of the unimportant, I found serenity and peace.

I spent my time cleaning, sorting and whitewashing over memories, attempting to consign them to a different life, but inside I was the same, nothing had changed. I knew that time would have to pass before I truly felt settled, but that didn't stop the occasional flicker of doubt. I couldn't deny that there was part of me that felt I should head back to the city.

Time had been spent organising the studio so that I could eventually resume work, everything had to be perfectly set in its place and exactly where I needed it to be. Though my living space was cluttered and unstructured, here in my working space I had to be able to reach a hand out without looking and find the exact thing I needed. I found the organising process cathartic and fulfilling, a ritual I had always completed since I began painting.

I set up my canvasses against the far wall, placed my easel where it could catch the best of the light. My paints were lined up alongside palettes, brushes, pots and knives on the old trestle table, the splashes of colour across the surface evidence of previous works. Now the room was ready for me to start work again and I felt as though at any time of the day or night, I could simply step through the door and begin.

As the light began to fade I curled up on the sofa with a glass of wine. It was an indulgence I didn't allow myself too often; alcohol was not one of my favourite things. I knew more than most where it could lead.

Where the carers at the home had been reluctant to share information about our lives, my foster parents had not. They had held me, patiently answering my questions and not shied away from the truth when I sought it. I knew it had been hard for them, to take my dreams of my absent mother and turn them into something dark and unwanted. There had been times when I was younger that I wished they had kept it to themselves. But now I was grateful for it. The truth, though painful, was easier to deal with than the uncertainty of not knowing.

My mother had been an alcoholic and I was taken away from her at 15 months old, severely neglected and underweight. I was alone when the police broke down the door and took me away. As far as my foster parents knew, she had never sought me out. I don't know if she wrote to the home, if she enquired after my whereabouts. The scant information I had was bleak enough to prevent me from reaching out for more. I knew that her name was Margaret and I knew that her addiction had meant more to her than I had. It was enough, more than enough.

A hand moved absently to my stomach and I pressed against it, feeling the flat, soft plane through denim. I cursed its lack of shape, longing to feel an answering kick from within; wishing things could have been different. I wondered how it could be that I had grasped so tightly to my mother's hostile womb yet my own longed for child had loosened her grip and died. Sighing, I tried to swallow past the lump in my throat. Tomorrow would have been my baby's due date and no matter how far I moved or how much I changed, there were some things I would never be able to leave behind.

I closed my eyes and let it wash over me like a

tidal wave. How long had it been since I had given the baby any amount of thought? I had pushed past thoughts of her and focused on the mundane. Now, as well as the grief, I felt the guilt of that dismissal weighing down on me.

All of a sudden I felt it was too close in the house. I felt trapped, hemmed in by the walls around me with the TV flickering in the corner of the room like a warning beacon. Throwing open the door I ran barefoot out into the dark garden.

I sank down into the too long grass, leaning forward to press my face into the ground. I cried for my lost baby and the sound filled the silent garden before fading into the night. The grass pressed against my face, cold and damp against hot skin as I drew ragged breaths that caught in my throat. How could this ever be alright? How could I have believed for one minute that I could leave this in the past? I had lost the one thing I had always wanted, a family of my own.

I flinched at the hands that suddenly touched my shoulders, gentle but firm enough to pull me to sitting.

'Are you okay, lady?'

I sniffed and smelled lavender and clean linen. I tried to answer but found I couldn't because I wasn't okay. Through puffy eyes I saw the woman who had been planting roses in the graveyard. Warm, blue eyes looked back at me with curiosity and concern. She knelt down next to me in the grass looking a little embarrassed as if trying to work out why she had come here.

'Who are you?' My voice hitched half way

through and I watched her gesture vaguely towards the hedge.

'I thought you was a wounded animal. That's why I came in, I thought you was an animal needing help.' A gentle West Country accent softened her voice, making it sound sleepy.

'I'm Lacey, I live next door.' She held out her hand and looked down at it as if it were an alien thing, as if it didn't quite fit there.

'I'm sorry, I'm fine really. I've just had a bit of a bad day,' I replied, shaking her hand. I could hear the awkwardness in my voice, the stilted words. Her eyes swept over me and I hurried to my feet taking a step backwards. I was uncomfortable with this stranger looking at me and seeing my vulnerability. I brushed myself down, feeling awkward as my clothes clung damply to hot skin.

The woman held up her hand, stalling me.

'Could you help me up please? My legs tend to hurt.'

I hesitated before reaching down to support her as she stood, stumbling slightly and I held on tight, worried that she would fall.

'Do you want to talk about it?' She looked away, her eyes gazing beyond my shoulder into the darkness of the hedges and beyond, as if she were uncomfortable at prying into something she shouldn't have been.

I shook my head, 'No, thank you.' My own words were clipped, polite but distant and she flinched from them before nodding.

'I have to go anyway, I've got Charlie waiting for me.'

She turned quickly and hurried down the path leaving me looking after her as the gate swung closed and she disappeared into the darkness. I went into the front room and sat for a while staring into space, all the emotion spent. After a while I stood and headed towards the bedroom.

15

Lacey

The letter came six weeks after she had been arrested. She didn't realise it was there at first because she didn't always check the box down by the hedge.

The weeks leading up to its delivery were tortuous and slow. She had arrived home from the police station, dropped off without fanfare to a house that looked exactly the same. Even the cat appeared unchanged, not seeming to notice she had been gone. But for her nothing could be the same.

She spent hours looking at the walls of her house, the sturdiness of them, the familiarity of them. They were her fortress, her anchor. They lived in symbiosis, her and the house. She brought it energy and kept it clean and the security of those walls kept her safe and rooted in the present. She could tell where she was in the year by the way the sun shone in through the windows, by the various hues that washed across the floor.

Apart from little trips into the village centre, she never left the cottage anymore, finding the world outside increasingly baffling and hostile. She had been born in this house and she rarely left it. Though her memory often failed her there were many things she could remember, images that stood out in sharp focus. She remembered other times she had left, other times she had been taken from here; confusing and chaotic images that put a tremor in her hands and made her stomach leap and turn. Nothing good ever seemed to come of leaving. She wanted to die in this house.

But now it seemed that something threatened that wish. What if she was found guilty? What if she was sent to prison? She knew it would be the end, that she would go from the court to the prison and never again set foot here, where her life had begun. The solidity of these walls became tenuous and uncertain, as if they could crumble and leave her exposed to the elements. She had never before doubted that she would always be here, but now she feared it would be prised away from her by strangers who knew nothing of her life.

By the time the letter arrived, Albert was in the ground next to his wife. She had been told to stay away from the funeral, she wasn't welcome. The vicar had come to see her, had cleared his throat and tried to explain it in his apologetic way, never quite meeting her eyes. She had understood, though she would have gone if she had been given the chance. Instead she had sat at the end of the lane and listened to the sombre church bells calling him home. She had wondered for a moment whether they would have the wake at Dove Cottage, but the hours passed and no-one made the journey to this end of the village.

She spent the day thinking about Albert and

the evenings they had spent together, talking about everything and nothing, putting the world to rights. She would miss him. Not just for the company on those occasions but for the smaller things. She would miss the way he would wave and say good morning when he encountered her, or how she could hear him singing through the open windows in summer. Sometimes his was the only voice she would hear in a day filled with silence.

As evening fell, Lacey went into her garden and gathered up some wild flowers and grasses. She tied them together with string and when it was fully dark outside and the night was about to shift to morning, she made her way down the lane and up the road to the churchyard. Moving towards the more recent graves, she glanced around her, afraid to be seen. But there was no-one out at this time and she picked her way carefully through the mounds that were hidden in shadows.

She approached the newest grave and sat beside it breathing in the scent of freshly turned earth. She talked to him for a little while, telling him about the police station, the ride in the police car. She tried not to imagine him down there among the cold and the worms. She told him about the mouse that Peachy caught that was still alive and ran around the house in panic. She told him that she was sorry she hadn't been there for him, that she would miss him because he was the only one who treated her with decency and kindness. She laid the flowers on the mound and clambered to her feet, wiping away a tear and leaving a smear of dirt across her face.

Sometime after that she found the letter. It was tucked in with a routine doctor's appointment that she wouldn't attend and a local nursery flyer. She looked at it with curiosity and fear in equal measure and then she sat at the kitchen table and stared at it while she drank her tea. She moved around the house, following her usual routines, gathering laundry, washing up. Each activity was punctuated by a step into the kitchen to stare at the white envelope and worry about what it contained.

When she sat down to lunch, the envelope rested near her bowl looking like a name tag at a wedding, *Ms L Carmichael*. She placed it upside down so she couldn't see the name and saw instead the return address of the Devon and Cornwall Police. She turned it over and over as she spooned soup into her mouth, watching as the sharp edges caught the light from the window.

With a sigh she opened the letter in one sharp movement. There among the black typewritten words, among the phrases and technical information that she didn't understand she saw the words *no further action*. She read them over and over, tried to put them into context with the rest of the letter that explained how in light of forensic evidence, there was no case to answer. She didn't understand it all but she knew enough to know that it was over.

It hadn't been simply the thought of going to prison that had scared her so much. There was more to it than that. It was those words, those simple words that had been typed up by a secretary who had no emotional attachment to them. For Lacey, the freedom wasn't just from the charges. Because now she knew, it was there in black and white. The forensic evidence showed that she had not been responsible for the death of Albert Allen.

She passed a hand over her forehead and intense pain followed. She frowned against it, but the buzzing started in her head. She winced from it, could feel her heart hammering and as her vision started to fade she felt herself stumble and fall into the black, black hole.

★   ★   ★

She woke in utter darkness and wondered where she was. It couldn't be her bedroom because there, even on moonless nights, there was a faint lightening around the edges of her window frame, from the streetlamp at the end of the lane. The smell was wrong too, vaguely musty and earthy. It was familiar but she was not yet aware enough to work out how she knew it.

She tried to remember and waited for the little clues to appear. The tiny fragments of memory, flashes of colour and conversation needed to coalesce to form a whole image that might make sense to her. Sometimes it happened, but sometimes they remained apart and those lost hours, occasionally days, disappeared forever.

She reached out her hand and it brushed against a rough wall that left her skin dry and dusty, she reached out the other hand and felt the same. And then she knew. She was in the cupboard under the stairs. She was glad that she had found out before standing up.

Carefully she pressed her palms forwards until they touched the door and moved them over the surface until she found the handle. It was dark and she limped her way on painful feet to the light switch, shielding her eyes as she flicked it on.

The letter still sat, half folded on the kitchen table. A sack of cat biscuits had been knocked over and some of the contents spilled onto the floor. Apart from that everything was normal. When she moved a sharp pain pressed into the soles of her feet, stretching up to her ankles and she winced. Sitting down, she looked at the thickened pads of skin and discovered several thorns like tiny spikes protruding from the pink surface; they looked like blackberry thorns.

The field next door to her house had blackberry bushes in the hedgerows, they followed the edge of the field all the way down to the old stable by the stream. Why had she gone there? What had she done? In that moment she felt exposed and afraid. Vague images jumbled in her head, a glimpse of a hand reaching for her, the cold stab of fear. They were gone before she could grasp them fully and she couldn't tell if they belonged in this moment, or from another time.

She moved towards the front door, as quickly as she could and turned the key, sighing with relief as the lock slid home.

16

Rachel

The air hung heavy and still over the field. From the five-bar gate at its entrance, the meadow looked like a picture. Nothing moved, and the sky beyond was cloudless, the light so bright that it brought everything into clear, sharp focus. Hidden among the blades of grass, splashes of colour like drops of paint nestled and around the edges of the meadow, fingers of light forced their way through tree branches and dappled the ground.

Knee-high meadow grass had dried to the texture of straw beneath the blazing sun and the flowers had begun to wilt, the deep red earth baked hard and cracked. The peace and stillness so total that even the insects seemed unwilling to disturb it.

In the far left corner of the field, where the trees grew thicker and provided blissfully cool shelter was a stream. Little more than six inches deep, it bubbled a shallow path over loose stones bringing with it a cooling breeze and the gentle melody of dancing water. Here, there was also an old stable. Open to the field on one side but so overgrown with blackberry bushes and honeysuckle, that anyone stepping beneath the beautiful scented blooms was rendered invisible to prying eyes. The light becoming green tinged as it seeped through the leaves that covered the opening. There were two stalls here but they had not been used for a long time, the plants finally claiming the structure for themselves.

The dramatic change in temperature as I stepped into the shadows of the trees brought a sigh of relief to my lips. My eyes adjusted slowly to the change in the light, seconds passing as the dark shadows retracted into hues of green, soothing and gentle beneath the canopy.

I sat on the shallow bank, the earth damp and cool through my clothes. Inside, I felt as though I was looking into darkness so intense I wondered if I would ever be able to fill it. In an alternative reality was there another me somewhere on the verge of labour, pain tearing through me as my baby fought to enter the world? Or would the result be the same no matter what reality existed? I wanted to believe that somewhere my baby had made it, that somewhere she was whole and new. It was so much easier than thinking she had never mattered.

Drawing my knees up, I rested my chin. I had dreamt of her, before the night I had woken to blood on the sheets. I dreamt of a baby crying, and I had gone in search of the source, moving from room to room in a mansion with too many hiding places. The crying had gotten louder, but every room contained only an empty crib. Then I had found myself in a garden with the full moon shining down and turning all the trees silver. The crying had been coming from beneath the branches of a cypress tree. I ran to it and stood among beautiful white lilies. I peeled back the petals from one of the flowers and found the baby there, tears all gone as she smiled up at me. Tiny hands rested on a round belly, legs curled up and crossed at the ankle. Sorrowful eyes looked up and met mine. I reached out a hand, but before my fingers brushed the soft skin, the petals began to close. When I pulled at the petals and opened them again she had gone, and I had woken up in a cold sweat.

After that, whenever I thought about her it was the dream image I saw. Chubby arms with folds at the wrist and dimpled cheeks beside a rosebud mouth, dark eyes framed by beautiful long lashes that fluttered contentedly into sleep; a light brushing of dark hair covering a soft pink scalp.

I reached into my bag and withdrew my sketchpad and pencil and began drawing tentative lines in the centre of the page. I drew the baby from my dream, tiny and perfect, surrounded by petals. The image took shape slowly at first, speeding up as my fingers gained confidence in their subject. The swell of full cheeks, the delicate mouth curved into a slight smile that seemed sad and lonely. Tiny crescent shape fingernails on folded hands. Beautiful and lost, realistic but never real enough. If I picked up my eraser and wiped it across the paper, my baby would be gone as quickly and silently as before. A dandelion seed floating on the breeze.

I laid my pencil down and carefully tore the sheet of paper from the pad. The drawing only occupied the centre of the page, my perfect baby but only three inches high. I began to fold the paper, tucking in the edges but being careful that the image was never covered. The shape of the origami boat formed easily beneath my fingers and when I was done I put a finger to my lips, kissed it and pressed it onto her graphite face.

I lowered the paper boat into the water. Holding it there for a few seconds as the scant current tried to steal it from my fingers. I opened my hand and let it go, watching as the boat bounced a little and twisted in the water. I watched as it caught for a moment on something hidden beneath the surface before the pull of the water freed it. Following a bend in the stream, it drifted out of sight.

A breeze had begun to stir the leaves above me and I added to it with a shuddering breath, drifting among thoughts of a little girl who would never be. I sat as still as a statue; a shadow on the river bank, and lost myself in daydream. The colours changed among the trees as the hours passed, until slowly the light faded and the day swept away.

17

Lacey

The months had passed and the house next door remained empty. She understood why, nobody wanted to live in a house where someone had met a violent, if accidental death, especially not the local people who had known him. And there were those who still did not think that Albert's death had been an accident, who still wondered about the woman in the house at the end of the lane.

She had phoned the police station in the end just to clarify, just to make sure that it was truly all over and she didn't have to fear another knock at the door. They had told her that, although they could not go into detail, there was evidence in the postmortem results to imply an accident. They had spoken to the Crown Prosecution Service about the fact that Lacey had left the scene of a crime, but because of factors relating to Lacey's age and vulnerability, they would not be pursuing any further charges.

It was over in that respect and the routine of Lacey's days returned to what it was before, with one exception. She didn't set foot in the house next door, there were no evenings with company, there was no-one to talk to. But she was free and she was glad of it.

She became accustomed to the silence from

the other side of the hedge. Dove Cottage loomed there, vacant and cold and dark. She felt sad about that. A house should be lived in. But no-one wanted it. The seasons changed and Lacey tried to keep track of them but sometimes they got away from her and she became uncertain.

She knew when it was Halloween, the night when she huddled inside afraid of the banging against the walls and the chants that sounded like banshees to her. The holly on the door of the shop told her when it was Christmas, the bells in the church told her when it was New Year and when it was Sunday. The buds told her when it was spring. And when the flowers started to grow and open she knew that Albert had been gone for a year.

Not long after that she had heard the truck come up the lane, she had become aware of the movement outside, on the other side of the hedge. She had spied through the branches and seen the car pull up and the pretty, dark haired girl had got out looking like a rabbit caught in headlights. And then last night, she had heard the crying in the garden and had gone to investigate, setting foot in the garden of Albert's house for the first time since she had seen him lying dead at the foot of his stairs.

Later, she stood at the window in her spare room, sweeping carefully at old cobwebs with a feather duster, trying her best not to hurt the spiders that were in the process of building new homes. She never liked to hurt anything and figured that she had more than enough room to share. Movement had caught her eye and she looked down to see the young woman. Her shoulders hunched up around her neck and her head down, face hidden by long hair. The woman walked towards the stream, towards the old stable that few were aware of, but Lacey remembered, even though she couldn't see it from here and rarely ventured down there anymore. Too many memories, too much regret lay there.

Lacey turned to where Charlie sat cross-legged on the bed, watching her in that quiet way of his, soft brown eyes that always carried a hint of a smile even when his mouth was still.

'She seems nice, Charlie. I reckon we could've done a lot worse for a new neighbour.'

Lacey turned and walked from the room, dust motes trailing behind her, heading towards the kitchen to put the kettle on. As she passed, she saw Charlie's eyes move towards the window, where the girl's shadow had disappeared beneath the trees on the far side of the meadow. He didn't reply.

18

Rachel

Darkness had fallen completely in the valley by the time I emerged from beneath the trees. Letting myself into the house I headed straight for the kitchen, I hadn't eaten since that morning and my energy was dwindling. I was crunching on a biscuit and waiting for the kettle to boil when there was a knock on the door. Brushing crumbs from my mouth and trying to swallow past a dry throat, I opened the door. The old lady from the night before stood against a backdrop of darkness, a purple headscarf tied over cotton wool hair and a fluffy pink dressing gown belted around her ample waist. She held a box of eggs in one hand and there was an awkward smile on her face.

'I saw you come back.'

I stared at her for a moment, discarding the expectation of bad news. She offered no further explanation and seemed content to simply stand and watch me, her eyes bright in a weathered face. I endured the silence for as long as I could before growing uncomfortable and asking, 'What can I do for you?'

She shuffled from one foot to the other and appeared unsure of what to say next. Standing in bare feet as she was, she barely reached my shoulders. She glanced downwards, looking at the egg box in her hand. She held them out to me, her eyes wider as though she had suddenly remembered. 'Eggs,' she said, 'from my chickens. I thought you might like some. I was going to bring them over earlier but then I saw you go out and I couldn't. I heard the gate squeak when you came back and I wanted to bring them over, in case I forgot tomorrow.'

There was something in her face then, she looked uncertain and I realised that she reminded me of someone much younger. In those moments she seemed like a child trying desperately to get things right, trying to make a good impression. Fleetingly, I saw myself in the stranger on the doorstep and in that moment I looked at her with different eyes. I took the eggs.

'I'm Rachel,' I said, and she smiled at me as if I had given her a gift.

'Lacey,' she told me again. 'I live next door, in End Cottage.'

'Well it's a little late, I was just about to head to bed.'

An instant apology fell from her lips and she looked a little forlorn, as if she hadn't thought of this time of night being associated with sleep. I found myself feeling sad for her, this funny little woman with her bright clothes and wild hair.

'Perhaps you would like to come over for tea tomorrow afternoon, just to say thank you for the eggs?'

She looked beyond me into the hallway, her eyes sweeping an arc from the front door to the back, lingering a moment somewhere behind me. As her face turned back to mine she was nodding. 'I'd like that,' she said, and there was a sincerity about the way she said it.

'Is two o'clock okay?'

She nodded her agreement and smiled up at me, a wide, toothy smile that lifted her face. 'I'll see you then,' she said and raised her hand to wave as, for the second time in twenty-four hours, she said goodbye and walked out of my garden gate into darkness.

19

Rachel

I spent the morning in my studio, planning, preparing and throwing some paint at a canvas in an attempt to drum up some enthusiasm for work. I painted flowers, abstract and strange, in many colours and when they dried I whitewashed over the whole thing until I was left with what I had started with, a blank canvas. By the time I had cleared up it was almost two o'clock and Lacey was due. I had achieved nothing more than stained hands and lost time.

I was in the kitchen putting the kettle on when she knocked at the door and I opened it to find her on the doorstep holding a bright pink cake and looking shy. I stood aside to let her in.

'I made this,' she said, and handed me the cake. She paused on the doorstep, staring at the doorframe and into the hallway beyond. With what seemed to be an effort she pulled her eyes back around to me and stepped cautiously into the house.

'You shouldn't have,' I said, indicating the cake in my hands as I walked into the kitchen and placed it on the table.

'Oh it's nothing. I love to bake, coming over here gave me an excuse really.'

The cake looked lovely and I told her so as I made the tea. I felt as if I moved like a marionette, stilted and uncomfortable. I wondered what it was that had possessed me to invite Lacey into my house, a woman I knew nothing about other than the fact that we were neighbours. I was beginning to wish I had stayed silent.

We sat at the table and tried to think of things to say. I had never been particularly good at small talk, it sounded insincere coming from me, as though I didn't really care for the answers.

'Have you lived in the village long?' I asked as I poured the tea and tried not to be embarrassed.

'All my life,' she said. 'I was born here, in the same house I live in now. My father was the village doctor for many years until he got sick and died.'

I remembered the graveyard and the rose bush she had planted and thought that it may have been for him. I couldn't imagine what it was like to live in the same place for so many years, to never be embraced by new walls or make somewhere your own by washing away the marks of others.

'What about you, why did you move to the village?'

It was like a dance, each step faltering and tenuous. She too was making small talk, following my lead but I didn't know how to answer and the conversation felt false, stagnant. I picked up my cup and took a sip of my too hot tea to buy me a few seconds in which I could think.

'I moved to Devon because I needed a change

really. I was fed up with living in the city and wanted something calmer, something different. All those people were starting to make me feel claustrophobic.'

Her eyes on me were heavy, questioning, as though she sensed that a lot was being left unsaid.

'I can't imagine what it is like to live in a city. Even Exeter, which is fairly small, makes me feel closed in and headachy. I need to look out of my windows and see the trees.'

Her gaze moved to the window and beyond, to a view that must be so similar to her own, a wall of green from the high hedges of the garden boundary. I cut two slices of cake and enthused about the flavour of it. Lacey beamed at me across the table and looked pleased before we lapsed into an awkward silence and continued eating. I racked my brain for something to say but floundered and came up empty.

'What do you do?'

I looked up and found her eyes on me, open and curious and I felt a surge of gratitude for this question. It was easy to answer, it was safe. 'I'm an artist, I have an agent back in Birmingham who sells my pictures for me and finds clients so that I can work from anywhere.'

'You work from here?' There was genuine interest in her voice and she glanced around her, as if looking for evidence.

'Yes I do. Well, I mean I'm supposed to. I haven't started work since I moved although everything is set up ready. Would you like to see my studio?' I relaxed a little as I spoke, feeling as though someone was holding up prompt cards in the wings and as a result I knew what to say next. The ground seemed more solid beneath my feet as Lacey nodded and we both stood.

I led her towards the dining room and turned at the door. She walked slower than me, favouring her right leg, and her eyes were staring at the floor. I watched her come closer and then she did a funny thing, a kind of a hop and step, as if she were stepping over something at the foot of the stairs. She looked up at me and smiled as though nothing was untoward and I thought that maybe she had simply tripped a little.

We walked into my studio and Lacey gazed around with curiosity at the jumble of colour and bristles and white, white canvas. It looked chaotic and random but I explained to her that even blindfolded I could find any single thing. The air smelled of chemicals and linen and paper, like an old bookshop, a smell that I found warm and inviting. I tried to see it through her eyes but could only see the familiarity that enveloped me every time I stood with a brush in my hand and prepared to create something new.

I suggested that we take our tea into the living room and I stood back as Lacey turned to leave the room. She did the same thing she had done before at the base of the stairs, the funny movement. Not a trip then. I was curious but I didn't ask why.

By the time I had gone back to the kitchen to pour two new cups of tea, Lacey was standing in the middle of the lounge, staring at the walls and spinning slowly as if on a turntable. Her eyes wide as they took in the kaleidoscope of colour and shape from the many canvasses and wall hangings.

'Some of these are a little bit mad aren't they? Look at that one,' she spoke in a kind of baffled whisper as she pointed towards one in particular, a mass of red slashes and purple swirls and shook her head. 'That's a bit disturbing if you ask me. I couldn't have it on my wall,' and then she paused and glanced quickly at me as if something had just occurred to her. 'Are any of them yours?'

I cast my eyes over the walls, thinking of the emotion, the momentum behind each one of the images before me. 'All of them.' I could hear the note of apology in my voice and I wondered at it.

She laughed then, the deep rumbling rush of a river tumbling over a waterfall. It rolled across her like ripples spreading outwards in water. She laughed and everything on her shook, her hair, her cheeks, the underside of her arms. The movement washed over me and swept me away until I laughed too, until we both laughed so much that the reason for it became obsolete. The sound swept away the discomfort of strangers and somewhere amid the laughter we became not quite friends but something close.

20

Lacey

The church stood against a backdrop of trees, the edges rounded by centuries of inclement weather. The old brown stone looked warm and comforting in the sunshine. Its tower stood strong against the blue sky, a sentinel watching over the dead. With stained glass windows and ancient studded wooden doors it displayed its age and history proudly.

In a small village like Winscombe, the church became a hive for the local community. Weekly events, jumble sales, children's days and writing groups were all regularly held there in the small community hall that had been built at the far end of the graveyard. The details would be published in a monthly newsletter and pushed by volunteers through every letter box in the village.

She always receives one but she never attends anything, she wouldn't like to see the faces of everyone else when she walked amongst them like an intruder. It was ironic when she thought about it. She had been born here, decades ago, long before the war had come along and taken the young men, changing everybody's future. Aside from a handful of residents she is probably the oldest in the village and yet she is the outsider, the unknown element. She had long ago given up wishing it could be different.

She picks her way through the gravestones, flowers in hand and stares down at the place where her parents lay side by side. As always, she places the flowers on her mother's grave first and tries not to hear the criticism that pours from the ground for her failings as a daughter, then she turns to her father's grave and begins her usual tirade. She says all of the things she never did when he was alive, talking a little too loudly over the reproach from her mother. She tells him he was a lousy father, that he was cruel, that he had destroyed her life. It is the same every time she comes. She tries to exorcise the ghosts he has left her with.

21

Rachel

As I walked amongst the gravestones, sketch-book beneath my arm and sunglasses firmly placed over my eyes, I turned my attention to the small details of the church, trying to decide where to begin. On the northern side of the building where the main door stood I saw, half hidden in the shadows beside an archway, a green man carved into the stone.

Sitting among the oldest gravestones with the grass tickling at my legs, I decided that this was where I would begin. As I gathered the stillness around me and began to draw, the headache that had plagued me on waking began to release its grip. Earlier that morning, I had turned over in bed and groaned, holding my head as I pushed myself up to sit on the edge of the mattress.

I couldn't remember noticing the afternoon turn to evening the previous day. Lacey and I had chatted about nothing much at all, snippets of information about the local area from Lacey and facts about city life from me, with neither of us touching on the personal details of our own lives. I had been surprised at how easy I found it to spend time in Lacey's company after that initial awkwardness.

We had progressed from tea to a bottle of wine, which had proved too easy to drink. I was fairly certain that the lion's share had been mine and my tolerance for alcohol was poor at the best of times. Somehow, after a little while, it had seemed easy to talk about the reason for my tears in the garden.

I didn't go into any great detail. I spoke from a place of calm acceptance as though the storm had passed and I was sweeping up the debris. I told her that I had lost my child, and that it would have been her due date. It seemed a simple story when it was broken down like that. She had surprised me by shedding a tear, one solitary droplet that had meandered down her cheek until she reached up and brushed it away with a look of surprise.

Neither of us had noticed the light ebbing away.

With some reluctance, Lacey had, a little unsteadily, gotten to her feet and announced that she had to be getting back to Charlie. I hoped that her husband wouldn't mind her being out so late, but when I voiced that, she corrected me.

'Oh, Charlie isn't my husband he's my son, and no he won't mind. I'd just hate for him to wake up and worry about me.'

I waved her off, waiting until I heard the soft catch of the door to Lacey's house close from over the hedges, before I went back inside.

★　★　★

I kicked off my sandals as I began adding shading to the lines on the page. I was so

98

engrossed that I didn't hear the approaching footsteps on the gravel path or realise that someone was standing behind me until they cleared their throat. I flinched and the pencil jerked across the paper leaving a dark, heavy line across the delicate shadows of the church door. I turned to look at the tall, reed-thin woman.

'I'm so sorry, I didn't mean to startle you. Are you Rachel?'

Nodding, I lay my pad aside and got to my feet, brushing myself down before holding out my hand. She took it, her skin dry and cool against my clammy palm.

'I'm Martha, your landlady. I was just coming to put some flowers on my dad's grave when I saw you sitting here, so I thought I'd come and say hello. I hope it's not ruined.' She pointed to the sketchpad in the grass.

'Oh no, don't worry. It's nothing special anyway, just practice.'

'How are you settling in? I've been meaning to come by but things have been a little busy.' Her steel grey hair was pulled back into a ponytail that reached just past her shoulders. She had a harsh, uncompromising look and carried herself ramrod straight, but her eyes and smile were friendly, her voice soft and delicate in contrast to her appearance.

'Most of the unpacking is done now so I'm almost settled in. I love the cottage, it's such a peaceful place to be.'

'My dad loved it there too, it was a haven for him really, especially after my mum died. I'm glad you've moved in. A house like that is meant to be lived in and it's been empty for a bit too long.'

'I can't believe it wasn't snapped up straight away. It's so much better than all the other properties I was sent details for.'

Martha's eyes slid away, moving over the gravestones before fixing on one of them with a frown. She was quiet for a few seconds and I watched her, trying to read her expression. 'Well, I guess people round here can be a little superstitious. Dad had lived in that house for more years than most people could remember. He was popular in the village and maybe taking on the cottage would have been a bit too much like stepping into dead man's shoes.' Her voice was hesitant and she looked down at the wild flowers in her hand, already beginning to wilt slightly in the heat. Martha turned back and smiled, 'It's a good place to live. We're lucky in so many ways. People are mostly friendly, whether they know you or not. I'd much prefer that to being among strangers in a city.'

While I had enjoyed the anonymity living in the city had brought I could see her point, there was something nice about the old-fashioned values that led to the courtesy of saying hello as you passed someone by on the street. Although I was reluctant to be drawn into conversation with strangers, I did get a feeling of warmth from the passing greetings, however small they may be.

'I'm beginning to realise that, although I've not met many people here yet, only John in the shop and my neighbour Lacey.'

Martha looked away again, but not before I

saw the skin tighten at the corner of her mouth.

'I don't mean to cause any alarm or tell you what to do, but you just watch yourself around Lacey Carmichael. She's not a good person to know. My father . . . ' her words trailed off as she glanced back towards what I assumed was his grave and she sighed. I waited for the rest of the sentence but it didn't come.

'Anyway, just be careful, that's all. The problem with that woman is that she's lived on her own far too long and forgotten what it's like to be around normal people. She lost her marbles a long time ago.' There was sharp emphasis on the word normal. The bitterness in her voice dripped like poison and I felt a stirring of discomfort. After the initial awkwardness the day before, I had found Lacey an easy person to be around, but I was also aware that Martha was my landlady. I didn't want to do anything that would jeopardise staying at a cottage that felt more and more like home with each day that passed. I let the silence grow for a moment, unsure of what to say. I glanced down at the ruined sketch on my pad and then out across the gravestones thinking that it was time to go home now.

Martha's gaze was unfocused as she stared off into the distance, lines between her brows and tightness still around her mouth.

'What's Charlie like? I've not met him yet,' I asked because I could think of nothing else to say to break the uncomfortable silence and I couldn't simply turn and walk away without saying anything.

'Charlie? I'm not sure who you mean.'

'Lacey's son, she's talked about him but we haven't been introduced.'

Martha's eyebrows rose sharply and she looked a little dumbfounded before she laughed. It wasn't a nice sound, and she looked at me with what looked like pity.

'Like I said, Lacey has lived alone for far too long. She's never been married and she certainly doesn't have a son, if she told you otherwise then it was a lie. She is a stranger to the truth that woman. My advice would be to stay away from her.' Martha shook her head and closed her eyes for a moment. When she opened them again her expression had changed, had become warmer once again as if she had pulled down the shutters to hide the sharpness. 'Anyway all that aside, I hope you'll be very happy here. Most people are. And don't hesitate to call if you need anything, I'm only up the road.' She reached into her bag and pulled out a piece of paper and a pen, scribbling her phone number down and handing it to me. 'Just in case,' she said.

I smiled and said thank you, then watched as she turned and walked towards her father's grave. I picked up my things before moving across the graveyard and out through the gate, curiosity following closely behind.

22

Lacey

It was nothing more than bad timing she would think to herself later, when the blood had stopped flowing and the tenderness on her forehead had bloomed into a lump that moved slightly when she pressed it.

From her place at her parents' graves she hadn't seen Martha. If she had, she would have stayed away, she would have known there could be trouble if they came face to face. But she didn't see her and she didn't know.

Lacey stands and looks at the flowers in her hand. There had been three bunches, now there is just one and she moves towards Albert's grave to leave them there for him, to remember. Just as she gets closer she sees her. She notices the expression on Martha's face change as their eyes lock together, from one of grief to the kind of anger that pushes reason aside.

Lacey stops walking and tries to turn away but it is too late, the taller woman bears down on her like a wave.

'How dare you, how dare you come here. Haven't you done enough?' The words force through shaking, thin lips as Martha reaches forwards and snatches the flowers out of Lacey's hands before hitting her across the face with them. They sting like a whip and she gasps, reaching her hand up to her face, feeling wetness there. She remembers the rose she put in the flowers, she wishes she had removed the thorns.

'You killed my father, you old hag and now you come here gloating. How fucking dare you. You might have fooled the police, but I know what you did, I know what you did, you murdering bitch. I saw you leaving the house, I saw you and then I found him, you killed him.' Her voice cracks down the middle and falls apart.

Lacey is crying now, holding her hands up against the onslaught of words. 'I didn't, I didn't,' she says, over and over again but her tears and denials seem only to enrage Martha further.

'If you come here again, if you come anywhere near his grave again, I'll kill you myself! Do you hear me? I'll kill you my fucking self!' And she pushes her. The small crying woman trips and begins to fall, she puts her hands out but her head still catches a glancing blow on a headstone. Pain blooms and for a moment she can't see, she can't move. She is on her hands and knees among the dead, dripping blood and tears onto the dry grass.

She gets to her feet and glances around her like a wounded animal, feeling hunted and afraid. She doesn't understand because the police said she hadn't done it, she hadn't killed him and she wonders why Martha thinks she did. Perhaps it is just because she needs someone to blame. But even so, beyond the rational thoughts an element of doubt creeps into

Lacey's mind. She struggles to her feet using the nearby headstone for support. What if the police got it wrong?

She looks around to find that Martha has gone. She puts her hand to her forehead and makes her slow, unsteady way back to the lane, back to her home. It takes her some time.

23

Rachel

When I got back to the cottage, the answer machine was flashing with a new message. I pressed play as I kicked off my shoes and smiled as the husky voice of Jane, my agent, called out too loudly into the silent room.

'I hope you're really out and not just ignoring the phone like the antisocial peasant we both know you are. I'm waiting . . . ' There was a sound of fingernails tapping against something hard followed by a dramatic sigh. 'Oh for God's sake, I guess you really are out. You live in the arse end of nowhere, where could you possibly go? Anyway, I just called to say that I'm coming down to see you, probably next weekend if I can swing it. Trust you to move to the country. Don't tell me I need to bring wellies! Call me when you've stopped communing with the sheep.'

There was a click as she hung up the phone and I smiled. Jane was a city girl through and through and believed all of the stereotypes of village life. Too much *Vicar of Dibley* had fostered that viewpoint.

I went upstairs to freshen up before calling her back and as I did so I wondered at the little scene with Martha in the graveyard. She seemed like a nice enough person and I couldn't help but wonder at the animosity she had displayed towards Lacey. There had been real venom behind her words and I didn't know what to make of it. Perhaps it was nothing more than a long-standing feud that had blown up out of nothing. Still, I couldn't help but wonder what it was all about. And I wondered about the mystery surrounding Lacey's son. Surely Martha had got that wrong.

I settled down onto the sofa and curled my feet beneath me, pushing the thoughts away as I dialled the number. She answered on the first ring.

'Jane Green speaking.'

'Sorry I missed your call, I was out sketching.'

'No problem, at least you're creating something instead of sitting on your arse. I just wanted to let you know about my impending visit and check that it fits in with your hectic schedule!'

I heard the sarcasm in her voice and smiled at it. Jane knew that I was taking it easy, getting everything sorted before I began 'proper' work again and she wasn't too happy about it. There were plenty of people that wanted my services at the moment it seemed. 'Stop being snippy, I'll get back to work soon.'

'Good, because I've got a few new commissions for you. Your councillor turned out to be a bit of a godsend, bless her. She's been singing your praises to all her friends so we've had a few enquiries. I'll bring the details down with me rather than send them.'

'That's fine, Jane, I'll look forward to it. How

are you, anything exciting going on up there in the city?'

'Nope, my life is as it always is, work, work and more work. Unlike some people I could mention, talking of which, how're things in the back of beyond?'

I told her briefly about meeting Lacey and about Martha and the contradicting information about Lacey's son.

'Well, why don't you invite her over for dinner when I'm down? I can usually read people pretty well and she sounds interesting. You could invite Charlie over too. That will give you a bit of insight into what's going on.'

'Good idea. Are you sure you wouldn't mind giving up an evening of nagging me to work harder?'

Jane's throaty laugh echoed down the phone, 'Cheeky bitch! No worries there, invite her over for the Saturday night, that way I can have all of Friday evening to nag.'

'I look forward to it.' I smiled, feeling brighter than I had in days.

'Me too, Rach, I'll call you before then anyway. Bye for now.'

Jane hung up her end before I had a chance to say goodbye in return.

★ ★ ★

After a lazy lunch of cheese on toast, I went out into the garden to gather up some flowers. I was fairly certain that most of the ones I picked were weeds but they looked pretty enough when bunched together and tied with a bright purple ribbon. I made my way up the lane. Lacey's house, like mine, was hidden by a tall, unkempt hedge. Whereas mine was straight, hers followed the curve of the track and the gate was near the upper end, impossible to see from the track until you were almost on top of it. The hedge had been allowed to grow over the gap and I almost walked straight past the wooden gate before I spotted it and slipped the latch.

Her house was similar to mine. White walls and a stable door made it look as though it came from another time, like something out of a fairy tale. There were windows in the eaves beneath a slate roof and I could see white lace curtains behind the glass. There were window boxes filled with bright colours that tumbled down over the walls. This house was bigger than my own and the garden wilder. The grass was almost knee-high with splashes of colour running through it, red poppies nodding in the sunshine. The path was little more than a vague meandering gap amongst the overgrown lawn with no visible stones to walk on. A huge oak tree cast a shadow over the front garden, an old-fashioned wooden swing hung from ropes tied to one of its branches. I loved how wild and lush the place looked, how perfectly it blended in to the surrounding countryside.

As I made my way to the front door, it opened. Lacey scurried out, a clash of bright colours. She jumped slightly when she saw me and her wicker basket fell from her hand, bouncing on the doorstep before coming to rest in the grass on its side. I bent to pick it up for her and smiled. As I stood up I saw the long scratch across her right cheek, curved and jagged edged, a bruise, the faint pale blue colour of a new injury, was beginning to bloom over a lump on her forehead.

'My God, what happened?' I put my hand on her shoulder and her eyes slid from mine.

'I fell,' she said quietly, 'in the graveyard when I was putting flowers on my parents' graves.'

There was something in the way she said it, she looked ashamed and in that moment I knew that for some reason Lacey was lying to me. I pushed it aside and forced myself to smile, not wanting to pry and make her feel more uncomfortable.

'I just came to give you these, to say thank you for the cake and everything.'

Lacey's face lit up, her smile reaching all the way to her hairline. She winced a little as the muscle contortion pulled at her damaged face. I looked at the garden and realised that there wasn't anything in the little bunch of flowers that she couldn't have picked herself from her own borders, but she seemed pleased nonetheless.

'That's really kind of you, Rachel, really kind.' In her smile I could see traces of youth, her pleasure in such a small thing chasing away the years and painting innocence on her skin. Again, she had the air of a young girl about her.

'I also wanted to ask you if you'd like to come over for dinner next Saturday? A friend of mine is coming down from the city and I wondered if you'd like to join us?'

Lacey's brows knitted together and she pulled in her bottom lip. 'I'm not sure about that one. I'm not really used to company you know. It's been a while.' The innocence remained but now it was shadowed, a look of genuine concern and uncertainty.

'Well it's nothing special, only an old friend of mine who's visiting for the weekend. Not a formal dinner party or anything like that. You'd be very welcome and you could bring Charlie along too, it would be nice to meet him.'

As Lacey's eyes swept back towards the house, to an upper window that looked out over the fields, she was silent and appeared lost in thought. After a moment she looked up at me and smiled,

'Charlie won't come, he doesn't like to leave the house much but I think I might like to.' The reply carried a shyness that came out in a rush, 'If you're sure that's okay?'

I wanted to ask more about Charlie. I wondered if he was unwell in some way. But it would have been impolite to ask and I wasn't sure what I could say. Lacey was looking at the basket in her hands and I realised that I was preventing her from going about her business.

'Well, you'd be very welcome. Jane's lovely and it will be very relaxed.' Something occurred to me then that I hadn't considered, 'I'm sorry to ask you this, but would you mind not mentioning to Jane about how we met, about the baby? I haven't told Jane. In fact, you were the first person I spoke to. I will tell her eventually but not just yet.'

'I won't say anything, Rachel.' Her eyes darted briefly towards the house again before she looked down and just for a moment she looked desperately sad. 'Secrets are one thing I'm good at.'

24

Lacey

She waits until she hears the gate latch before turning back to her front door and opening it. She makes her way through to the kitchen and digs out a vase from the cupboard beneath the sink. Her eyes are misty and she reaches a hand up to brush a tear away.

'Daft old bugger!' She mutters.

It seems silly, to be moved to tears by such a little thing. She knows that she would never be able to explain to Rachel why it means so much. A tiny bunch of flowers that grow everywhere hereabouts, anyone could pick them. But that doesn't matter, it is simply that someone has picked them for her.

Lacey fills the vase and places the flowers in it, not bothering to remove the ribbon, she likes the way it looks. She takes a doily from the drawer, puts it on the farmhouse table in the kitchen, placing the vase on top.

She stands for a while looking at them, hands clasped to her chest and eyes still damp.

'Daft old bugger!' She says again, this time with a small smile on her face. Then she turns to pick her basket up and makes her way to the front door, a bubble of warmth filling her chest. To Lacey, it means more than Rachel could possibly realise, it means the world. Nobody has ever given her flowers before.

She hates having to lie to Rachel about the injury to her face, but she can't bring herself to tell the truth. Losing Albert had plunged Lacey back into the solitary world she had lived in for such a long time. Just hearing the voice of another person has once more given Lacey a less tenuous grip on her day to day life. She finds that, when she focuses on conversations she has had or on memories of people's expressions, her mind is more inclined to stay in the here and now. The dark moments take a step backwards.

She can't tell Rachel the truth, she is too afraid she might believe Martha. She is too afraid that Rachel will look at her with the scorn she has seen on Martha's face, that awful, awful hatred that tears at Lacey's skin.

25

Rachel

By the middle of the week almost everything was ready for Jane's impending visit. The house was tidy and the spare room had been sorted for her to sleep in. I frantically juggled boxes trying to clear the space out entirely, but had run out of places to store them and only succeeded in moving them from one side of the room to the other. I threw the rugs over them and topped it all off with a vase of dried flowers that I'd blown the dust from. Jane knew me well enough by now not to expect perfection.

By Thursday all I needed to do was venture out to buy food for us all. I hadn't left the village since I had moved in and had been reluctant to do so, but as it turned out the trip to Exeter was uneventful and brief. In no time at all I was heading back to the cottage, the car laden with bags.

It was the road sign that I saw on the way home that knocked me for six. Something so simple, just metal and paint that told me it was eight miles to Dawlish, eight miles to the past. In my head I saw the beach, I felt the heat and heard again the conversation that changed my life and had torn me kicking and screaming from a reality I wanted so desperately. Was this the road we had taken then? It didn't look familiar, there was no sense of déjà vu as my foot unwittingly eased up on the accelerator.

In a twist of synchronicity it had been the other sign, the plywood sign that had first set me on the journey that would finally lead to that childhood holiday at the beach. Everything had changed for me after the other children had burst into my room and dragged me, terrified, into the corridor. The security my room had afforded me had vanished in that moment. I felt vulnerable, more alone than ever and I knew then that somehow I had to get away.

Occasionally people would visit the home. Foster parents looking for a child to take away with them and I had often wondered what magic these people possessed. I would sit on the sidelines and watch as the care kids transformed into kind, happy creatures. They would hug each other and laugh out loud, putting on a great show of perfection so that they would be chosen, the best sweets in the candy shop.

Up until then I had never pretended. I didn't want to be taken away or how would my mother be able to find me? I would sit watchful and silent, scowling at the couples who came to make their choices and praying that they would take away with them the worst of my tormentors. I sat in the furthest corner and pulled faces, turning my back if their eyes dared to fall upon me. I knew what I looked like to them, a skinny waif of a child with a mass of tangled dark hair and eyes like bruises. I was never chosen.

The lessons I learned that caused my change of heart were painful ones. I knew that there was no point hanging on and waiting for a mother that had forgotten all about me, I knew that the bullying would continue until I found a way to end it. And I knew that from that moment on I would be just like everyone else, I would pretend until finally it would be my turn, the door of the home would close behind me and I would be safe.

I practiced smiles in my little mirror for when visitors came. I brushed my hair and held it back with hair bands or ribbons so it didn't fall over my eyes. I did what I could to look like happiness came naturally but it sat awkwardly on me, a mask that didn't quite fit. I tried anyway.

Not long after that some visitors came. The other children sniggered when I walked into the room, elbowing each other and pointing at me. I was wearing my best dress and had put a pink ribbon, lopsided, in my newly tidy hair.

It turned out to be a waste of time. The middle-aged couple with frown lines between their eyes and brown clothes were only interested in boys. They left without a name to pick up later and nobody seemed sorry about that.

One of the older boys, Michael, cornered me after dinner in the TV room. At eleven he was three years older than me. He had mousy brown hair that poked out in every direction and a face like a cherub, all dimples and shining innocence. The care workers seemed to adore him and thought he could do no wrong. The children knew differently. He was mean and cruel with a darkness in his eyes that frightened me sometimes. I had once seen him with his shirt off and there were circular scars across his back and on his chest. Curiosity had got the better of me and I asked him what they were. He sneered at me. 'Cigarette burns, bitch. Do you want some?' I tried to avoid him after that.

He pushed me up against the wall and held me there with a rough, grazed hand.

'What the hell were you doing today? You think you've got a chance of getting out of here, freak?' He laughed and it spread around the room like a disease. But as the laughter washed over me, and my cheeks burned with fire fed by humiliation, I felt my teeth clench. I felt my fear take a step backwards, becoming smaller. I lifted my head, tilting my chin back until I stared him right in the eyes.

'I'll be out of here before you will, shithead.'

There was a sharp intake of breath from the others and his eyebrows rose into his fringe. He pulled his fist back and I didn't look away, didn't flinch from the impending blow, I just stared right at him and saw something falter as he glared at my defiance. As he brought his hand towards me he opened it. Instead of the punch I tensed against he delivered two small slaps onto my cheek, patronising and stinging but not what I had expected. He slowly lowered his arm and his eyes slid from mine, the room was silent. I pushed him aside and walked from the room feeling that in some way I had scored a small victory.

As it later turned out, I was right. It was a Saturday and I had done my chores, as we all had. I'd had laundry duty, which I hated, collecting bed sheets that smelt of ammonia and sweat and had stains that I tried to keep away from my skin. After lunch, we were told to get our glad rags on and the house became a hive of activity, excited chatter and sounds of drawers slamming coming from the upstairs rooms.

It was the third time we had had visitors since the incident in my room and I was no less determined to find a way out. I didn't sleep too well anymore. The first people had been the brown clothed couple that left empty handed. The second had been a young couple that had been totally charmed by a little four year old called Astrid. All the children were unhappy about that one because Astrid had only been at the home for a couple of months and it seemed so unfair. I understood it though. She was a sweet thing with confusion in her big brown eyes. She looked lost and afraid so who wouldn't want to take her away from that house?

We all stood around the dining room fidgeting and looking like we didn't quite fit when they came in. I still kept my place in the far corner but at least I looked at the grown-ups when they arrived which was more than I had done before. Diane and Richard Parks were in their forties. He was a round jolly man who kept his arm around his wife's back. She had a cloud of greying blonde hair that was cut above her shoulders and didn't quite sit down flat. As she looked at us all, her bottom lip pushed out ever so slightly, as if she couldn't believe we all had no-one to love us.

I smiled at that bottom lip and as my lips

curved up her eyes met mine and she smiled in return. She turned and whispered something into her husband's ear and made her way over to me. I felt the eyes of the other children like needles and glanced away as she approached. Mrs Parks crouched down until she was in my line of vision.

'What's your name, sweetie?' She smelt nice, like sunny days, and when I answered her I wanted to beg her to take me with her. I told God that I would eat all of my vegetables and do all of my homework if Mrs Parks took me away. Please, please, please, Amen.

I was told the next day that I would be going with them to their home in Marham, a village a few miles away that I'd never heard of. I packed my pitiful belongings over and over again while I waited and put a wedge firmly under my bedroom door every night. It felt as though it took forever but finally the paperwork was all completed and I could leave. I never saw the house again.

It seemed a lifetime later that I sat in my car staring at the sign, wondering what would happen if I took that road. Would my life unravel as it had then? Would everything change? A blaring horn dragged me back to the present and I realised I had slowed the car almost to a crawl. I held up my hand in apology as the other car pulled past me. I put my foot down, keeping the car pointed towards Winscombe, towards home.

26

Lacey

She sits at the table. The dim light pushes against the window and the bare branches of the trees beyond whisper winter into her ears. She feels the chill in the room, sees it in the breath that blossoms in front of her lips and she thinks that this winter will be particularly harsh and cruel; even here in Devon, where the snow rarely falls and the lambs are sometimes born in time to greet the New Year.

There is a noise near the door and she jumps towards it, startled. Her mother is alive again and she walks into the room, looking younger than she has seen her for some time. Her hands are full of cutlery and the silverware clatters against the table before they are steadied. A deep breath tells the tale of her mother's nervousness. It quivers a path through her airways leaving her shoulders rigid, her hands shaking. Her mother's eyes steal quick glimpses towards the door and she flinches at the wind, at nothing, before she turns and leaves the room.

She sits and waits, staring at the grain of the table, at the darker furrows that make her think of the farmers' fields in springtime. She follows the marks with short practical fingernails and watches as decades of wax and polish fold black and tacky beneath the edge of her thumbnail.

She can hear the clock ticking and the faint sound of her mother's trembling sigh from beyond the doorway.

She swings her legs back and forth, one after the other, feeling her feet snag against the floor and the hem of her dress. She runs her hands down her thighs and thinks, it must be Sunday because she is wearing her best dress with the lace and the embroidered flowers.

She wonders where her father is but realises he must have been called out to someone because of the way her mother glanced at the door and looked worried. She begins to sing quietly to herself,

'One, two, three, four, five, once I caught a fish alive. Six, seven, eight, nine, te . . . ' She looks up and sees that her mother is standing in the doorway, her shadowy eyes marching across the room and the reproach in them chases the words back into silence. She thinks, 'swing my legs, scratch at the table, but don't sing'. Is it because her voice is an alien thing, here where words are spare and never more than practical? How difficult it is to remember everything. There are so many rules, so many things she can do, so many things she can't do, so many things she can only do when no-one will see her, like laugh and skip and breathe lightly.

The front door opens and slams suddenly and she sees the aftershock engulf her mother, who flinches away briefly before she rushes to greet him and take his bag. She snaps her eyes away from the hall and back to the table, feels her spine become straighter, her stomach pull inwards, her legs become still. She holds her hands together demurely in her lap and does not glance up as he comes in. So many rules. She barely even breathes as he walks to the table, pulls out his chair and sits down, every movement exaggerated as though he were too big, too important for the space he finds himself in.

Does she feel his eyes upon her? For a moment there is the sensation of a spider web touching lightly across her cheek. She wonders if she has imagined it as she fights the urge to see if both of her feet can touch the floor at the same time. She wonders if she has become invisible, if her father even realises she is in the room with him, in her pretty Sunday dress and with her dirty thumbnail. Or is there merely an empty space where she thinks she is?

Her mother once again bustles into the room, shaky and desperate, trying to do everything right and yet failing simply by being there, by being anything other than still and perfect. She places his plate in front of him and then waits beyond his right shoulder as he looks at it. The silence becomes thicker, heavier and she feels the three of them push against it, her mother's hand fluttering at her chest as if the stillness is no more than a fly that she can waft away.

She can see from her end of the table the curling edges of the bacon, the shiny patches where it has begun to dry as they waited. She can see that the food looks unappetising, old and she knows that her mother sees it too, she sees it in the way her lips move in quiet contrition. She

123

wants to tell her mother that it is not her fault, that the blame lies with the patient that called him away from his freshly cooked breakfast, or it's her father's fault for being so unreasonable, cruel. But she doesn't, she sits within her hidden void and wills him not to notice her.

She stays statue still as the plate is snatched up from the table. She doesn't flinch as it flies just above her head and shatters against the wall. She tries not to hear the high pitch of her mother's fear as he takes hold of her arm and drags her from the room. She feeds the lace of her hem through trembling fingers and hums quietly to herself, as quietly as she can so they do not hear her.

She hears heavy footsteps, the dragging slip of her mother's feet against the boards of the stairs. There is the sharp sting of flesh on flesh, palm on face, a muffled cry of pain. She hears the throwing down, the squeaky sound from the bed, her mother's submission.

After a short time she gets to her feet and goes to the cupboard under the stairs to fetch a brush and as quietly as she can she cleans up the crockery, the grease stains, the ruined food. By the time she hears footsteps on the stairs again she is sat back in her seat as though she never moved at all. He walks into the room and she forces herself to be still, to not react to his presence in any way. He does not look at her.

She sees his eyes move to the space where his plate hit the wall, to the floor below it and all the while she keeps her gaze on the emptiness of the wall opposite her. She wonders if she will be punished too, simply for being there. Perhaps she left a dirty spot on the wall, a sliver of porcelain on the floor. It seems forever that they remain still and silent.

She feels the beginnings of a tremor in her right leg and the more she thinks of it the harder it is to keep still. She closes her eyes and concentrates, her legs are the trunk of a tree, they will not bend or move in any way, they will not betray her and make him see she is there. When it seems under control, she opens her eyes and he has gone. She did not hear him leave the room and has to look around her carefully before she is convinced that she is indeed alone. She feels her shoulders sag, her heart calm. In that moment she is so relieved that he did not see her, that she is the invisible one.

★   ★   ★

Later, when they go to church, her mother does not go with them. She imagines the darkened form hunched beneath the bed covers crying silent tears against the cloth. She imagines the bruises painted across her mother's skin. She sits beside him in their pew at the front and wonders if he feels her loathing for him, wonders if she despises him enough that it will take tangible form that will billow from her and engulf him.

At the end of the service she overhears him talking to the vicar, kind Father Alan who gives her a strange, sad smile if he happens to catch her eye. They speak of nothing in particular and their words blur and run into each other as she stands statue still beside them. But then she hears her father say, 'One of her turns, you know.' And she raises her eyes from the ground long enough to see the vicar nod sagely, she sees him turn in her direction and meet her gaze and behind the sympathy she can see shadows and suspicion. For the briefest of moments he places his hand lightly upon the top of her head, a blessing to comfort her, and she feels tears threatening to spill as her father turns and begins to walk away. Quickly she catches up with him, wanting him to have no excuse to punish her.

One step, two steps, three steps. She watches the ground as she walks and doesn't look up. The tips of her toes come into her line of sight and then disappear, get replaced, reappear. She sees the lace of her skirt sway back and forth, like a bell. She feels the tension in the back of her neck as her chin grazes her chest. She knows that later, when she is alone in her room, she will feel it like a knot between her shoulder blades.

But she has no choice. He is watching her and she dare not give him reason to punish her, she dare not let her eyes rest on anyone who may be passing. She remembers a time before when she dared to break the rules, when he caught her. She remembers the punishment, the fear; she remembers that for days every movement reminded her not to do it again. So she keeps her eyes on the ground and the rest of the world passes her by unnoticed.

She sees the rough surface of the lane and glances slightly, ever so slightly to the side. His feet keep pace with hers, she sees the shine of his shoes and there is pride in each step. He clears his throat and she thinks that maybe he is about to speak to her, she waits for whatever harsh words, whatever orders or censure may come but there is nothing else. She thinks that maybe it was just the dust from the lane catching in his throat; the summer has baked the ground hard and dry and the dust dances in the sunlight. When she breathes in she can taste it on her tongue.

She frowns and becomes confused, surely it was winter that morning, when her breath clouded from her lips and a chill was in the air. She stares at the dry, dusty ground and fights the urge to run as fast as she can so that she is home quicker and doesn't have to walk on the strange surface that changes in an instant. She keeps her steps measured and even, more afraid of the man at her side than the rapidly changing season.

One step, two steps, three steps. She counts them in her head as she watches her feet. She has done this so often that she knows exactly where she is. She knows when to turn, she knows when to bend beneath a low branch. She reaches for the gate and holds it open for him before walking up the path slightly ahead of him, and she does the same with the front door. She sees the grass growing between cracks in the path.

Inside when the door is safely closed behind them she finally lifts her head and looks around, seeing that she is alone. The house is silent. Catching sight of herself in the mirror she gasps and her hand flutters to her chest. She turns from her reflection and looks around at the empty room hearing nothing but the sound of her own startled breath. She puts her face in her palms and starts to cry, huge racking sobs that force through the silence as she remembers that she is old now, and her father is long dead.

27

Rachel

By the time Lacey knocked on the door on Saturday I was already in a flap about the food and Jane had calmly taken over in the kitchen. One side of her mouth curved up in a wry smile, which alternated with a look of bafflement at my ignorance.

'Honest to God, how can anyone be so crap?'

'I studied art not cooking, remember! You don't moan too much when you get a nice little commission.'

She smiled at me over the smooth table surface and handed me a bundle of cutlery. 'Here you go, take some of your artistic talent and make the table look pretty. I'm sure even you can manage that one.'

I huffed in mock anger and stuck my tongue out, 'I don't know why I invited you,' I said sulkily and she laughed.

'You didn't, I invited myself!'

The previous night had passed too quickly as we sat into the early hours. We talked over a bottle of wine about work, which for most people would be off limits on a Friday night, but not in Jane's case. She was passionate about what she did, her love of art matched only by her genuine interest in people and it showed in every syllable that she uttered. I wasn't immune to her excitement and as we talked I could feel the lethargy of the previous weeks evaporating into excitement at the thought of picking up my brushes and getting started.

She told me about her latest discovery, a sixteen year old boy that she had met at an art exhibition. Taylor, she explained, did the most amazing abstract art. As a child he had been diagnosed with ADHD and prescribed Ritalin. What he found hard was that he could only really let himself go and paint the way he did if he stopped taking his medication. He fought a daily battle and felt that in the end he was always disappointing someone, whether it was himself, his teachers or his exhausted and desperate parents.

Jane thought it was this angst that gave him his edge; it seethed across the canvas. She wanted to nurture him, to give him the platform he deserved to show his work. But she worried that by doing so she would be encouraging the internal battle within him. By the time we headed up the stairs to bed, slightly tipsy and a little unsteady, Jane was no closer to making a decision about Taylor and I had been no help whatsoever.

As Jane filled mismatched cocktail glasses with pre-shredded lettuce I went to answer the door. Lacey had obviously made an effort to tone down her usual dress sense. Instead of the normal riot of clashing colours, she had opted for only one, though in several different shades. Her dark purple skirt skimmed the ground, the hall light reflecting from the tiny mirrors sewn into the material. She wore a pale lilac tunic that reached over her generous hips and was tied in at the waist by a purple scarf. Her hair was held back by a glittery lilac headband. A fortune-teller in a carnival tent. The only thing missing was gold hoop earrings and a crystal ball. She looked amazing and I told her so.

'Thank you,' she muttered, her voice barely there. She seemed ill at ease, a little unsure. She glanced nervously over my shoulder and I placed a hand gently on her arm, leading her through into the kitchen.

'Jane, this is Lacey.'

From where Jane was bent over, peering intently into the oven, she stood and turned in one graceful, fluid motion. Her eyes briefly scanned Lacey from head to toes before her face lifted into a huge smile. 'You look fabulous!' She took the distance between them in three short strides and wrapped her arms around Lacey's shoulders, kissing her on both cheeks, 'It's a pleasure to meet you.'

I saw the faint blush spread across Lacey's face and after a second, her own arms, held stiff at her sides came up and she lightly returned the hug. Jane looked genuinely delighted at the image before her and as she lowered her arms and stepped back, still smiling, I picked up a bottle of wine from the ice bucket on the table and offered to pour.

Over the starter, Jane once more returned to the dilemma of Taylor, this time directing her comments at Lacey and asking her opinion.

'What does the boy want to do?'

'He wants to paint,' Jane replied, 'he's a typical artist in that he only seems to feel alive when he is working. I think that for him painting is an escape from his difficulties, even when it is his difficulties that he is painting.'

'Then let him paint. If it is where his heart lies then he absolutely has to go for it. He can spend a lifetime thinking what if and what would that achieve? If he stops his medication and it all goes horribly wrong then he has lost nothing but a few months of difficulty. But if he doesn't stop his medication and he doesn't paint, he could spend the rest of his life unhappy. In the end it's nobody's choice but his.'

Jane slid her thumbnail between her lips and bit down on it lightly, something she always did when she was deep in thought. 'You're right, of course. Maybe I should try harder to see it from his point of view instead of getting all maternal and protective. I just don't want to be responsible for making life difficult for him.'

'It sounds to me like his life is already difficult but that's not down to you, it's his disorder that causes that. And maybe it won't be as a bad as you think, the result could end up being the best thing that's ever happened to him. You can live a life without risk, lovey, but it seems to be that you risk not living at all if you do that.'

I could see on Jane's face how delighted she was with Lacey, it showed in the warmth of her eyes when she looked at the older woman. 'That's wise advice, thank you.'

Lacey's eyes moved to her wine glass and her

hand followed, lightly holding the stem as she pulled it towards her mouth and took a noisy gulp. 'It's not wisdom, I just think it's better to have regrets about a wrong decision than to live a lifetime wondering what could have been.'

'You sound like you're talking from experience there?' I said.

'Oh yes, I am. Maybe when you get to my age you just have more time to think about the things you could have done differently, too many opportunities to ask yourself what if.'

I knew what she meant, the what if game was one that I played with myself more often than was healthy. Jane pushed her chair back and began to clear away the empty dishes to make space for the main course. The conversation paused as she began to dish up, but it was a pleasant silence without awkwardness or discomfort.

I refilled the three glasses and Lacey smiled at me from her seat as Jane brought the salad bowl to the table, along with a serving dish full of vegetables and potatoes. When we all had our plates in front of us we began to help ourselves.

'So,' Jane began, 'Rachel tells me you have a son.'

Lacey's eyes softened and she smiled, 'Yes I do, his name is Charlie.' She looked like any proud mother talking about her child. It made me wonder again about my conversation with Martha in the churchyard. Was it simply that she was mistaken about this, that she didn't know Lacey well enough? It didn't seem very likely in a village this small but it wasn't unheard of for people to keep big secrets. Who knew what went on behind closed doors?

'And your husband, is he still with you?'

Shadows leapt into her eyes and I was fascinated watching the play of emotions across her face. It was open and easy to read, as though she had never learnt the art of hiding how she felt, or had never been bothered to try. Her shoulders sagged a little as though a sudden weight had pushed them downwards and the mood in the room lost some of its lightness. 'I never married.'

'You didn't marry Charlie's father? That must have been incredibly difficult for you, things being what they were.'

Lacey was silent for a while after Jane spoke. She seemed to be looking inwards, and I could sense that Jane's reluctance to interrupt her matched my own. After a time Lacey's eyes focused again in the present and she looked self conscious to find two pairs of eyes on her. She gave us both a tentative smile. 'I'm sorry, I've never actually talked about this before, not to anyone. It was such a huge secret you see and nobody has ever been interested enough to ask before, I suppose. After all this time I'm not even sure if it's a story I could tell.'

'Well I'd like to hear it if you can.' I smiled encouragingly at her, hoping that she would talk to us. For some reason I felt a strange sense of responsibility for the sadness of her words, for the lonely picture she had painted of herself. Across the table from me I saw Jane smile in reassurance as well.

Lacey was silent again as we looked at her sat between us. She gave a slight shrug and nodded. 'Alright then. I'm sorry if it's a little boring for you both, like I said it's a bit of a long story.'

28

Lacey

She remembers. Looking back she can see a thread pulled tight and leading into before. This story . . . this story is different, tantalising, compelling. Because this story she remembers with clarity. It is an anchored ship in a sea whipped by storms and for her it has held her safe. Warmed and comforted her when the tempest rages and she cannot remember where she stands.

These memories are linear, formulaic. They stand apart, separate from the others, they are proud, strong. There is a start, a middle and an end like all good stories. But it is not a good end, not for her. It is a tragedy this tale, a tragic end that tears her heart from her body.

All these years later, when everything else has faded and gone, it is that tragedy that reminds her how to feel. It tells her that she loved once, that she was loved. She wonders if she can tell this story and do it justice without it ripping into her. Without her feeling those emotions expand outwards beyond her until they envelop the two faces that watch her with calm expectation; until they are all swept away.

But even as she thinks this, even as she thinks that her life is mist surrounding the island of this one collection of memories, she knows that she

136

will try. She knows that she will share it. After all this time she wants someone else, someone other than her to know that once she was loved, that once someone looked at her as if she were the only other person in the world. And so she begins.

⋆ ⋆ ⋆

She had named her son after his father, Charlie senior, and she had known from the very first moment she laid eyes on the man that she would love him. Perhaps she had known even before that. She remembered overhearing a conversation between her parents about him, about how he had come down from Exeter to stay on his uncle's farm and work, because his heart was too weak for him to go and fight in the war. As soon as her mother said his name it was like a bell ringing in her head, ever so faint but definitely there. At the time she hadn't paid it any attention, barely even noticed it. But afterwards, after that first moment she looked upon him, she remembered it and just knew he was for her.

She couldn't say what it was about him, even now. She would wonder about it, try to think what it could have been. He wasn't good looking, not in any conventional sense. He was tall, a little pale and thin, with big hands that looked like they had outgrown the rest of him somewhere along the way. His face was long and slightly lopsided and his hair was crazy, no matter how short it was cut there was always a little tuft that stood up at the back.

But to her there was something special about him. He had the deepest blue eyes she had ever seen, with laughter lines at the corners even though he was only young. Those lines had made him look as though he never stopped smiling. He was warm and gentle and all the girls seemed to love him a little.

He had been a flirt. He loved making all the girls blush and she had hated it. From the moment she fell for him, that first time they met, she found it so hard to see him reduce the local girls to giggles. Years later, when he existed nowhere but in her memory she would understand it more. There were so few men around then, only the old and the sick, the young boys not yet grown into themselves. It was no wonder that all the girls loved him. He had brought a little sunshine into all of their lives. He seemed so worldly-wise compared to the country girls even though he had lived only a few miles away, his self-awareness appealed to her, she found him interesting, exotic.

She was set apart from the others because of her father and what he did for a living. She had been a pretty thing back then. Her hair, when it was down, was thick and dark, hanging just above her slender waist. When all the other girls started copying the city styles and having their hair cut off to their shoulders and curled into rolls, she had left hers alone. And she never wore make-up, her father would never have allowed it. He said that make-up made women look like painted dolls or whores.

The only time Charlie ever seemed to be

serious was when he spoke to her, and she had taken that as a great insult. He never seemed to turn on the charm if she was there, which was rarely. His tone became more serious, and he looked at her respectfully because she was the Doctor's daughter. She could never be seen as one of his pretty girls. She desperately wanted him to notice her the way she had noticed him, but he seemed indifferent to her and that hurt.

He had been turning on the charm for Rosemary Westcott one day when Lacey had raised her eyes and seen them. He still had that dopey smile on his face when she had walked up with the apples she'd just been picking. He turned towards her and the smile just slipped away, it cut her to the bone that she wasn't even worthy of a smile. She felt the threat of tears behind her eyes and thought that she could either cry or lose her temper. Before she had given it much thought she raised her hand and slapped him, good and hard right across his cheek. Rosemary had looked at her in shock as Lacey turned and walked away, her eyes on the ground with tears spilling over.

Later, Charlie would tell her that when she slapped him he knew for sure that one day he would marry her. He would explain that the only reason he never flirted with her was because she was the one who mattered. He felt awkward around her because she was something precious, too precious to make light of.

Her father hated him. Thinking that he was a good for nothing layabout and that he should be fighting like all the other young men, despite his weak heart. She found it difficult to understand how a doctor could judge him so harshly for something he couldn't help, but then her father was often cruel and thoughtless. He wouldn't have cared that Charlie felt a failure because he wasn't out there fighting with all his friends. He didn't care that the young man worked so hard on the farm, as if he were trying to make up for his weaknesses by helping the village as much as he could.

Her father thought him a coward, but to her there was nothing cowardly about him, in her eyes he was brave and strong-minded, even though his body let him down. She knew that if he could have lied his way into battle, he would have, but her father wouldn't see it and always spoke down to him, greeting him with barely a nod and a frown of disapproval.

They had both known that he would never give them his blessing. Charlie would never be good enough for the Doctor's daughter. And so they met in secret, barely acknowledging each other in the street when they passed so no-one knew how they felt. She found it tortuous seeing him talking to other girls and feeling unable to go up to them and say 'Leave him alone, he's mine!'

She saw the looks they gave her, she knew that they all thought her a little odd because she barely looked at him. She shrugged off their stares because Charlie loved her and one day they would know it, one day she would marry him and their opinion of her wouldn't matter anymore.

Her father had always been protective, possessive even, but in those days when she wasn't doing household chores or going with him on his visits, she was out in the fields and hedgerows collecting food. She would go gathering berries, nuts, even dandelion leaves and roots, fresh eggs from their hens. The outbreak of war had given her a strange kind of freedom that she was unused to, she could go out without a chaperone as long as she did as she was told and came home with a full basket. It made it easier for her on the days she met Charlie.

They would meet at the top end of the field, near the stream. The branches hid them from sight and few people went there anyway, even then. They would sit by the water and hold hands, sometimes talking nonstop, sometimes not talking at all. It was simply enough to be together away from prying eyes. He told her all about his life in Exeter, where he lived with his mother who was still struggling to get over losing his father so young to a heart attack.

She felt a real shiver of terror when he told her that. She knew Charlie's heart was bad too; would she lose him the same way? She couldn't imagine her world without him in it. He had given her a taste of what it was to be loved, to be heard. He had filled a space that had left her not quite so cold, not quite so alone. How would she ever cope if that void came back now?

It's strange what hindsight does. If only she had known then that there would come a time when she envied his mother the time she had shared with his father, even though it was all too short.

She hated the weekends more than anything else. These were the times that she would sit in the darkness of her room and pray and hope that he would come back to her, that all would be well. At weekends he'd get on his bike and ride the eight miles to Exeter to spend some time with his mother and take his turn on fire watch. There'd been a few bombs dropped on the city, and the community left behind were taking it in turns to watch out for incendiary bombs, to put them out before they could spread.

During the week they would see each other for as long as they were able to without drawing suspicion. On the occasions when it was pouring with rain they would meet beneath the sagging roof of the old stable in the field near her house. She could still remember, even now, the feeling of her hand in his. The roughness of his skin against her palm, his hand folded around hers like a big paw. She loved hearing him talk but she loved the silence too, it was comfortable and simple. She found it so easy being together, so hard being apart. She would gather up her basket and head back across the field as Charlie jumped across the stream and headed out the other way, so no-one would see them leaving from the same place. He knew what her father was like, a dour, proud man who believed women had their place and it was where he told them to be.

Charlie was protecting her from that, in his way. He wanted to be able to approach her father and ask for her hand. She knew that it would never be accepted. No matter how many hours Charlie would spend wracking his brains trying to think how he could impress her father, Lacey knew there would never be a chance of success. She doubted that even a Prince would have been acceptable.

One day by the stream, when the day was cold but clear, they sat and talked about nothing and everything. He had woven a little ring out of grass, a messy thing that started coming loose immediately. He had taken his time over it, a little frown on his face as he concentrated to get it perfect. When he was satisfied, he had solemnly got down on one knee, taken her hand in his and asked her to spend the rest of her life with him.

She had cried and felt foolish. It was what she wanted more than anything, for Charlie to be hers and for everyone to know it. No more sneaking around, no more pretending. He slipped the woven grass onto her finger and she told him that yes, she would marry him.

He had stood then, a smile lighting his whole face. He took both of her hands in his, pulling her to him and kissed her, deeply. It felt as though there was nobody in the world but the two of them. In that moment she forgot about her father, the war, everything but him. They stood in a little bubble and nothing else existed beyond that.

He led her to the little stable and pulled her into his arms again, kissing her long and deep. She was lost in him completely; it was magical and perfect, just how it was always meant to be. She had felt invincible then, as though nothing could ever stand in their way. The love she felt for him was so strong that surely her father would see it when he looked at her, and realise that this was meant to be, he would give them his blessing, perhaps even be happy for them.

She did not remember how they went from standing to lying on the floor, wrapped up in each other. At that point everything went cloudy. There was a vague memory of noise that made her wince, of hasty movement, of a twisting and turning and a sharp stab of fear. But she couldn't remember any sense of wrongdoing.

Looking back, those moments seemed surreal and indistinct. When Charlie moved over her it felt like the most natural thing in the world. They were together, how they were always meant to be. Afterwards they had cried, kissing each other's tears away and tasting the salt. They were silent and she didn't want to speak because she was so afraid that if she did, it would burst that bubble and the outside world would be allowed back in. She wanted to stay in that moment forever, to grasp it tight and hold it safe. But slowly the realisation came that she couldn't, she had to get up and go home and the thought crushed her, squeezing the air from her lungs.

Charlie reached up, gently pulling twigs and leaves from her hair, brushing at her clothes until she was presentable, though she wondered at the point of it all. She was a woman now and surely all the world would see it, whether she wanted them to or not.

He held her in his arms, as tender as could be and told her that he would see her on Monday. She had forgotten that it was Friday and he was riding to Exeter. For the first time she had begged him not to go, she worried about his heart as he rode; she worried about the bombs, about everything. The bombings had increased in the city towards the end of April and she was so afraid for him, even though it had been quiet for days and the worst seemed to be over. Maybe it was just that every time he went away from her she felt a little part of her paused, until he returned safely.

'I'll be back on Monday and I will come and see your father and ask him for your hand in marriage. I love you, Lacey Carmichael, I have loved you from the moment I first saw you and I will love you till the end of time and that's a promise.' He kissed her then and he left. She stood in the stable and heard his footsteps as he jumped the stream and walked away.

How many times had she lived that day over and over in her mind? That one moment of perfection that she locked away inside to keep her company in the hundreds, thousands of nights that would follow.

The weekend disappeared, passing by at a horribly slow pace. She thought of him constantly, alternating between fear and excitement at the thought of him approaching her father. She had prayed and prayed that her father would accept them, all the while believing, knowing, deep down that he never would. She had vowed then that if he refused to accept them, then they would run away, go somewhere, anywhere, just as long as they would be together. She even went so far as to imagine their escape, imagining how she would get outside without notice and where they would go. At least she had some semblance of a plan and it comforted her in some small way, she would never have to be without him again.

That Sunday afternoon she could feel the butterflies taking flight in her stomach. Wondering what time he would set off from Exeter, wondering when he would be safe back on the farm, and what time he would come calling the following day.

She didn't know then, that early that morning there had been air raids in Exeter. She had slept soundly the night before, deeper than usual and she had heard nothing in the skies. She always wondered afterwards whether those were the reasons he stayed an extra night. Did he decide to return the following morning in case he was needed? She was sure the unsettling noises from the sky would have frightened his sensitive grieving mother, so perhaps he had stayed for her. These were the things she would never know the answers to, though she did find out later that Charlie had been on fire duty on that Sunday night.

She didn't know what woke her that same night, just that she was thrust from dreams to waking instantly with her heart hammering in her chest. She went to her window and looked out, it was a beautiful, clear night, the moon looked to be just beyond full, but there was something strange about the colour of the sky. She raced as silently as she could down the stairs, trying not to wake her parents as she went.

She ran into the garden and stood in the chilly night air in just her nightclothes. Looking northwards she could see in the distance that the sky was glowing orange with dense clouds hanging above it all. She was mesmerised, not even aware at first that her parents had come to stand behind her and that they were also staring into the night sky. Exeter was burning. They stood helplessly watching as the smoke rose miles away, filling the sky until it looked like the worst kind of storm coming.

'God help them.' Her mother's voice small and filled with emotion, broke the silence and she looked at her with tears on her face.

'What God?' she said and turned and ran into the house leaving them looking after her in the strange light. She ran to her room praying over and over again that Charlie was safe and that he was back at the farm, that he had left Exeter when he was supposed to. He would turn up the next day and ask her father for her hand in marriage and her father would say yes and she would get her happy ever after just the way she was supposed to, the way she had dreamt it.

She had sat up in her bed for hours, arms clutched around her knees, rocking slowly backwards and forwards. The night seemed everlasting and sometime, in the darkest hours, she had felt him leave her. She never could explain it, not now and not then but she felt it happen over and over even though so many years had passed. It was an absence. She felt it and she just knew. Charlie was gone.

She didn't sleep that night, the sun came up and her eyes felt full of sand. She rose and began her chores, moving like a zombie through the hours. And all the time there was part of her that was waiting and hoping. Perhaps she had been wrong the night before; perhaps it was fear that had made her feel his absence so sharply.

She waited and waited, making excuses not to venture too far from the house. She spent time out in the garden tending to the vegetable beds and the hens, her eyes constantly looking to the gate, willing it to open. When she went into the house she looked to the windows as often as she could without raising suspicion and the minutes passed like hours as she hoped and prayed and waited. Her parents said nothing to her about her strange behaviour and she was glad of it. Perhaps they had blamed her strange behaviour on the events of the night before; they saw her as a tender girl who would have been shocked by what they had seen. And of course she was, though not for the reasons they thought.

Slowly the time passed and the hour got later and later. If Charlie didn't come then it could only mean one thing, that he never made it out of the city. She didn't imagine that he was in a hospital getting better somewhere.

She felt cold and empty, her heart a lead weight in her chest. She couldn't feel his presence anymore; he was dead and she knew it and couldn't even cry. She had crawled upstairs to her room and lay down on the bed. She stayed there for days and days, not crying, not feeling, not sleeping, just a shell with nothing left inside. Her parents came and went like ghosts in the shadows. She was barely even aware of them, even when mother tried to coerce her into eating. She wanted them to leave her alone. Perhaps if she lay there long enough she would die too.

It was a long time later that she learned what had happened. Twenty Luftwaffe bombers had flown up the river and dropped incendiaries on the city. Charlie had been on fire watch with several others near the street where his mother lived. The fires had burned out of control and Charlie and several others were trapped by the blaze. Only one of them made it out. The others all died along with Charlie's mother.

If only he had listened to her and not gone that weekend. It was his sense of duty that killed him, he couldn't fight in the war so he had done what he could. It seemed such a small thing to him, so trivial, nowhere near enough. But it was too much. He died for it and left her alone to face life without him. His death would be lost among hundreds of others, just one more casualty of a hateful war.

There was a memorial service for him in the local church. The local girls all sniffed into their hankies as though they had a right to. She had sat on the fringes next to her parents with dry eyes and a broken heart, now never able to say that he had been hers. They glanced at her throughout the service and saw her blank expression and lack of emotion. She saw the raised eyebrows, the questions in their eyes. She knew they thought of her as cold but then it wouldn't have come as any surprise to them. After all Charlie and Lacey had never really spoken to each other and she was the one girl who didn't get to receive his attention and his laughter. If only they had known the truth, if only they had seen for themselves the way he looked at her when nobody else was around. Now they would never know what she knew and she would grieve forever in silence as they, in their ignorance, believed their tears to be just and their feelings more important than hers.

She kept the grass ring he had given her, pressed between a folded piece of linen. It grew dry and brittle over the course of time until she was scared to look at it anymore, in case it broke apart and crumbled into dust.

She had thought that apart from the little ring, all she had were memories. But after a while she realised she was wrong. She had been so ill with grief that she hadn't been eating and had lost a lot of weight, her curves vanishing and her face becoming pinched and drawn. Her mother treated her like the most fragile thing imaginable and she wondered if on some level her mother sensed what she was going through. Maybe she had her suspicions about the loss of her lover because her mother was certainly more gentle and kind with her for quite a while afterwards. Her father thought she had some strange ailment and would get her to swallow mouthfuls of some foul tonic he had concocted. Her stomach rebelled against it and would gripe and clench afterwards, though she was never actually sick.

Through the perpetual fog she lived in, Lacey started to realise that she was feeling stranger even than her poor diet should allow for. She was exhausted all the time and her shrinking breasts felt sore and tender. It was only when she counted back over the previous two months that she realised she had missed a couple of periods. Lost as she was in her feelings and desolation she hadn't even noticed. She was horrified, scared, exhilarated when she realised what it meant. Some part of Charlie had stayed with her after all and the moment when she realised she was carrying his baby, she clawed back a little of her former happiness. Suddenly she had a little hope for the future. He hadn't left her entirely alone.

29

Rachel

The wall clock ticking gently against a background of silence pulled me away from the images conjured up by her words and I realised that Lacey had stopped speaking. I glanced up and met Jane's eyes across the table and saw reflected in them the poignancy of the story Lacey had shared. I understood. I too was moved to the verge of tears by the tragedy that Lacey had gone through sixty years before.

She stared down at the table, her eyes half closed as though unaware of what was in front of her. She looked sad, yet strong and proud and I didn't know what to say, what words would fit into the silence around us. Jane's hand reached across the table to take Lacey's and I saw the older woman start, before glancing around her and shaking her head a little as though to displace the memories that had risen to the surface. For a moment no-one said anything. Slowly, as if being woken from a trance, Lacey's expression lifted and she looked from one of us to the other, her face solemn and still.

'Thank you, both of you, for listening to me. You know I've never told anyone that before. It's lived inside me all this time. I wasn't even sure I would get the words out but now I feel so much better, so much lighter. It's as if I've just lost fifty pounds.' She began to giggle. A light, girlish sound that was surprising and contagious enough to break through my reverie and curl my own lips into an answering smile. I felt my own laughter bubble through my chest and catch in my throat before spilling out to join Lacey's. How easy it was to laugh with her.

Before long Jane had joined in too and the three of us sat there laughing and holding hands until tears ran down our faces and I no longer knew — could no longer tell — if they were tears for the tragedy of Lacey's story or simply a welcome escape from it.

When the tears had been wiped, the glasses had been replenished and the dessert placed on the table, Jane looked at Lacey with curiosity.

'How come you've never told anyone about Charlie before?'

Lacey scooped up a big spoonful of pavlova and chewed on it with obvious delight before she answered. 'I've always been something of a social outcast as far as the others in the village were concerned. My father was as far removed from the stereotype of a friendly village doctor as he could be.' Lacey chewed at the corner of her mouth, as though the question had puzzled her, had caused her to think more deeply than she wanted to about this. 'Back then people thought that a doctor's word was second only to the word of God, they all looked up to him. What he said went, and I suppose I was touched by that too. I think people thought I was set apart from them because of who my father was, so I never developed any close friendships like the other girls did. He was also possessive. He didn't really like me associating with what he called the riffraff. My relationship with Charlie only drove the wedge between them and me even deeper.'

'A lot of years have passed since then though. Has it never even come up in conversation?' I saw the shy young girl reappear in Lacey's expression and she began to fidget, tugging at the hem of her tunic as her eyes sought inspiration in the grain of the table.

'That's the funny thing about small village life, reputations often last longer than the person themselves. In the eyes of people who knew me, and even those who never knew me — those who weren't even born — I'm the same person I was back then. They are part of the community and I'm not. I'm just a strange old lady. Some of the children think I'm a witch.' She gave a funny little half smile and there was a world of loneliness in it, a shadow of acceptance that this was just the way things were and nothing could change that.

'What about Charlie, your son I mean, did no-one ask you about his father?'

A shadow crossed Lacey's eyes, fleeting and dark and she turned away from us, her lashes sweeping down and hiding her eyes. Her voice was little more than a whisper as she answered, 'That one is another long story Jane, definitely one for another time. I don't think I could cope with digging up those memories right now.' She lifted her head and smiled up into Jane's eyes but the shadow cast a grey wash over the laughter of moments before, 'All I can say is that people

154

only ask if they want to know, and nobody asked.'

'There must be someone surely, friends or other members of your family?'

'No family. Not anymore, it's just me now. I was an only child you see, so after my mother and father were gone there was no-one. And Charlie was the only person I loved, nobody else came close.' She brightened a little, 'I do see people occasionally. The vicar pops in every so often for a cup of tea. He's a lovely chap, bit of a mad old fruit but that's probably why we get on. And the headmaster up at the local school, he calls round too and asks me to make cakes for whatever school fête or fundraiser they've got going on. Not that he comes round only for that, he picks up shopping for me now and then and helps me out a bit. He set up my internet connection for me and showed me how to use the computer so I can order shopping and bits and bobs.'

I could see her thinking deeply about who else she had in her life, as though she wanted to dispel any impression that she had given of total isolation. But the seconds ticked by and the well came up empty. When she spoke again her voice was smaller, less certain and she glanced around her as if she were making sure no-one could hear.

'There was Albert. He was my closest friend. After his wife died we used to keep each other company a bit, cook dinner and play cards, that sort of thing. That got right up Martha's nose that did. I think she thought I was trying to take her mum's place but that was ridiculous thinking. I've never so much as looked at another man since my Charlie died.'

I explained to Jane that Martha was my landlady before turning back to Lacey. 'It must be a bit lonely since Albert died then,' I said. At least now a bit of light had been shed on Martha's obvious dislike of Lacey.

'It has been.' She turned and looked towards the open doorway, beyond to the hall, her eyes wide and her movements becoming stiff and stilted for a moment. It reminded me of rust, of clocks winding down.

'He died here,' she pointed towards the door, 'he fell, he fell down the stairs. It broke his head.' Her hand reached up to the back of her head and rubbed it gently. I looked behind me to the open doorway, imagining in the shadows an echo of the lost old man. I wasn't sure how I felt about him dying here. Maybe a little sad at the thought of it and maybe a little uneasy too. I remembered Lacey's funny little hop over the foot of the stairs and understood it now.

'He was such a lovely old chap was Albert. Spent almost his whole life loving the same woman and when she died his own life was a shell of a thing. It's like he was just biding his time after that, waiting until he could join her. I miss him all the time but I can't begrudge him that at all, they're together now. Just like me and Charlie will be one day.'

If I'd had a brush in my hand then I would have painted her expression, the purity and emotion of it. She looked determined, defiant

156

and again she reminded me of a child who had not yet learnt to hide their true feelings behind an outward pose of calm. I envied her for it and couldn't help wondering if she would stamp her foot if she got cross, or roll around on the floor screaming if she was frustrated. I wondered if that would make me like her any less and decided that it wouldn't, it would only add to the rich and interesting tapestry that Lacey unfolded before me.

30

Rachel

I know now that the barriers that we erect, the walls we build around ourselves to stop others getting in, are nothing more than smoke and mirrors. I always thought I was safe as a child when I hid behind my hair and looked away so no-one could see my eyes. I thought my every action helped weave around me a cloak of invisibility to protect me from prying eyes. Later, when I was wrenched from security and surrounded by strangers, when the family I always wanted was torn from me before I was old enough to understand why, I used silence as a weapon to push people away, to prevent them from getting too close. To me it had seemed a solid, impenetrable thing; I thought nothing could get through. But one puff of air and like magic, the barrier was gone.

Where did the air come from that left me exposed? Was it the sign on the road from Exeter, or was it Lacey's story? Perhaps it was both things combined that made me realise it might not be too late to make amends and undo the bitterness and regret.

In fifty years time would it be me standing where Lacey was, with the past eating into me from the inside? I recoiled from the idea of experiencing for myself the stark loneliness that had been so apparent in Lacey's eyes. In that moment I wanted little more than to undo past wrongs and to apologise for the way I had behaved. I needed forgiveness and it had been so long since I made any kind of confession.

After we had walked Lacey home, we sat in the kitchen, lost in our own thoughts,

'I think that was the saddest thing I ever heard.' Jane broke the silence that hung over the table and stared into her newly poured wine with a frown.

When I didn't reply she leaned forward and gave me one of her looks, chin down and eyes peering up through her raised eyebrows. 'What are you thinking about?'

'I don't know. It's just the thought of her keeping that inside for all this time and never breathing a word to anyone. It just sounds so lonely.'

She nodded her agreement and we drank in silence for a while.

'She reminds me of you.'

I looked at Jane but said nothing in reply, waiting for her to continue. Her words were discomfiting because they mirrored the thoughts I'd had only moments before.

'Don't look at me like that, you know what I mean. You're pretty tight-lipped about your past. Whenever you talk about it, I always feel a bit cheated, like you're deliberately missing out the most important bits.'

'I don't like talking about it.'

'Oh I know, that's my point. Maybe if you stay silent about it long enough people will stop asking and you'll end up with a story you never shared, just like Lacey.'

I slurped at my drink a little too enthusiastically and coughed as it went down the wrong way. I knew she was right and felt embarrassed by it. I had never been forthcoming about my past. I still carried the scars from the judgement of others. I still blanched from the scorn in their eyes as they looked down on us care home kids from the lofty heights of the wanted. The more time went by the more difficult it became.

Jane knew that I had grown up in children's homes, that my mother had neglected me, that I had been unhappy. But when I talked to her about it, I barely scratched the surface. I didn't really talk about how I had felt at the time. I had never told anyone about Diane and Richard other than their names and that they had once fostered me. I only ever mentioned them in passing, as though they were little more than an insignificance. Yet they had been so much more than that. I had mourned them for years, as if they had died suddenly and I had been left with the grief of it.

★   ★   ★

They had driven me away that day and I sat in the back of the car looking at the curve of their heads, seeing only sky through the windows and the tips of the trees. I felt tiny, afraid, relieved. The leather seat was cracking a little and I picked at it with my stubby, bitten fingernails as I began to worry about the changes ahead of me.

160

I pushed my hot face against the plush fur of the pink rabbit that sat on my knee. Diane and Richard had given it to me after I climbed into the car seat. I had clutched onto it as I sat and looked up at them watching me through the door of the car. I felt like an animal in the zoo and despite the warmth on their faces, the obvious delight I could see there, I closed my eyes and tried to shut out a world I didn't understand. I remember the smell of that toy rabbit, a new clean scent that I buried myself in.

We pulled up outside a cottage in the small village. I could see the church tower from the driveway; it was closer than I wanted it to be. I didn't trust graveyards then, every horror story I had ever been told curled from the gravestones like smoke. The cottage, though, looked sweet and welcoming and as I took a step towards it Diane bent down beside me and gently cradled the back of my head with her palm.

'Your new bedroom is a little bit empty at the moment. It's got a bed in it but it isn't painted like a little girl's room should be. So how about tomorrow we go shopping and buy the things we need to decorate it just how you would like?'

I felt excitement bubble up through my stomach and fill the space beneath my ribs until I thought I would pop. The thought of being able to choose, the idea of colour and fabric and newness was overwhelming. I hadn't even set foot in the house and already I was thrilled beyond measure. Diane reached down to hold my hand. I smiled and held on tight as we walked to the front door.

I expected my bedroom to be like the inside of a shoe box, bare walls, floors and windows. But it wasn't. It was painted in neutral tones, with a warm brown carpet that didn't look and feel like the sandpaper I was used to, and simple pictures of flowers hanging on the wall. The curtains were lacy, frothy things that looked to me like a waterfall tumbling over the glass. The bed was made with a proper quilt, with patterns of squares and diamonds.

Right from the first, that room felt like home to me, in the proper sense of the word, not a Home where forgotten children were. It felt like somewhere I could be cared for, somewhere I could fit in, and best of all there were no other children there, no-one to be a source of torment. A sense of security crept over me, wrapping around my shoulders.

The rest of the house was lovely too. Mostly neutral like my bedroom but the cushions scattered around the place, the haphazard rugs and the randomly placed pictures added a softness that I felt myself sinking in to. There were magazines on the coffee table, a half finished jigsaw puzzle on the dining table, slippers tucked beneath the edge of the sofa. Signs that the house was lived in, that the occupants were relaxed, that I didn't have to worry if I dropped something as I often did. I stood in the centre of the lounge and stared around me, turning slow circles as Diane and Richard stood to one side and smiled.

'What do you think?' Richard's voice was as warm and soft as the decor.

162

'I think I love it,' I said and heard my voice crack on the last syllable. My eyes grew wet and the tears spilled over. I tried to quickly mop them up with Rabbit, but Diane was beside me in an instant and took the toy from me, replacing him with a clean hanky that smelt of washing powder.

I tried to apologise, I didn't want to spoil this moment by crying and being a baby and I was so scared that they would think I was unhappy with them and send me back. Diane took the hanky, wiped at my nose and told me she understood. As she sat me on her knee and rocked me gently back and forth I remember thinking that everything was going to be okay.

That feeling stayed with me until I couldn't easily remember a time without it, although it took a little time before I could relax completely. Those first few nights, I wedged a towel along the bottom of the door so nobody could come in while I slept. Eventually, Diane sat me down and told me that I was safe, that I didn't need to barricade myself in, but if it made me feel happier then she would buy me a bolt for my door. The offer alone made me feel better and slowly the urge to wedge the door vanished.

As promised, we painted my room. The neutral tones changed to soft pink walls and lilac rugs. I kept the patchwork quilt and the flower pictures. They bought me an easel, which was placed in the corner of the room. There was a tray of paints that looked like a solid rainbow, I loved to look at them, to touch their powdery

163

bright surfaces and see the film left on my fingertips.

What may have been the most mundane of things for most people became a source of fun for me. Washing up and raking leaves became a pleasure as they earned me pocket money, sweets or kisses, sometimes all three. Going shopping for new clothes was a novelty, one that was always punctuated with a trip to a cafe where we slurped on strawberry milkshakes and ate huge choux buns with fresh cream oozing out of the sides. It would become a routine thing for Diane and me, one that I treasured.

Richard worked as a manager in a local factory and every day he would head off in the morning leaving Diane and me at home. We would pack a picnic and head off to visit the old castles in the area, climbing among the fallen stones, scrambling about the ruins before sitting down on the sloping ground to eat hard-boiled eggs and juicy oranges.

For the first time I didn't feel like a misfit. I was no longer that person standing on the outside looking in. For the first time I felt normal, part of something greater than just myself. I got used to the spontaneity, the affection and the night-time stories before sleep; quickly making the transition from feeling like a visitor to a sense of belonging, as though the house itself could no longer be complete without me in it.

I started going to the local middle school when the summer was over and I found it easier than my previous experiences. The village was so small that most of the other pupils knew I was fostered but somehow it was more accepted here.

I had brand new clothes that I had chosen for myself as there was no uniform at my new school. My shoes shone and my hair was neatly brushed. I made more of an effort to look nice because I no longer felt like a stray and Diane would help me to brush and plait my hair.

I made friends with other children. A little girl called Sophie had just moved to the village too. She was an American, one of the RAF children from a nearby camp and was opposite to me in almost every way, she was blond, blue eyed, chatty and confident. We became best friends, and hers was the first birthday party I was ever invited to. I was so excited I wanted to burst. I ran home and showed Diane the printed invitation with balloons and clowns on the front. She laughed and clipped the invitation into a little frame to put up on my bedroom wall.

I started to call my foster parents mum and dad. It felt strange at first, like a hard toffee in my mouth that slowly softened against my tongue. The first time I asked if it was okay, Diane's eyes grew misty. 'Of course you can, I'd love that.' She threw her arms around me, squeezing me tight for a little too long until I squirmed in her grasp and wriggled free.

My days became more and more like everyone else's family life. I would make mistakes, get told off and run to my room sulking. It was normal, I was normal. The days began to merge into each other and I got used to everything until I began to take it all for granted.

That first Christmas, we made paper chains and decorated the tree with beautiful lights. On Christmas Eve I got to hang my first ever stocking at the end of my bed. I can't even remember now what I found inside the following morning, but I remember the excitement of trying to sleep the night before and waiting for Father Christmas to come.

I remember the piles of coloured paper more than I remember the contents of the presents and I remember sitting down to a proper Christmas dinner with crackers to pull and funny hats to wear. As I was tucked into bed that night, exhausted and full of chocolate, I felt sad that the day was over and I remember that feeling of regret even now.

It is moments like that first Christmas that stand out in my memory when so many other things have got lost somewhere along the way. The memories that seem to last, are the moments when I began to feel like everyone else, a first sleepover, birthday party, or funfair. All the images roll in to one and seem to take place immediately one after the other, rather than stretched out over several years as they were. In my mind, that first Christmas is remembered alongside the beach holiday and yet the reality is that those events were more than two years apart.

They took me to Devon when I was eleven. We went for two whole weeks and stayed in a holiday cottage near Dawlish Warren. I could see the beach from my room, could hear the sound of the sea as I drifted off to sleep at night. I loved it there. The sun shone almost every day and we crammed the hours full.

There were boat trips, sand castles, fairground rides and candy floss. I remember the feeling of my sunburnt skin, the coolness of the cream rubbed into my shoulders, the tangle of my hair after a day of sea breezes and the taste of salt on my lips when I poked my tongue out at Richard for splashing me. Years later I would try to capture it in acrylics but I could never do it justice. The memory had become almost mythical to me, a step outside reality.

There were other reasons that holiday would stay with me. It was on the last night that adoption was first mentioned. They asked me how I felt about it, whether it was what I wanted and for a little while I found it hard to speak. In some ways I felt sad because the question reminded me that my place with them wasn't permanent. I had never really thought up until that moment that it could all end and I could be made to go back. I realised that the thought of being adopted by them was the most important thing in the world. I told them as much.

'We want that too, Rachel. We'll phone up next week and see if we can get the ball rolling.' Richard reached across the restaurant table and held my hand. I didn't want to let it go because I suddenly felt afraid that I might fade away, that I was nothing more than temporary, but I smiled up at him anyway and his smile met mine half way.

That was the moment that everything

changed. I would wonder for years what would have happened if we had not sought the adoption. Would everything have worked out better? Would I have stayed in that little cottage that I thought of as home, with the only parents I had ever known? Maybe it was my fault for being greedy and wanting more than I had. I would torment myself with thoughts like that for years afterwards, wondering what would have happened if only I hadn't agreed to the adoption.

I didn't know that some time before that holiday, Diane had found a lump in her breast and that it was being investigated. I didn't know that the lump came in the shape of a question mark that was stamped onto my paperwork.

Weeks after the holiday, when everything was settling back down into a now familiar routine, I came home from school to find two strangers and a flood of tears that had caused devastation to the place I called home. Two grey-faced, grey clothed people, a man and a woman, had washed away the colour from the lounge. Diane rushed to me when I walked in, her arms sliding beneath mine and holding me tight as could be, her wet face pressed against my own which was flushed from running in the strong wind outside. I looked over her shoulder and saw two pairs of eyes looking back at me, bland and expressionless as they prepared to tear my life down with words I wouldn't understand.

They spoke and I heard them, but when I look back the only thing I can remember is the crushing weight of their words. They were heavy, solid things; I felt them in the air all around me as they were pushed into my ears by Diane's sobbing. I felt myself shrinking beneath them and I turned and ran, my feet flying across the carpet and up the stairs two at a time until I burst through the door of my room and threw myself onto that beautiful patchwork quilt. Sharp words like machine gun fire cracked from below me, followed by gentle footsteps on the stairs and the red, distraught face of my foster mother as she came into my room to pull the jigsaw apart.

'Breast cancer,' she said. 'Unsuitable parents,' she said, and I sat and listened and broke. I felt my own cheeks wet beneath the fingers I tried to cover my face with. I don't know how long I had been crying. But when she told me I had to go with the strangers, that I couldn't live with them anymore, I became hysterical, slapping at the hands of the social workers who were stealing me away.

My life was quickly thrown into bin bags. The sense of belonging that had taken years to complete was dismantled in minutes by careless hands. The clothes had my name on them this time, they had never belonged to anyone else, but did it really matter? The end result was the same, my new life was torn apart around me and I knew then that it had never belonged to me. I had merely borrowed it for a while.

As they drove me away I banged against the window until my hands hurt, pleading to be let out, screaming and begging the strangers to take me home. I watched as Diane and Richard clung to each other, their faces desolate as we drove away and they got smaller and smaller through the glass. I reached for the door handle but was roughly pulled away from it and told to stop being so silly.

Eventually I had fallen silent. My tears had dried, my feelings shrinking into a hard mass that sat at the bottom of my chest. I felt everything inside me wither, and pulled a mask down over my face until I felt invisible, encased in stone. I stared at the headrest in front of me and never once looked out of the window, not caring where I was being taken. It didn't matter, it wasn't home. As the car ate up the miles and the two halves of my life grew taut and snapped apart, I sat silent. I stayed still as the car moved onwards to the outskirts of Birmingham, before being swallowed up among the huge buildings and concrete spaces.

We pulled up outside a house in a leafy suburb and still my eyes didn't move. I stared in front of me and didn't look around even as I was half led, half pulled from the car by emotionless fingers that left a red mark. I walked the corridors and ignored the sounds of other children, another life. The old, familiar smells rushed up my nose and pushed tears to the corners of my eyes; it was all too real and at the same time too far removed from what my life had become. Everything closed around me and I shut myself away from them. I lost myself in the dark places inside me where I felt nothing.

For a long time I was sure it was my fault. I had no right to a family of my own. I should have left things as they were and then the authorities wouldn't have asked the questions about Diane and Richard's health. They wouldn't have found out about the breast cancer, they would have left me with my family. If they had been my real mum and dad the authorities couldn't have taken me away, I would have stayed there with them and faced whatever was to come.

But, as time went on and I settled into the new home, my feelings began to change. Within two weeks I received a letter with my home address on the back. I stared at the lovely curling script. It looked soft and gentle; so familiar, the same writing and the same envelopes that had always sat on her desk in a neat pile. In that moment it seemed that nothing had changed for them. Everything about their day remained the same. It was only me that had been torn apart by my removal, only me that stared at four bare walls and had no colour around me.

I could picture her sitting at her desk, ankles crossed, looking to the window as she thought about what she could say. How dare she write to me and remind me of all I had left behind? How could she print the old address on the envelope without a thought as to how it would torment me? A bitter resentment began to flourish. I tore that letter to pieces without reading it, and the ones that followed met with the same fate.

As time passed the letters came less frequently and the anger festered inside me every time I saw one of them. I was hurt and eventually I wrote back. Four little words shaped by grief. Four little words that built a barrier that looked like concrete, but was nothing more than smoke. *Aren't you dead yet?* I posted it before I could change my mind. I didn't receive any more letters.

31

Lacey

The room is cool and calm and she feels as if she has been here forever. The walls are closing in and as the hours pass she is sure that the room is becoming smaller. She wonders what is happening outside and, ignoring the aches in her muscles and bones, moves to the window. She thinks that if she focuses really, really hard she will be able to hear the stream that runs through the field. It has rained a lot and the water is higher than it should be. It would soak through her dress if she walked through the meadows.

She thinks that if she holds her breath until her head goes dizzy, if she holds it past the point where her senses shift, then she will be able to fly. She can hover over the wet grass and be with the birds. Then she will see for herself how high the water is.

She draws the air in deep, deep, deeper still, until the blood rushes in her ears. She holds fast, holds tight and hears her heart loud inside her head. It sounds like a drum and her fingers move to her lap, her head begins to nod and her fingers tap along with the beat. She begins to hum softly in the back of her throat, forgetting about holding her breath, forgetting that she meant to learn how to fly.

Her closed eyes open quickly as the door to

her room crashes against the wall. Her father stands there, his expression cold. She has mastered the art of pretending to look at him while her gaze is turned inwards, away from his orders, his demands, his scathing bitter hatred. She does it now and he is a ghost to her, standing in the doorway, invisible, nothing more than a current of air that bends in the shape of a man.

'Give me your arm.' He barks like a dog and she wonders why he never wags his tail, why he never seems happy. But while she questions this, she doesn't question his orders and she holds her arm out, it looks mottled blue, bruised like an apple. She does as she is told, she is a good girl. She feels the sharp stab and winces. She wonders at it, looks at it and then her vision fades out into a blackness that is total and complete, where she doesn't fly.

When she opens her eyes again he is not there, but there is pain in his place. She tries to sit up but as she does so a burning, tearing sensation rips through her.

She catches sight of towels in the corner, they are white stained red. She lies back down and wonders how long the pain will last. It comes in waves like the ebb and flow of the tide and she wonders if she counts them, which wave will be the biggest. She drifts away and dreams that she is a bird hovering above the ocean.

32

Rachel

I stood beneath an early morning sky that grew ever more overcast and looked across an empty stretch of sand towards the horizon. Far in the distance I could see two jet skiers crossing each other and from my vantage point, they seemed to be perilously close to colliding. I moved my eyes away and stared out to where the sea was empty and growing darker.

Perhaps it was inevitable that sooner or later I would stand here again, the place where I had buried my childhood happiness in the sand. The temperature was cooler than the day before and a spiteful breeze caught at my trousers, whipping them against my skin.

There were no families playing as there had once been, just a couple in their twilight years strolling hand in hand by the water's edge as their dog ran in and out of the breaking water.

This time, when I drove along the road towards Exeter, I had turned at the sign for Dawlish, I had followed it and looked for the familiar in the trees that rushed past the windscreen. As I stood halfway between then and now, I felt shame crawling beneath my skin. For the first time I saw past my apparent abandonment, to the Diane and Richard I had known then, the warmth on their faces, the hugs and the kisses they had swamped me with, the subtle emotions reflected in their expressions that I hadn't understood then.

How awful I had been, how self-absorbed. I looked out at the sea and blinked against the sudden downpour as the clouds broke and sent hissing, spitting raindrops into the parched ground. The distant couple moved quickly away from the water's edge but I stayed where I was, the rain drenching my clothes and plastering them to my skin.

I had been so angry, so beyond rationality. I could look back with adult eyes, and see I should have done things differently. I had been too young to know better. I was hurt. I wondered if the solitary life I had lived was a product of the person I had been then. If my childhood had set me up for nothing more than a life of holding people at arm's length for fear they may leave anyway.

I watched the clouds roll across the sky and felt the weight of my anger draining into the cooling sand. I looked at the emotion behind it, examining the strands and threads that had bound my mouth and prevented me from asking the questions I should have asked years before. I let my adult-self step into the space vacated by the grieving angry child.

I could acknowledge that behind all the anger, there was fear. What if I wrote to them and discovered that Diane had succumbed to her illness? What if I found it was too late and there was nothing I could do to make things right? It was so much better to embrace that fury in ignorance, than to find out I had to grieve for her, knowing I could never say sorry.

I thought of Lacey and the loneliness, the isolation she had lived with. Of the loss she had faced with such courage. I wondered if Richard too had been left alone to face life without the person he loved. Or was Diane still alive and healthy? Were they both alive? Or both dead? Did they both lie beneath the ground in the graveyard I could see from my old bedroom window? Suddenly I found that I desperately wanted to know.

I returned to the car and drove back to Winscombe. The rain had stopped but the clouds still hung low and threatening over the hills. It was still early when I let myself into the house and there was no sign of Jane, she was probably still sleeping off the night before. I spooned honey into hot milk — a taste from my youth — and stepped out barefoot onto the cold rain-drenched grass.

I thought of Lacey and the way she had talked the night before. She had lost herself in her past, holding each moment as though it were a precious jewel. It helped me look back with different eyes. As I moved across the lawn, I saw in the dark trails I left behind me a snapshot of the last time I saw them. Richard's arms around Diane as she sobbed and turned away, the devastated look on his face as he watched the car disappear down the road, a broken man trying desperately to console his devastated wife.

How had I buried these images so effectively? How could I have pushed them to one side until they no longer existed for me? I was slowly spinning, looking at the sky and the way the clouds blurred as I turned. I was trying to work out how I could get in touch with them again when Jane called to me from the door.

'What the hell are you doing, you mad bitch?'

I stopped mid turn and took a final sip from my almost empty cup before bowing theatrically. 'Reminiscing and dancing like an idiot, is that okay with you?'

Jane smiled at me. 'Of course, do you want a cup of coffee to wash down those memories?'

In answer I twirled across the garden and handed over my mug, which was received with a faint head shake and a single raised eyebrow. I smiled and realised that I felt lighter than I had for years.

Over coffee and toast I told Jane about my foster parents. I didn't go into all of the details, I didn't share with her the insignificant things that had made the couple a family to me. I talked about how I had felt, about how I had belonged. She sat and listened without interruption, and as I talked I watched the emotions play across her face. I told my tale laced through with contrition, guilt painting my speech a dark tone and I felt her hand slide into mine and squeeze as my words reached into the present and added another route to my map.

'How come they took you to Birmingham, instead of back to Norfolk?'

I shook my head a little. 'I'm not really sure, nobody bothered explaining anything to us back then. Maybe they were worried that if I was too close to my foster parents then I would try and go back. I was glad of it though. I think it would have seemed worse going back to the home I had left. At least in Birmingham I was a new face and no-one knew my history.'

'So what are you going to do now?'

'Try and find them, I guess. Write to the old address and see if I get a response. I'll look online later and see what I can dig up. It's strange really, I've tried to avoid thinking of them for years but now I've started I feel really impatient to find out.'

Jane squeezed my hand again then stood and brushed at the crumbs on the table, sweeping them into her palm before dropping them into the bin. 'Well, I've got to head off home anyway, I'll just go and grab my stuff. I've left the commission details on your easel, it's about time it was used for something!'

I flicked her retreating backside with a tea towel and listened to her laughter echo down the hall.

33

Rachel

An hour can easily go by unnoticed. It could pass in the blink of an eye, nothing more than a fragment, a whisper. Yet it was more than enough to create a different future, it was more than enough to take my trepidation and stitch the rags and feathers of other emotions to it. How quickly things could change, how seamlessly I could traverse the chasm from ignorance to knowledge and how strange my world seemed as a result.

After more than half an hour of lightly skating across the surface, I had come across a website that promised good results. I had put in Richard's name, wary of searching for Diane's. I added the village Marham, Norfolk and I clicked Enter. That was all it had taken, little baby steps that stumbled and grabbed at my past pulling it instantly into the present.

First, Richard's name appeared, followed by the same address they had lived at all those years ago, the place I had called home. And there, beneath that information were the simple words: other occupants Diane Parks. I looked at the date and saw that the information was from the 2007 electoral register, only two years previous.

I considered picking up the phone and hesitated, pacing the floor as I thought of a million reasons why it was not the best idea.

Perhaps a better plan would be to write a letter. The written word would be less of an immediate shock. I knew that I was being a coward, that writing seemed preferable simply because it was impossible to hang up on a letter. They could take their time to digest the contents, to evaluate their feelings and decide if they would be as dismissive of mine as I had been of theirs.

When I was sat with pen in hand, I could get no further than my address and the opening line. Beyond that, the page stayed infuriatingly blank and I felt powerless as I tried to discover the way forward.

Dear Diane and Richard...

I sighed and got to my feet again, I would make a cup of tea and think some more, I would walk in the garden and seek inspiration, I would go to the shop and buy some biscuits. I would go to the stream and watch the water disappear from sight, taking my indecision with it, I would sit in the churchyard, paint a picture, tidy up, change the bedding, have a bath, plant some seeds, trim the hedges. Suddenly everything seemed more appealing than sitting at my desk and trying to apologise for a lifetime of silence. I didn't know how to begin and the more I thought about it the harder it became. I knew what I wanted to say, but it would take pages and pages for me to spell the word sorry.

Dear Diane and Richard, I'm sorry that it has taken me so long to write to you.

Dear Diane and Richard, surprise! I bet you weren't expecting this.

Dear Diane and Richard, I wish I had a magic

wand that I could use to turn back the clock...

I needed to say them all and none of them. But then another thought occurred to me, what if they never thought about me? What if they had just accepted that I was gone and got on with things, seeing me as nothing more than a brief interlude? I became suspended as much by this wondering as I did by my lack of words to explain the years away. I continued my pacing, my procrastinating, my mental paralysis, each step leading me in circles back to the start until I ground to a halt and pushed bunched fists against my cheeks and screamed through gritted teeth.

I screwed up yet another piece of paper, added it to the growing pile that drifted like snow against the edge of the bin and took deep breaths until my frustrated heart rate returned to normal. I thought that perhaps I could go into my studio and throw some paint at a canvas, massive swirls of red, orange and black that would be the perfect representation of my aggravation. It made me feel better to take charge of the moment, and I moved towards the room with a spring in my step. I shook the tension from my shoulders and lost the rest of the day in spirals of colour while the writing paper sat pure and white against the varnished surface of the table.

34

Lacey

How much time passes before her father notices something is amiss? It seems only yesterday that she had been at the memorial. She wonders what has happened in the spaces between then and now. If she concentrates, if she thinks really hard she sees image after image of her hands folding over her growing abdomen while she desperately hopes he won't see. She hides herself behind doors and tables, coats and scarves, and he turns his eyes from her and fails to see.

She swallows her nausea and tries to ignore the quizzical looks her mother gives her as she throws herself into her chores, and does what is expected. Perhaps if she carries on as normal, no-one will notice. She could give birth in the fields like the cows do and make her home in a barn somewhere. She could keep her baby safe.

Her clothes grow tighter and she adjusts them in the night but soon it isn't enough, nothing will fasten and the panic rises like bile in her throat as she grows more afraid. She conjures up fairy tales to keep her safe, makes worlds within her world and she becomes uncertain of what is real, what is now. She is almost convinced that someone will ride to her rescue. And if not, what then? She will run away.

She squirrels away little bits of money here

and there, not much because there is little around, but she does what she can. It is pitiful but the action cushions her, pushing aside her fears. She feels the baby move inside her and it makes her think of dragonflies. She presses her hand to her stomach and wills her child to stay inside where it can't be seen.

It all unravels though, so fast, so frighteningly. Arrow sharp in her memory, she sees it all again, she sees it all the time and it never grows old. She will see that moment forever when she is in the garden, when she collects eggs, when she drifts.

She is in the garden, seeing to the chickens, heading back to the house with the eggs when her father walks up the path. She moves to turn her back on him but she loses her footing, she stumbles and he reaches out his hand to steady her. How the Fates must have laughed to themselves as they conjured up this little catastrophe.

She will always see the look on his face as his hand brushes her swollen abdomen. For just a moment he looks genuinely puzzled as if something simply doesn't add up. But he reaches his hand out again and presses it hard and flat against her and she cries out as his fingers curl inward like iron claws and the truth falls over his eyes.

His face grows stormy and dark, a hurricane threatening to sweep them both away, but it is gone as soon as it begins. She sees the calm descend as he takes a slow breath and reaches forwards gently to cup the back of her neck as he stares into her eyes and reads the questions there. His hand pulls back and punches her hard in the stomach and her knees go weak. She nearly falls, she would have but his other hand curls around her hair, holds tight, holds her up. She swings from the hand that holds her. Please father, please. And he slaps the words from her mouth. They break on the floor along with the eggs and she sees them there, swimming among the smeared yolk.

Her mouth fills with blood and she spits. It hits him in the face and bloody saliva trickles across his lips, down across his chin. His face is cast from stone. She loses time as she stares at him, before he beats her to the ground where she curls up around her baby and hopes that if it has to be this way then they will die together.

35

Rachel

A week goes by during which I work, I paint, and I fail to write a letter that has waited for years. I go back to the beach again. I even go and stand outside the house we stayed in, it is painted a different colour now but I remember sitting inside and looking out into the sunshine.

Whatever hold I believed the beach had over me was exorcised now, and I realised that it was only the people that held tight in my memory not the place, the place only mattered because of them. There was no inspiration for me here among memories, and so I returned to stare once again at the paper and will the right words to appear.

I held the pen as it stayed still and silent in my hand. I became edgy and uncomfortable until I could stand it no longer. Grabbing my keys and pointing the car towards the city, I sought distraction in the shops and eventually, as the screens were brought down and people made their way home, I found myself outside the cinema. I decided to kill a few hours there before going home to the paper that was beginning to feel like a haunting.

★　★　★

I can't remember now what I watched; I stared blankly at the screen and tried to get lost in it, but all I could think about was the uncomfortable seat, the vague smell of body odour mixed with popcorn, the occasional cough and giggle. By the time I walked away with the handful of people I had shared the film with, it had started to rain and I felt more despondent than I had when I arrived.

On the drive home I thought that I would just write the first thing that came into my head even if it was rubbish. It would be a beginning, a possibility.

By the time I headed up the lane the darkness was complete, especially here beyond the circles of the streetlights. I pulled the car onto the verge outside my gate and stepped out. As I shut the door, I caught sight of something, something lighter that broke the darkness towards the head of the lane.

I turned slowly towards it and let out a tiny scream, a short, sharp sound that broke off abruptly against the night sky. It took me a moment to realise that it was Lacey. She was looking towards me and I raised my hand in greeting, a smile growing on my lips. As I waved I could see her mouth moving.

'Hush little baby, don't say a word.'

She stood so, so white against the darkness, the rain blurring her edges and as I moved closer to her and said her name, I realised that she was completely naked, her generous breasts and stomach hanging in folds. I could see scratches, black, ragged lines on her arms and ankles, and her eyes were staring past me, through me, into nothing as she swayed where she stood and sang her lullaby. I hurried to her, removing my cardigan so I could wrap it around her chilled shoulders and as I did so she urinated. It ran down her legs and before I could jump back out of the way it splashed onto my feet, where it was washed away by the rain.

36

Lacey

How long has it been? It could have been moments or hours, before a voice screams at him to stop. She hears the fear in the higher pitch of the words and she tries to look at her rescuer through swollen eyes. She is hunched on the floor still curled around her baby and so very scared for this little life inside her, this little heartbeat that gives reason for the blood in her veins. She feels the wind from his trousers as he passes, hears a door slam. She realises through the pain that this is the first time that anyone has stood up to her father, and then she realises that she is still alive and she wants to weep.

She drifts in and out of dark spaces as hands float in the air before her and reach out. She cringes away from the touch as pain lances through every part of her. How can this hurt so much without killing her? Maybe she will die after all. She waits for the release.

When she opens her eyes she is in her room. The curtains are closed and the darkness is welcome. Not dead then. Her mother bends to her and she feels coldness against her forehead, feels water run across her cheeks and behind her ears. She lifts her hand and finds that even her fingertips hurt where they brush against her mother's wrist. She meets her mother's eyes and sees submission in them.

'You silly, silly girl!' she says as she turns and places the cloth back into the bowl, as if she is berating her for nothing more than spilling the milk or breaking the eggs. She wonders where her father is. She is terrified that he might come in and start again. Her mother leaves and she lays there too terrified to move. Maybe if she lays still, the baby will be okay, maybe his fists missed, maybe his kicks landed wide. She stares at the ceiling and crosses her bruised fingers, telling her baby not to leave, she can't lose him too.

She lays there as her mother brings more water, as the evening fades to night and the owls begin to hoot. And as the minutes stretch and she breathes through her fear she feels a fluttering across her belly, a tiny movement that opens her eyes as wide as the bruises will allow. She curls her hands up around the baby and strokes through her skin until she falls into a sleep where she winces every time she moves.

37

Rachel

I guided Lacey's unresisting body towards the gate leading to her home. I opened her front door, took her by the hands and led her inside.

Lacey sat down on the hard wooden, floor. As I turned to shut the door, she was sat with her legs crossed, immodest in her nudity, rubbing absently at the deep, oozing scratches on her ankles. She rocked slightly back and forth and I tried to work out what I should do. As her fingers moved over the wounds they came away bloody, tacky and I searched for dressings that I could cover them with.

I found kitchen towels near the sink, and filled a bowl of water to begin cleaning her up. As I did so I smelt ammonia and dank earth and realised that if I could get her in the bath that would be a good place to start. I talked to her as I moved, as a mother would to a child. I wanted to get her comfortable, and then I would see if I could get hold of her doctor. I was scared for her, unable to work out what might have happened and how she had come to be standing naked in the lane, covered in scratches. Perhaps Charlie could shed some light on it.

I opened the door to the living room. This was the first time I had been inside Lacey's house and normally I would have loved the chance to look around. The lounge was in darkness and I rushed to the other downstairs room to check if Charlie was in there, but I found that was empty too.

I looked towards Lacey, still naked, still rocking, and I grabbed a towel from over the radiator and placed it over my cardigan on her shoulders. I reached behind her and locked the door, worried that if I went upstairs she might leave the house. All the while my head was spinning with concern and a sense of helplessness.

It was late now so perhaps Charlie was sleeping, it would explain why he hadn't heard the movements from downstairs and come to investigate. As I took the steps two at a time I was surrounded by silence and the house felt empty around me. End Cottage had four doors upstairs, one more than my house. The first door I came to was closed but faint yellow light spilled from beneath it and I knocked gently. I opened it when there was no response. The light from a bedside lamp illuminated a pretty, airy bedroom with pale walls and a rose covered bedspread. The room smelt of lavender and fresh linen, it smelt of Lacey.

I rushed over to a chest of drawers against the far wall and dug around until I found clean underwear and a pair of pyjamas. Stepping back into the hallway I paused, listening for sounds from beyond the other doors, from the hallway downstairs. I could hear Lacey humming tonelessly, a sound of fingernails tapping against a hard surface but other than that there was silence.

The next door I opened revealed a small room filled with boxes, an old covered sewing machine, a tailor's dummy. The next was a bathroom. I went to the last door and knocked lightly on it. There was no response. I knocked a bit louder.

'Excuse me,' I said, my voice loud and jarring in the silence. I didn't want to knock too hard in case the sound disturbed Lacey but there was still no response. I reached for the door handle and turned it. The room beyond was in darkness and I hesitated before pressing the light switch, feeling awkward that the sudden glare from overhead might wake Charlie up with a start.

As I stood there at the threshold trying to peer beyond the faltering light from behind me, I could hear nothing but silence and my own heartbeat. There were no sounds of breathing, gentle snoring, no rustling of bed clothes. I flipped the light switch and blinked rapidly as a bare bulb illuminated the blue walls in the last of the bedrooms. It was empty. An unmade bed with a bare mattress sat against the far wall. A chest of drawers beneath the blue curtained window had lost their sheen beneath a film of dust. I walked to them and opened the top drawer to find nothing. There were no personal touches in the room, no books anywhere, no clothes on the bed or the chair in the corner. The room felt as though no-one had lived in it for a very long time.

38

Lacey

As the dawn breaks and the birds tell her it is morning her father comes in. She cowers, pulling back against the bed covers and curling around herself. He looks at her with disdain.

'You will get up and go about your chores. Under no circumstances will you leave this house. Is that understood?' He doesn't wait for an answer and she nods at his retreating back. He is hiding her away. She is sure it is not just because of the pregnancy that he is locking her inside, not just the shame of it. He is hiding away the damage that his anger has imprinted on her skin.

When she struggles down the stairs, limping through the aches in her body he stands in the hallway with a blank expression. He points to her stomach and tells her that if it still lives, she will be heading up to Bristol, to a distant cousin who runs a convalescence home. She will stay there until the baby is born and they will take it from her, it will be adopted. She will be alone. And she will come home with empty arms. She will have nothing.

She does not protest, but she knows in her head that she will run. When her baby is born, when it is placed in her arms, she will be gone. Scoop him up and steal him away and run far from here. She will make a new life for herself; create a new past, a different her. She could be a war widow in a strange place. They will understand, they will sympathise, and they will embrace her. No-one will take her child.

She stares at her father, at the thin line of his mouth, the sharpness of his face and she hates him. He is a monster to her. An evil shadow. She lowers her eyes and says, 'Yes, father.' He turns and leaves the house, his coat over his arm and his bag in his hand.

She sits on the bottom stair and waits for the tears to come but her eyes stay dry. She feels her heart shrivel towards the parents that have made these decisions for her, that have stolen her life and given her a pathetic substitute. She knows that her mother, too, is at the mercy of her father, that she feels his cruelty, his coldness. But in that moment she hates them both; one for his malice, the other for her weakness.

Within days her bruises have faded, become nothing more than shadows that are easy to overlook. She comes in from the garden to find her bags packed. Sitting on the train she imagines a female version of her father waiting for her at the other end of the line. But the truth is different. Mary is a dear thing, a middle-aged spinster who seems to find the charade delicious in its scandal.

She decides almost immediately that she will stay in Bristol. Perhaps with the small amount of money that she has, she will find somewhere to stay, somewhere to work. Perhaps it will be somewhere her father will never find her. The thought comforts her as she becomes enormous and finds breathing difficult. She dreams of a little boy and cannot think of the baby as a girl after that.

She screams through her labour, the pain so great that she feels removed from herself, as if she has stepped outside her body and has become little more than a casual observer. The midwife tells her not to make such a fuss but the pain seems to go on forever and her body is pulled apart inch by inch until she falls through the cracks and feels strange and distant. She watches herself push and push until he finally slithers out into silence and the frowning face of the midwife who reaches for a blanket and busies herself.

The woman walks towards the door and she calls after her. At the doorway she turns and looks gravely at the exhausted woman on the bed, she shakes her head and walks away. There is a residual image in the space where she departs, a tiny bundle silent and unmoving, a little hand, pale and blue that is visible through the folds of the fabric.

When Mary comes in, her cheeks are wet. She says that some things aren't meant to be. Everything inside her dies right there, on the bed amidst the blood and waste. There is no pain, no tears. Everything is frozen and that is how it will stay for years to come.

39

Rachel

I placed my hands under Lacey's chilled arms and helped her to her feet. She was compliant and allowed me to lead her to the bathroom like a meek lamb. There was a wet stain in the hallway that showed where the water had run from her skin as she sat and rocked. Her eyes stared straight ahead as we climbed the stairs, but her feet lifted as we went.

She stood in the bathroom as I ran the water and checked the temperature before leading her to the edge of the bath. She was still humming beneath her breath, becoming sluggish in her movements as I encouraged her with a singsong gentle voice to get into the warm water.

To my relief she lifted her leg and stepped gingerly into the bath and sat down. I picked up a sponge and washed her with the rose and lavender scented shower gel that I had found at the edge of the bath. Her eyelids became heavy, her song slower and quieter as sleep waited to grasp and pull her down. I finished quickly and reached for the towel, wanting to get her out of the bath before she fell asleep completely. I was afraid that I wouldn't be able to wake her again.

She stepped from the bath leaning on me for a moment, and I wrapped the towel around her. I led her to the bedroom where she sat silently on the edge of the bed. I rubbed her dry, casting frequent glances at her expressionless face.

She lifted her arms and feet for me as I put her pyjamas on her. When I had finished she lay down without protest and I covered her with the duvet, her eyes once more growing heavy and beginning to close. Her breathing grew heavier as I tucked her in and she didn't respond at all as I bent forward and kissed her lightly on the forehead.

I looked at the calm, relaxed face half hidden by the duvet and felt overwhelmed by a feeling of complete sadness. As I walked towards the door and reached for the light switch a whisper followed me, 'Goodnight, Charlie.'

I wondered at it and at the story behind it as I flipped the switch and pulled the door shut behind me.

★ ★ ★

I wiped the floor in the bathroom, scrubbed at the wet patch on the hall floor, put the soiled towels into the washing machine and searched for some food to feed the increasingly vocal and attentive cat that seemed to materialise from the woodwork. By the time I finished I realised that my reserves of strength were totally depleted and tension banded across my forehead like a vice.

I rubbed the palms of my hands against gritty eyes. I felt numb, uncertain as to what I should do next. I looked at my mobile phone and realised that it was almost midnight. I knew I couldn't leave. Should I phone a doctor? Or could I leave it until morning now that Lacey was sleeping? It was too late to phone Jane for advice, too late for disturbing anyone it seemed.

I went into the kitchen and put the kettle on to make tea, a job made slower by unfamiliarity. Sitting on the sofa with the hot mug in my hand, my mind skated around the evening's events, trying to make sense of what had happened. I was haunted by how fragile and helpless Lacey had been. How different. I had seen no awareness or recognition in her. I didn't know where her wounds had come from, where she had been, what had happened. I was out of my depth and filled with worry.

I took my tea into the lounge and went to the telephone table, searching through it for some clues, some answers as to what I could do next. But all the time I searched I could hear Lacey's voice repeating in my head that there was no-one but her, no friends, no family. I remembered her saying about the vicar, a mad old fruit she'd said but it was something for me to grab onto, something I may be able to use.

I found a little phone book and went through its pages; the entries were pitiful, highlighting even further a life with scant company. It didn't take me long to find the entry for Father Thomas and I tapped the digits into my mobile, knowing that it was too late to call him now but that I could make use of it in the morning. I needed someone to shed some light on what had happened, someone who could give me guidance and tell me what needed to be done.

I decided not to use the number I found for

her doctor just yet. She was calm and sleeping and I was worried that if I called someone out they would wake her, confuse her further. I worried that a stranger in her house might scare her and make her retreat further into her fragile state. I copied the number down but only intended to use it if there were no other way. I would see how she was in the morning and go from there.

I wondered about Charlie. That mystery only seemed to get deeper as time went on. It was obvious that no-one other than Lacey lived here, and yet she had seemed so forthright, so genuine in the way she spoke about him. I still held on to the belief that somewhere along the way there had been a grave misunderstanding. I thought about the evening's events, the empty bedrooms, the layers of dust in the room that should be his, but the more I tried to focus, the more the images evaded me. I curled up into the sofa and finished my tea, placing my cup on the floor as my eyes grew heavy and I drifted off to sleep.

40

Lacey

She is lost. There is water around her ankles, fish with sharp teeth beneath the surface that bite at her. She feels them tearing into her skin and side steps quickly and finds herself on dry land, in a fog so dense she cannot see her own hand in front of her face. She falls to her knees, feeling harsh fingers grab for her, she reaches up to brush them away and her hand closes around thorns that mark her palm with droplets of red.

She feels heavy, so heavy and she cannot resist the lure of the ground as it twists and shapes itself into a pillow. She lies down and the fog closes in around her, she feels it almost solid against her skin. She drifts and floats and then she is gone and the darkness takes over. Only this time when she wakes she is safe in her bed. She is warm and dressed in her pyjamas, it is different and the fear and confusion seems less. She wonders if any of it was real and looks at the palm of her hand, at the scratches that tell her she was somewhere else — somewhere other than this — for a while at least.

She goes down the stairs and Rachel is there. Her stomach becomes a black hole that her heart plunges into, as she stands barefoot and dishevelled. She feels like a stranger in her own home. She stands and twists her hands together, waiting for the sleeping girl to wake up, waiting for her judgement. She wonders if this young woman who has come to matter to her, has borne witness to her absence.

She fetches a blanket and places it over the sleeping form, wanting her to stay comfortable, to stay asleep. She doesn't want to face judging eyes that will condemn her now as so many have done, she doesn't want to be alone again.

She feels caught out, vulnerable. Did she say anything as she floated in the blackness and this girl held her hand? How many stories has she told? How many lives has she lived that aren't her own? She isn't even sure anymore what her life is, how to define the truth, what she has become.

She looks at the sleeping girl on the sofa and wonders for a moment if she is real. She is sure that she is but she can never really be certain. She cares about her as if she is real but sometimes she wonders where the truth actually lies. She thinks about the empty room upstairs, of brown eyes and sadness, of a tiny cold hand taken quickly from view. She thinks of what it means to love and to feel, she thinks of the vastness of nothing. She thinks of an orange glow on the horizon and bruises that bloom on pale skin. Sometimes she wonders if anything is real.

41

Rachel

When I woke up light was peering round the curtains and a soft blanket had been placed over me. I shook my head a little to rid myself of any remaining sleepiness and sat up, as I did so I noticed Lacey sitting in the chair near the window, her features soft and indistinct, darkened by the light behind her. Her shoulders hung heavy and her chin lowered. She looked defeated.

'I'm sorry if I woke you.' Her voice was subdued but rational, and I felt a lurch of relief in my chest. The air hung heavy with her shame and I watched as she turned away to look out into the garden, seeing the pinch of her lips. I sensed her hesitation, her lack of certainty in not knowing where to begin. She stood and walked to the kitchen. I heard her rattling about, heard the kettle boiling, the stirring of the spoon against china. She returned with a cup of tea that she placed in my hands before sitting down again, this time on the opposite end of the sofa to me.

I didn't know what to say. I didn't want her to be embarrassed but had no idea how to avoid it, how to make it alright. So I sat nursing my cup and waited for her to fill the space left by my contemplation. She cleared her throat and I waited for her to speak, but the moment dropped away into nothing and the silence remained. I sipped at my tea.

'Charlie junior died just before he was born.'

The words emerged in a tumble as they clamoured over each other, louder than they needed to be. I turned towards her quicker than I should have and made her flinch a little. Reaching out my hand I brushed it against her forearm, offering comfort as my mind raced through the things she had said previously about her son. I saw the truth and the lies, separate strands that I failed to understand. I was no less confused. I watched a tear roll down her cheek as she clasped her hands together and squirmed beneath my confusion.

She stood and left the room before returning with a box of tissues. She looked at her hands, at me, at the window, before taking a deep breath and looking somewhere else.

42

Lacey

She returns home still aching and sore to a dark, quiet house and a different life. Her father tells her that everything is in the past and won't be mentioned again. She thinks he is trying to be gracious. She meets his eyes and refuses to look away and eventually his eyes slide from hers. She says nothing. She is determined that she will never speak to him again.

The days become uncomfortable as the silence grows like a spectre that haunts them all. Her mother buzzes between them like a bee. Everything has changed. Attempts to draw them both into conversation falter and die and the silence becomes greater than they are. She watches her mother's fluttering hands and pale skin and she pities her, but it is not enough to make her speak.

In the days that follow her father speaks to her directly and she turns from him, slowly, deliberately. He takes his belt to her. She flinches as it bites into her but she is still silent. Her mind travels beyond him and the pain becomes subdued. He cannot hurt her more than he already has. She fixes her eyes on a mark on the floor and pretends that she is somewhere else. When he has finished his breath is heavier and as he puts his belt back on she straightens up and walks away without looking back.

Over the following weeks it happens again and again until she loses count. Wounds and welts pile up, half heal and split open, fade and renew until eventually it all stops. He no longer tries to speak to her, he no longer beats her; he couldn't find the way to break through the barrier she placed around herself. She feels as though she has won, as though she has proven that he has no power over her. She believes it for a long time. She believes it for years.

The silence stretches and grows, the house becomes a shell in which they move and breathe. When her parents talk, they use hushed tones and worried eyes, as though someone died here and they must stay quiet out of respect. She drifts through it all, through the mist of it, the quietest of all of them.

Time passes and she barely speaks to her mother too. This time it is not out of ignorance or anger. Her voice simply turns inwards. As she speaks less and less in the physical world her voice grows bigger in her emotional one. The voice in her head becomes louder, more real somehow, because there she can say what she wants, she can talk about what matters to her. She is the only one who cares about what she has to say.

She spends hours with nothing but her own company and she talks to the poor, dead little boy. He becomes real to her and as she thinks about him, he takes on physical characteristics. She can see the greenish blue of his eyes, the soft pink of his lips. He is perfect and she can see him vibrant and smiling and alive. She forgets about a blue hand in a worn blanket.

She drifts through the days, she does her chores, sings nursery rhymes, and moves from place to place, room to room. She pays little attention to the world around her and it begins to drift. Her mind is a happier place to be. She barely notices that people start to cross the street to avoid her on the rare occasions that she ventures out; it wouldn't matter to her if she did. All that matters is Charlie junior and she holds him in her head while her arms stay empty.

She doesn't notice that the lines between her life and her mind are blurring, that her hold on both is tenuous. She exists in both places but in neither is she solid and real. When she reaches for something tangible it is like grasping at cobwebs. She thinks that maybe they are all ghosts.

Her mother becomes sick and she barely notices. She will feel bad about that for years to come, in the moments when she notices her absence. She will wonder if her mother cried out for her, if she felt her distance. She cleans her up but cannot remember speaking. She is nothing more than a shape that moves at the edges of her mother's failing vision. She does not remember saying goodbye, she does not remember if she held her as she faded away. But she remembers the wetness of the cloth in her hand as she wipes it across her mother's pale face, she remembers the tears on her mother's cheeks as her eyes screwed up in pain.

She will remember the graveyard and the voice. She will remember that it was the beginning of a different time. And she will feel disloyal. She knows that her mother deserved more than a callous, cold husband and a silent, drifting daughter. She knows that she would do things differently if she could.

Sometimes she drifts and she imagines that she has, that she changed things and painted a different past. She sees herself tell her mother about Charlie, about love and about how he was wrenched from her with bombs and fire. She tells her about blood on towels, about her father and needles. She sees her mother holding a warm, pink baby, cooing softly. She tells her of the old stable and a sound like thunder in her head as she lay on the floor. They sit by a fire, smiling and sharing some time together. She looks up at her mother and she tells her that she loves her, because she knows that in the end, love is the only thing people remember.

43

Rachel

How painful the sunlight was as I walked back down the overgrown lawn towards my own house. The rain of the previous night had faded, leaving glassy surfaces and crystal clear skies. I had spent the morning with Lacey and as afternoon approached she had insisted that I go home for some proper rest.

When it became apparent that she could remember little of the night before I chose not to tell her how I found her, opting instead to tell a little white lie to save her embarrassment. I told her simply that I had called around to her house and found her hurt and confused. She didn't need to know more than that. I found that I cared for her very deeply, that her vulnerability had somehow pulled me closer and I carried her words, her story, like a heavy cloak about my shoulders. She had a way about her that I couldn't define but when she spoke I found it easy to get lost in her past. I could feel for myself the utter weight of her sadness.

Her memories came home with me. Walking straight into my studio, I mixed them with acrylics; different shades of blue and deep, swirling turquoise that I threw at the huge canvas as I painted her sorrow, a raging, tumultuous thing that, when I was finished, left me breathless and empty.

When I was done I cried for her, an achingly painful feeling as I thought of her, alone and lost with no-one to turn to. I had thought her similar to me in some ways but the more I learnt from her, the more she opened up, the more simple my own story became by comparison until I felt self-indulgent for ever thinking there were similarities.

I picked up the receiver and dialled the number I had taken from Lacey's house. It rang so many times that I was about to hang up when the receiver was snatched up by a breathless voice.

'I'm sorry to disturb you, is this Father Thomas?'

'This is indeed he.'

'My name is Rachel Moore, I moved into Dove Cottage a little while ago,' I began.

'Ah, the village's new blood! How may I help you?'

I explained about the previous night's events avoiding mention of the way I had found her. I felt disloyal somehow, as if I were telling tales and indulging in little more than petty gossip. I tried to explain how helpless I had felt and how concerned I was that I hadn't managed the situation very well. He was silent for a moment before speaking.

'Of course, you understand that I am limited as to what I can tell you without speaking to Lacey herself and getting permission. Confidentiality, you know.'

'Yes of course, Father, I understand that completely. What I am concerned about is that I should have handled it differently. Called a doctor perhaps, I'm not sure. I just felt at a loss really.' I could sense him nodding at me down the telephone line.

'The only thing that I can tell you without fear of Lacey's privacy being breached, is the stuff that is already common knowledge around the village, the truthful aspects of it of course, not the gossip mongering rubbish. Several years ago — hmmm well actually I should say decades, it was in the sixties after all — Lacey suffered a rather significant brain injury during an operation. It took her several years to recover from it. She now has what she refers to as blackouts, lapses of reality, so to speak. It sounds like that is what happened yesterday.'

'But what happens to her during these blackouts? How long do they last and how often do they happen? Does she ever become angry or noncompliant even? I'm just concerned because if it should happen again I want to make sure I do the right thing, call her doctor perhaps.' The words came out in a rush and were greeted with the sound of teeth clicking together.

'They don't happen very often to my knowledge and I've never known her to be angry with them, it's more like a kind of absence, like her mind has tootled off and left her physical self behind. I think the worst that happens is she wanders off if the door isn't locked. I've had to come out a couple of times before because I've been called by someone in the village who's seen her, dishevelled and confused. I usually just take her home and wait until she comes out of it. I don't know what medical help she receives and I know that she is incredibly distrustful of doctors, so I find that the best thing to do is keep an eye on her until it passes.'

'So what I did was the right thing then?'

'It certainly sounds that way, my dear. Often there isn't any problem because Lacey has a kind of early warning, in the form of a migraine or a severe bout of tinnitus, something like that. She gives me a ring then and either myself, or April, that's my wife, will come out and give her a hand. Sometimes though, there is no warning and that's when she's been found out and about. In that respect it is probably a little like dementia. Perhaps it would be easier if you thought of it in those terms.'

'But it doesn't happen often?'

'Once or twice a year if that, less so without warning, there seems to be no rhyme or reason to it that I can see. I couldn't tell you exactly how long it's been going on because I've only been the vicar here for twenty something years, but certainly as long as I've known her she's had this little problem,' he says, as if she has nothing more than psoriasis or restless legs.

I couldn't think of anything else that I could ask him without feeling as if I were prying into Lacey's business, so I thanked him for his help.

'You're more than welcome, my dear. Just let me know if I can help in any other way, won't you?'

I said goodbye and hung up the phone,

staring at it for several minutes while I tried to get my thoughts in order. But in the silence that followed all I could think of was Lacey, of her mother and a painful death in a darkened room.

44

Rachel

Dear Diane and Richard

I do not even know where to begin. I am lost for words and I know that no matter what I write, it can never be enough.

I am truly, truly sorry for everything. For my ignorance so many years ago and for the last letter that I wrote to you which was so totally unforgivable. All I can say is that my words came from the mind of an angry child and were never meant. I am older now, wiser perhaps.

I think about you both so often that I can't believe I have left it so long to get in touch. Put it down to guilt. I am ashamed of the way I behaved and the silence in between got longer because I didn't know how to break it. Again, I am sorry and again, I know it is not enough.

There is so much that I want to say to you, so much that matters a great deal, that I want you to know but I am at a loss as to where I can start.

I want to say thank you for fostering me, for letting me know what it felt like to be a part of a family. And thank you for telling me the truth about my birth mother when no-one else would. Words seem to let me down here because I can't explain how important these things were, saying thank you seems too small somehow. What else? A million things, I am an artist now, it is how I make a living and so I should also thank you for the easel that you put in my room not long after I moved in, who knew where that would lead? Sometimes, it seems it is the smallest things that have the biggest impact.

The village I live in is beautiful. It's very different from Birmingham, which is, as you know, where I lived when I left Marham and where I still lived until very recently. I haven't yet decided which place I prefer. I'm slowly falling in love with the peace of the countryside but when I fancy a decent curry or pizza at three o'clock in the morning the lack of options is a little frustrating!

I don't know what else to tell you, there is so much and surprisingly so little of any significance. I just wanted you to know that, as I said, I am older now, perhaps a little wiser and I can look at the past with much greater understanding.

I hope that one day you will forgive me for what I said and the fact that for years I have said nothing.

With love,
Rachel x

I posted the letter before the gum on the envelope had even dried. It felt insignificant, as if

I had tried to seal an amputated limb with some antiseptic cream and a plaster. I thought of the silence and I thought that maybe it would stretch on forever. I could see me never getting a reply, and always wondering what had become of them. I felt that it would be no less than I deserved, there would be a kind of poetry in that, a symmetry in their silence.

45

Rachel

When I lived at the home in Birmingham I shared a room for a little while with another girl my own age, called Sarah. She was only ever to be a temporary fixture, her mother was a single parent and had been injured in an accident and Sarah was a resident at the home while her mother healed. We were different in that sense and therefore we were never really friends; we never broke beyond the barrier of polite conversation into the realms of secrets and laughter. But we were never enemies either. We talked, we passed the time, we breathed the same air. That was all.

One night, after lights out, she told me about her dog, Mitzy. She told me that Mitzy had been in season and had managed to escape the house. They had gone out to search for her, eventually finding her in a field at the end of the garden locked together with a scruffy greyhound from up the road. Her mother had taken Mitzy to the vets and she had an injection to stop her from being pregnant, the morning after pill for dogs. I had laughed at the thought of that.

About three months after this, Sarah had gone upstairs to bed and found some of her cuddly toys missing. She found them in the spare room. Mitzy had scraped up the duvet on the spare bed into a big bundle and the cuddly toys were on top of the pile with Mitzy curled around them, as if she had built a nesting place for the little puppies that would never be. I had found the story so poignant, so sad and at the time I was too afraid to ask what had happened to Mitzy now that her mum was in the hospital and Sarah was in the home.

As I walked up the path to Lacey's house, I thought of Mitzy. I don't know why. I knocked on her front door and she opened it, her expression nervous and I reached forward and took her by the hand, wanting to look after her, to make sure she was okay and wondered if what I was doing was building a nest around her. Was she my substitute?

She stepped aside and gestured for me to come in, she looked resigned as if I had come to deliver bad news and she already knew what it would be. We went into the front room and took separate ends of the sofa again. It felt familiar, but not from that morning. There was something in the awkwardness, the stilted speech that reminded me of the first time Lacey had come for tea.

'How are you feeling?'

She raised her hand, gestured needlessly then shrugged and said she was okay. Her eyes slid to her lap and she ran out of words.

'Is there anything I can get for you?'

She shook her head, 'I'm sorry, Rachel. For last night, I'm sorry that you had to deal with it.'

'Please don't do that, don't apologise. I didn't have to deal with it at all; I could've called someone. I stayed because I was happy to stay.'

Some of the tension drained from her shoulders but not all of it.

'Lacey, I know about the blackouts, and I want you to know that I understand. That's actually why I've come. I want you to keep my phone numbers, mobile and landline, by your telephone. That way you can contact me at the first sign that you are going to black out.' Her emotions played across her face as I spoke, from shame to surprise. 'I'm serious about this too, it isn't just an empty gesture, okay?'

'Why would you do that? You don't have to do that.'

'I know I don't have to, I want to.' I handed her a piece of card and she looked at it for a few moments. She studied the numbers I had written so intently that I wondered if she was trying to commit them to memory. Then she stood and went over to the telephone table and placed the card next to the phone. She turned to me and smiled, a weary smile that lacked vitality.

'Thank you,' she said and came back to sit down. 'I don't know what to say. There aren't many people that would have done what you did last night.'

'I didn't do much, I'm sure others would have done the same.'

'Not in my experience,' she said with a slight shake of her head, 'it's like mental illness, you see. People can't see the cause, only the symptoms and the symptoms scare them. That's one of the reasons people avoid me, they think I'm mad.'

'Albert didn't though,' I said and she smiled.

'No, Albert didn't. He took the time to get to know me, I suppose. Most wouldn't. Like I said to you before, people seem to have long memories and once they have made up their minds it is hard to change them.'

There was nothing I could say in response to that because I couldn't contradict her. I knew how cruel people could be about the things they didn't understand. I knew how careless they could be with other people's emotions.

'I grew up in a children's home.' I told her and her head swivelled slowly towards me. 'My mother was an alcoholic and they took me away from her.' She blinked at me, uncertain as to how to treat the information I was giving her.

'I guess I'm telling you because I want you to know that I understand what it is to be different. The other kids at school treated us care kids a bit like lepers, like we were less than they were. I always felt like I didn't quite fit anywhere.'

She nodded her understanding. 'How long were you in care for?'

'Forever really, until I grew up. I haven't seen my mother since I was a baby; I only know that her name is Margaret. It's not much is it? I was fostered for a while but that placement didn't work out and there wasn't any more after it. The problem with being in care is that once you reach a certain age there are less people that want to foster you, especially when you hit your teens and the hormones kick in.'

'What about your father, did you ever meet him?'

'According to my foster parents the father's name part of my birth certificate was blank. I know less about him than I do about my mother.'

'How awful for you,' she said and I could see that she meant it.

'What about siblings?'

I shook my head, 'None that I know of. I was alone when I was found and no-one has ever mentioned that there was another child there, it was just me.' I could see in her face she knew how I felt; she knew what it was like to be the only one. It was why I had told her. I sensed the barriers that she had put in place after the previous night. I knew how awkward, how different she felt as a result of what had happened and I didn't know how else I could tell her that in some way I understood.

'Have you ever tried to trace your family, through your birth certificate perhaps?'

I shook my head at the question and explained that I had never seen my paperwork, had never asked for it. Perhaps I had always been too wary of discovering too much about the person I could have been had I not been taken away.

We sat with our heads turned to each other, mirror images as we each took the other's eyes and looked through them. Seeing the world differently; seeing the subtle nuances of another's path, the blemishes, the fractures that ran down the middle. She reached across the sofa and took my hand and we sat in silence for a while as I tried to find ways to let her know that she no longer had to feel alone.

'I'm sorry about what happened with Charlie, with both of them.'

She smiled at me and nodded. 'Thank you,' she said simply. 'You know, even though it all ended the way it did, I'm still grateful. What would I be without them? What would my life be? It would have been an awfully empty place without the memories I have of the two of them.'

I wondered at the years between then and now, at how long those memories had kept her company. I thought of the little bedroom upstairs and couldn't help wishing that everything had worked out differently for her.

46

Lacey

He is dying. She knows it. She can sense it in his laboured breathing, in the paleness of him. He has shrunk on the bed, turning in on himself. His middle is gone, the big dark heart of him, and he shrivels into the space left behind.

He refused to let her call anyone for help, he is afraid to go into hospital, she sees it in his eyes, a shadow behind them. How small he is, how pathetic. She watches him and wonders if the part of him that made her afraid — the part of him that took her life and moulded it, shaped it into something it shouldn't have been — was the first thing to die; it is no longer there and she no longer recognises him without it.

She thinks that she will find that part of him, take that black and dark and rancid part and place it in a little cardboard box. She wonders where she can bury it. Not in the garden where it will poison the earth, where it will fester and spread rotten roots through the soil, not in the graveyard where it can taint the purity of the ground. She spends days thinking about what she can do with it, where she can put it that will do no harm.

She goes into his room and feels his eyes on her as she moves around the bed with warm water and clean towels. As she bends to clean him, his mouth opens and the smell of rot fills the space between them.

'You hate me, I can see it in your eyes.'

A cloud billows from his cracked, dry mouth and surrounds her. She looks back at him with eyes that hold nothing. She sees no trace of the man she hated. She sees skin that looks a bit like her father stretched over a shrunken skeleton that cowers from hands that try to keep him clean, that try to keep the rot from spreading. She says nothing because there are no words in her just now.

She finishes what she is doing and leaves the room. She goes downstairs and can barely hear her own footsteps as she moves. She wonders if she is the one that has died. Perhaps this is her penance for being the way she is. Perhaps this is her Hell and she will spend eternity looking after the man who stole everything from her.

She rushes to the mirror and sees her own reflection staring back at her with wide eyes and a mouth that gasps for the air that reminds her she is alive. Her hand lifts, touches her face, feels the warmth there, the softness that yields beneath her fingers and she feels gratitude race the blood through her veins. She is solid, complete.

She heats soup on the stove. Not too hot, not too cold. She tests it on the delicate skin inside her wrist before placing it on a tray and taking it upstairs, careful not to spill a drop, careful not to awaken the vindictive part of him. She walks into his room again and helps him to sit up. As she reaches out he flinches, expecting the seeds of who he was to take root in her. She sees the expectation hang in front of her, but does not react.

She feeds him, and when he is finished and she helps him to lie down again, he meets her eyes. 'You just want me to hurry up and die don't you?'

She looks down at him, puzzled, at this man who looks like her father but isn't anymore. 'But you already did,' she says, and he closes his eyes and turns away from her as she gathers the tray and leaves the room.

47

Rachel

I told Lacey what Father Thomas had shared with me. Careful to point out that he had kept her confidence and that he hadn't spoken out of turn. She nodded and thought for a moment, as though she were weighing something up. She stood up and moved away from the sofa towards the window.

'When my mother died, my father didn't really know what to do with me. I think while she was alive he ignored me quite easily but after she was gone, I became too much for him.'

I watched as she lifted her hand and rubbed it across her eyes. 'I hadn't spoken to him for so long and Mother had always been a bit of a go-between. With her gone everything changed.'

She turned to look at me and I saw the uncertainty in her eyes. It stood side by side with her resignation as if she had already decided to speak and nothing would stop the words now even if she was unsure. She walked across the room and sat back down, hunching into herself and raising her shoulders until they framed her face and half hid it from sight.

'It started with electric shock treatment. I don't remember much about it just bits and pieces really, little flashes of memories. I can recall three or four times when he took me to the hospital, telling me it was for my own good. I never remembered the journey home. When the shock treatment didn't change anything he had me lobotomised.'

Her voice faded against the expression of horror on my face and she looked away from me. I was stunned. In my ignorance I had thought that lobotomy was something that only really happened in films and stories. I thought it belonged in the past, with archaic medicine and body snatching and I told her so. She shook her head.

'It was far more common then I think. Not an everyday thing but it was accepted in medical circles as a treatment for people with problems in their heads. There were a few quite well known cases.' She smiled then and it failed to reach her eyes.

'Not me of course, I don't think anybody knew about me. That was probably how my father wanted it.'

'But, why would he do that?'

She shrugged, as if I had asked a question that she herself had puzzled over for years. 'Perhaps because I never spoke to him, or because I spent all my time daydreaming. I wasn't normal to him, I was a source of shame. He was a doctor so it was probably easier for him to arrange than it would have been for anyone else. Maybe he genuinely thought it was the best thing, maybe he thought it would help.' She rubbed at her forehead again, as if assessing the damage done all those years ago. I found myself studying the space she touched.

'That is what Father Thomas was talking about when he said the brain damage was done during an operation of some kind. He just didn't tell you that the operation was done specifically to cause damage.'

I shook my head. 'I don't know what to say. I mean, is that why you have the blackouts then, because of the lobotomy?'

'I think so or perhaps because of the shock treatment. I don't know really, maybe it was both. My memory was affected quite badly by one of the treatments, I'm not sure which. Some things I can remember really well but a lot of it is very hazy. I can't remember the shock treatment but I can remember the hours leading up to the lobotomy and part of the operation itself. Though it took me years to understand what my memory was showing me. Everything afterwards is a bit absent though.'

'You remember the lobotomy?'

I think that she heard the disbelief in my voice. I had heard of people dreaming that they were awake during operations, I had even read that some people had perfect recollection of what went on in the theatre, but I had never met anyone who experienced it. She smiled at me, a sad parody of a smile.

'I know how it sounds but it was done while I was awake. I wasn't anaesthetised. I think it was quite common for that kind of operation.'

'Oh my God!' I shook my head again, unable to think of anything to say that would fit inside that moment. Knowing that there was nothing I could say that would take from her the terror of what she had been through. I was horrified, fascinated, and appalled all at once, that someone I knew could have been through something so terrible. I looked at this woman before me, at her independence, her vitality and I found it incredible that she had made it so far.

'I remember being on the table, I remember the thingy, the instrument, coming towards my eyes . . .'

'Coming towards your eyes?' I asked and she nodded.

'It was what was called a trans-orbital lobotomy. They went in above my eyes, through the back of the sockets. That's why I don't have any scars.'

I felt sick at the thought, disgusted by it and it must have shown on my face because I saw the sympathy cross Lacey's features and she reached out and patted my hand.

'I don't remember much after that. Little flashes of pictures really that might well have been dreams. All I know for sure is that I lost a year somewhere. I remember that it was 1962 when I went in to hospital for the op but the next date I remember is in 1963. I'm not totally sure what happened between those times.' She looked away from me then, her eyes moving slowly, her face still.

'I don't know how your father could have done that.' I stared across the room and the world seemed a slightly different place than it had before, slightly more tainted somehow because I had once again been reminded of the horrible things people were capable of.

'He wasn't a very nice man,' she said with a shrug and a slight shake of her head.

I looked back at her and saw acceptance of what her life had been, of the horrors she had been through. She smiled at me, a genuine smile this time that lifted her eyes.

'I take after my mother,' she said and then she leaned over and pulled me into a hug. She rubbed my back as if trying to give me comfort, as if I were the one who had been damaged, as though I were the one who needed to forgive the wrongs she had suffered. I hugged her back and then we sat for a while in silence. Her story filled the space between us until it seemed, in that moment at least, that there was nothing left to say.

48

Lacey

She stands in the bare room and looks out of the window at the lane that joins the last two houses. Sometimes she stands here and the walls feel light and welcoming around her. Sometimes, as now, there is an emptiness that chills her to the bone.

She looks around and sees the dust across the furniture. She sees fingermarks where someone rested their hands and carried that dust away with them. Ashes to ashes, dust to dust. The room is empty and she knows that if she turns to the bed she will see it unused, unmade. Her son will not be there because he never was and some of the time she knows that. And even though she can see him in her mind's eye, even though she knows exactly what he looks like and what he sounds like when he laughs, in lucid moments like this she knows that he has never been more than her imagination. He is the little boy who never existed.

She thinks about Rachel and the conversation they had that morning. Whenever she looks at the younger woman she sees dark eyes full of kindness and compassion. If she'd had a daughter, Rachel is what she would have wished for. How sad for them both that they had to grow up without loving families. She thinks about it until the edges of her thoughts grow insignificant. She draws patterns in the dust with her finger until most of it is gone, until there is only a thin trail that looks like smoke and then she turns to leave the room.

'See you later, Charlie,' she says and to her ears her voice sounds tinny and loud; it falls through the air like the dust brushed from her fingertips. She doesn't expect an answer as she pulls the door closed behind her.

As she walks down the corridor she thinks of the horror on the younger woman's face as she shared the story of the operation. She thinks of eyes open wide and dirty fingernails and a year that ceased to exist. That lost year is gone forever, fallen into the dark space left behind when they broke through the fragile bone and stole her memory. She thinks about what she shared with Rachel, how she said she wasn't sure what happened during that time and her conscience stabs at her because she knows there is an element of a lie in what she said. Had Rachel seen it in the way that Lacey's eyes slid to the floor?

It is true she doesn't remember. Not all of it, certainly not the immediate aftermath when her eyes were surely blackened and her mind woefully absent. The beginning of that year she does not see at all through her own eyes but through the words of another, someone she remembers vaguely, someone she knows she had seen before. When did she find those words, black and smooth against paper yellowed with time? Sometime after he was gone and the house was heavy and empty around her.

In the bedroom that she had rarely set foot in before, the bedroom she had stripped and painted and made her own, she had found it all those years ago: the ledger with the torn page, the ragged edge, the smudged ink; worn and used as though it had been read over and over again. She had pored over it, followed the leaning script with her fingers as if she could absorb the memories that way, as if they would become part of her if she touched them. And in those pages she had read the story of her lost year. Those pages with the front sheet that stated boldly: Miss Lacey Carmichael — Record of Convalescence.

How odd it was to read about herself in the third person, how strange to be told of things she had no recollection of. Her name a sharp reminder that the book was her story, her days, a fraction of her almost complete life and yet the words themselves seemed little more than discarded clothing, ill fitting and forgotten. She had been afraid at first to read further, to discover who she was, what she had become.

How many entries were there in the beginning that recorded 'no change', the words surrounded by a blank expanse of paper? They had appeared daily at first, after the initial entry that informed her that she had been vegetative, unresponsive, and incapable of independent movement. But after a while they had become a weekly entry as if the writer had become bored repeating the same words over and over again, 'no change'. She had frowned at them as if her displeasure were enough to force those words to curve around on themselves and say something different, something better.

How many hours had she pored over those pages and looked for variations in the script, mistakes, a drop of ink that changed the landscape so that it looked different from the others that said exactly the same thing? How many similar pages did she turn before the story changed and became one of improvement?

'Lacey responded to my presence today. I noticed that her eyes were open and they followed me across the room as I set about her bed bath. The changes are subtle but noticeable. She seems more aware somehow. And, rather obscurely, I am more aware of her being in the room with me.'

And not long after that:

'Lacey sat up today. She still does not move independently but I held her hands and pulled her upwards and there was little resistance. Once sitting she remained so, she did not fall backwards and return to a laying position. She remained seated until I guided her to lie back down.'

She hurries to her bedside table and finds the ledger and with shaking hands she opens the pages part of the way through. The leaves fall open as though to a much-visited page. She does not look at those earlier entries, at those moments that are like a stuck gramophone going over and over the same worn furrow. She moves forwards to where the words stretch into sentences and onwards into paragraphs that paint a scene that she cannot remember. The words dance before her eyes, crowd around her and mix up in the confusion of her awareness, until she cannot recall if the images they paint are memories that truly belong to her, or not. She is a puppet dancing at the whim of a book that tells the tale of a life she has lost.

Her hands shake as she forces herself to carefully turn the pages. She is afraid that she will damage them, that the book will become worthless, broken, more like the real woman than the paper copy that taunts her with knowledge she does not possess. If she loses this, what then? She knows that after a while it will all be gone again. She will remember nothing of that time. Without the script in front of her she will lose completely the part of her that she never knew. The thought makes her so afraid that she gasps at the air as if drowning. She already forgets so much. She doesn't want to lose this too, this part of her that is not her, this part of her that is someone else.

Turn the page, turn the page.

'Lacey continues to improve in some ways. If I take her hand and guide her to her feet she can stand adequately, though she is inclined to tremble a little as though her muscles have atrophied. Because of this I make certain that she receives exercise of some kind every day. This usually involves being led by the hand around the house. She takes the stairs with relative ease and will continue to move if there is a gentle pull on her hand or wrist. However, Lacey stops moving altogether if her limb is released. Only time will tell if she will regain her ability to move independently.'

She lifts her hand in front of her eyes and wriggles her fingers slowly, close enough to her face that the digits blur, becoming doubled. Time told, she thinks to herself, time told and I am fine, look. She cannot resist using those fingers, the ones that move independently, to press at the skin on her face, to feel the sinking in, the softness. And she wonders how much time passed before she could do this, before she could move on her own. She thinks that she could count through the pages and that she could work it out for herself but she is afraid to do so. She is afraid because then she will know for sure how long it was that she was at the mercy of someone else. She will see the bend and stretch of the helpless little puppet, the wires that held her up, the hands that controlled them. She will feel the insidious fear coil through her that she was ever that person. That she could become that person again. It is a fear that sometimes jolts her awake at night.

'Lacey's physical condition continues to improve week by week. She is stronger in herself and indeed now when I lead her around, I feel some measure of resistance in her movements. I take this as a good sign and it allows me some positivity about her continued recovery.'

She skips through page after page, turning them quickly as again she sees herself stall and stagnate on the paper, no change — no change. And then she comes to an entry that she stares at through the fleshy pads of her fingers, like a horror film that she doesn't want to look at but she cannot turn away and she feels herself begin to rock back and forth, one hand across her eyes, the other pressed to her chest trying to slow her quickened heartbeat.

'My prior concern for Lacey's ability to regain her independence has now been replaced by something else altogether. Lacey is a perfectly capable helper around the house and does as she is asked with few reminders. Many of her movements appear automatic and stiff but despite this she is very helpful and in this way she is a positive asset. However, Lacey appears to have lost any autonomy that she previously possessed. She does as asked but no more and if the request is deficient of any important information, Lacey seems unable to complete the task requested.

I am also increasingly concerned about Lacey's lack of emotional response. This was highlighted in depth to me today when we both witnessed a scene that should have caused some distress. One of our patients went into labour today and I took Lacey with me to the labour room to assist if need be. After a reasonably lengthy and arduous labour the tragic infant was stillborn. The young mother was clearly dis-tressed and the situation was indeed upsetting for all of us, however, Lacey did not respond in any way. She continued to stare at the young woman on the bed until Lacey herself was led from the room.'

The words push at her memory, nudging her to remember, to see clearly. She feels them crowding her, making her claustrophobic. But the images are not lucid, the spaces between are blank, faded and she screws her eyes shut tight as she tries to force the images forward. Tension bands across her temples as she pleads with her damaged cells to divulge the awful pitiful images that the words describe. But all she can remember, all she can see, is a blanket and a tiny still blue hand.

★   ★   ★

She snaps the book closed and thrusts it back into its drawer. She knows the rest of the book almost by heart, she can see the words clearly against her closed eyes. The entries tell her of long-term memory loss, impaired judgement. They tell her that she suffers from time and place disorientation, confusion, and her mouth twists into a sad, ironic smile.

She doesn't have to look at any more of the pages to know that shortly afterwards the book's memories merged with her own. That the words marched from the pages to join with the images that belonged only to her, that she is no longer seeing that time in her life through someone else's eyes. She knows when the written word catches up with her. She remembers returning home to a different world, a world where she does as she is told, where she sees the satisfaction on her father's face. She speaks when she is spoken to, does as she is asked. She is the perfect little daughter who never puts a foot wrong. She wonders if her father went to his grave believing that he had done the right thing.

Feeling drained, she slowly makes her way down the stairs and into the kitchen. She sees the two teacups near the sink and as she washes them she thinks some more about the woman next door and the little card with the numbers on. She feels tears damp against her cheek and berates herself for them, feeling silly that she is crying when she isn't sad. She dries her hands on the tea towel and takes a bowl of scraps out to the chickens; they greet her excitedly and their voices wash over her. She has done these chores so often that she no longer has to think about them, which is good because her thoughts are elsewhere as she puzzles over what move to make next.

When she is finished she stands and stares at the telephone. She wonders what she should do, what she can do. She takes in the shiny curve of the receiver, the roundness of the enlarged buttons. She lightly strokes her finger along the edge of it, thinking, thinking. Finally she opens her address book to the right page and lifts the receiver to her ear. Dialling the number carefully she hears the ringing on the other end followed by a greeting. She begins to speak.

Ashes to ashes.

49

Rachel

The days passed slowly, becoming average, routine. The rain came often to wash clean the fields and leaves. I learned to breathe more softly, with less urgency. The hectic pace of the city faded from my blood and was replaced with a calm that became evident in the somnambulant flow of my paintings. Somehow when I took more time to relax, more time to pause, I became more productive. Jane was thrilled.

In between time in the studio I shopped and cleaned, I went for walks across Dartmoor and never failed to be astonished by the landscape that stretched, dramatic and sharp, before me. Father Thomas called round for a visit under the pretence of checking that Lacey was okay. He was a jovial man who sounded pompous but wasn't. He had thinning grey hair, a small stature and a smile in his eyes. Over tea he asked if I would be joining the congregation. I declined, somewhat embarrassed, and explained that I had little belief in God.

He smiled, 'Oh I don't care about that, Rachel, I just need to get a few more arses on the pews.'

I laughed, appreciating his honesty. I told him I would think about it and both of us knew that I wouldn't, but he accepted the pretence with good humour and a smile and that was fine.

I saw Lacey fairly often during those days. I did little chores for her, taking my grass trimmer to her lawn and cutting her hedges back. She rewarded me with eggs and simple friendship. I found an easy contentment about my life that had been lacking for a long time and I relaxed into it, finding a measure of peace and ease of being.

One night I had finished painting long after the sun had gone down. I was scrubbing my hands at the kitchen sink, watching swirls of green and brown spiral around the plughole before disappearing, when there was a knock at the door. My heart stayed slow and steady as I reached for the tea towel, I had become used to Lacey's lack of awareness regarding the time and I was often up late anyway.

I glanced up at the clock as I dried my hands hurriedly and saw it was almost midnight. I opened the front door and was greeted by a wide smile like a child's.

'Have you seen it?' she asked breathlessly, her voice tinged with awe.

My mind raced through possibilities but came up empty. 'Seen what?'

She leaned forwards and grabbed my hand, pulling me outside into a clear night. I followed her, smiling and curious, as she led me down my path into the lane and up into her own garden where the house stood in total darkness. She stopped and turned her face to the sky.

'Look!'

I followed her gaze upwards, towards a sky

liberally scattered with stars and constellations. Here in the garden the sky looked beautiful, startling and I told her so. She gave my hand a squeeze and I could feel the shake in her arm as though she could hardly contain her response.

'It's not that, just wait,' she told me, her eyes still fixed on the sky. She was holding her breath. She gestured again and I turned back to the stars, and as I did so a shooting star blazed across the darkness and fizzed out to nothing. I felt her jump up and down next to me.

'Did you see it?' she asked and I nodded. 'Wait, wait, wait, there'll be more.'

We stood there for more than an hour, watching the sky as the stars moved around us. Our necks became stiff and the night's chill seeped up through the ground, into our feet and higher. Subconsciously we moved to stand closer together as we watched the meteor shower light up the dark dome above us. Lacey's enthusiasm was contagious and I felt myself start and thrill at every bright line that left a residual image on my retinas.

Soon enough though, the chill of the night became more obvious than the natural firework display above us and as one, it seemed, we began to move our feet more and fidget against it. Eventually we looked away from the sky and at each other.

'Thank you for coming to get me,' I said and she smiled at me across the darkness.

'Isn't it beautiful?'

I nodded and gave her a hug before saying that I had to go to bed, it was getting late.

'Goodnight, sweet dreams,' she said as I began to head up the path, as if I was a child and she was tucking me in. It made me smile more and I turned back to return the sentiment. After I had done so I saw her pass her hand across her forehead.

'I've just remembered,' she said, 'I was wondering if you'd be able to give me a lift into Exeter the day after tomorrow? I have an appointment in the morning.'

'Of course. Maybe afterwards we could grab a bit of lunch?'

She looked pleased at the idea and nodded. 'Okay then,' and with a final wave and smile she disappeared into the darkness of her house, and a light came on in the hallway.

I found myself smiling as I walked back home, at the simplicity of Lacey's joy. I moved around the house and switched off the lights as I went, taking one final look at the painting on the easel that displayed my subject — who I knew to be a bank manager — as a muscleman in a forest surrounded by wolves. Satisfied with what I had achieved that day I made my way upstairs to bed.

It was only as I lay in the darkness with the quilt pulled up tight around a body still trying to push the late night chill away, that I realised that the Perseid meteor shower occurred in mid-August. The days were blending into one another and I paid little attention to the date unless something reminded me of it. In that moment I became aware that August was half way over and I had still not heard from Diane and Richard.

I rolled over onto my side and rubbed absently at my cheek, wondering how long I could wait before giving up and accepting that my apology had been meaningless to them, and the past would remain where it always had been, immersed in regret.

50

Lacey

She remembers. She sits at the front of the church and listens as the vicar talks about the wonderful man that lies dead in the box in front of her. She wonders if she is at the wrong funeral. She can sense the crowds behind her, almost every seat filled. They are like a wave pushing against her back and she wonders if she will be able to stay seated or if she will be washed into an undignified heap on the floor. She can see herself lying there, her mouth opening and closing as she gasps for air; a fish washed up on a strange and hostile shore.

She knows the church is full. She can tell it in the rustlings that punctuate the vicar's eulogy. There is one behind her right ear, one over to her left somewhere. There is a sigh, and occasionally there is a sniff and the sound of someone delving into a bag before a nose is blown. She knows that people cry in that room where the angels hear prayers and take them away, where the flagstones hide important graves and the bones decay somewhere beneath her feet.

She knows that they cry and she wants to jump to her feet and scream at them to stop. She wants to ask them why they cry for him, that cruel, vindictive man who stole his only daughter's life and gave her a pitiful substitute for company. But she knows, beneath her anger and frustration, she knows. They cry for the longevity of him, for the familiarity of him. They cry for the times he saved them, for the times he healed them. They cry because they did not know the man behind the mask and they believe him worthy of their grief.

Her eyes stay dry, empty, another funeral without tears. She looks to her sides and sees the shine of the wood, old, old wood worn smooth with age. She sees the spaces where no-one dares sit, the spaces either side of her. She is alone on her pew and she would have to turn and draw attention to herself if she wanted to see the faces of those who mourned in her stead. She keeps her eyes forwards and listens, as the vicar's words become a bee buzzing in her head. She wonders why she wasn't asked to speak, to say a few words. Surely that would be customary. Perhaps they are afraid of what she might say or do.

She buries him in the churchyard next to her mother. She imagines her mother turning on to her side, away from the new arrival as his coffin is lowered. Again she senses behind her the faceless, ignorant mourners. She watches the birds in the trees and doesn't realise she is supposed to throw a handful of earth to mar the wooden surface that reflects the rectangular hole of sky above it. The vicar moves to her side, prompts her, and she bends to the sound of muttered questions that she knows are about her.

'Ashes to ashes,' he says and she wonders what that means. The Earth is not ash, her father will not be ash, and her father will not be dust. He will be rot; he will be mould, liquid, rank and foul. He will be on the outside what he has always been on the inside and nobody but her will see it, just as it has always been.

She stands at the graveside long after everyone else has gone. She feels someone touch her arm — the vicar most likely, he is the only one that dares to come near her — she hears him speak but it is indistinct and she does not respond. She stares into the ground and wonders if it is truly done with, if he has truly gone. She waits and waits for the sense of freedom. She waits but it doesn't come. She will never be free of him; her life is his creation. She is alone and untouchable, because of him.

She turns and makes her way out of the churchyard, over the road and up the lane. She keeps her head down out of habit and halfway towards home she forces herself to raise her chin, to ignore the voice that echoes in her head. She feels triumphant just for a moment but as she looks around she realises that the trees look strange, overwhelming. They tower above her and seem to close in as she moves. She shies away from them and lifts her hands to block out the sight. Slowly her eyes slide back towards the ground, she cannot stop them and she doesn't fight it. She begins to count. She knows exactly when to turn, exactly when to bend to avoid the branch.

She makes her way home and when she gets there and closes the door behind her, she cries.

51

Rachel

She sat silently beside me as we drove towards Exeter. The roads were narrow and winding, the hedges grown bigger now that the rain had come to provide sustenance. I had to concentrate far more on my driving here than I had in the city and sometimes I became aware of my knuckles gleaming white as I gripped tightly onto the wheel. I wondered if I would ever get used to it as a lorry thundered around a bend forcing me to brake hard.

From the corner of my eye I saw Lacey's hand grip the edge of her seat and asked if she was okay.

'I'm fine, just a bit of a nervous passenger that's all.'

I wondered at how many times she had made this journey. Would I be able to count the number of times on my fingers? Would there be some left over? I didn't ask, but I eased off the accelerator a little.

Once we got to the main road the traffic increased significantly. Cars laden with luggage until the drivers were blind to all behind them, caravans slowing down the flow as they went up vast hills. I moved into a lower gear, welcoming an excuse to go slower and let Lacey relax.

'Whereabouts do you need to go once we get to town?'

I felt her eyes move onto me as I negotiated the road ahead and then she turned away again.

'I have to go to my solicitors in Southernhay. There are just some things I need to sort out. It shouldn't take long.'

Her tone was quiet, embarrassed and I chanced a quick look at her. She was half turned away, her bottom lip nipped between her teeth as though she tried to stop herself from saying more. I changed the subject.

'There's an art exhibition on at the museum. Nobody well known, I think it's just local artists showing off their work. Would you like to have a look with me after lunch?'

I felt her eyes move back to mine, saw her cheeks lift in my peripheral vision, 'I'd like that,' she said, and her hand relaxed a little more on the seat as we moved closer to the city.

★ ★ ★

Tucked behind the bustle of the main street, Southernhay was like entering a different world. Vast buildings, many of them old and covered in vines, housed the financial and law firms, as well as the more upmarket estate agents. Gardens ran down the middle of the streets, ringed by the road that stretched in an elongated circle from the top of the street to the bottom.

'Whereabouts do you need to go?' I asked and she gestured vaguely left and up. Parking spaces were few and far between but I found one further up the road and slid the car into it.

'Is this close enough?' She nodded and moved to hurry out of the car. 'I'll wait here for you.' She leaned in through the open door and grabbed her shopping bag.

'I don't think I'll be very long, Rachel. Thank you for giving me a lift.'

I smiled and said it was no problem as she straightened up and scurried off, still chewing at her bottom lip.

I waited until she was out of sight before I got out of the car and stretched my legs. The clouds had parted and the sun was shining, the earlier rainfall combining with it to make the air humid and close. I filled the waiting space up with trying to decide where to go for lunch. I didn't know Exeter well, but I had read something in the local paper about a new restaurant opening up near the Cathedral, so maybe we could go there.

I sat down on a nearby bench and squinted into the sunshine, watching people in suits move up and down the roads and pathways. Bustling little worker ants with a mission to complete. I didn't envy the rigid structures of their working life. I looked down, at my long dark skirt and my Victorian style boots and I thought that I didn't quite fit in here. City life was almost totally purged from me now and I was glad of it.

I watched them bustle around talking amongst themselves and I sat on the peripherals like a ghost, an observer, wondering at their lives and the thoughts they hid behind the masks of professionalism. I didn't see any of them smile. I was still wondering about this when Lacey came back, looking relieved. I stood up, tucked her arm through mine and followed the signs to the Cathedral.

We found a restaurant with tables outside, huge umbrellas shading us from the autumn sun as we sat and watched the people picnicking and playing on the grass surrounding the Cathedral. On a bench near the low wall that surrounded the green, a man of indefinable age lay sleeping. His face had a ruddy glow to it, weathered and cracked as he snored softly and occasionally shifted against the hard surface. We watched as he opened one eye and looked at the floor next to him before reaching down and picking up his bag, moving it to his lips and drinking deeply. Nobody paid him any attention.

Children ran in circles, laughing and chasing after pigeons that always seemed to scoot out of the way just in time but never flew far, landing a few feet away, as if they too were enjoying the game. The whole scene was busy but peaceful and I was glad we had come.

While we waited to be served, we talked about nothing of any importance. It was an insignificant conversation that faded with time, becoming nothing more than a stitch in the fabric of growing friendship.

We both chose a stir-fry that when it was put in front of us, piled high in the centre of our plates, looked almost too good to eat, like a piece of art. I picked at it delicately, unwilling to disturb its perfection. Lacey picked up her knife and fork and pulled hers apart like a miner looking for gold. We laughed, drank wine and enjoyed the moment. Afterwards she insisted on paying. I couldn't imagine that her pension stretched far, but her face was set, determined and I didn't argue.

After lunch we spent some time wandering around the shops. The differences between Birmingham and Exeter were vast and despite the presence of major shopping chains, Exeter retained the calmer air of a market town. We walked the long line of the High Street and Lacey pointed out St Stephen's Church, which according to the sign outside was a thousand years old. It bumped its majestic, worn shoulders with modern shops on either side, looking out of place and slightly uncomfortable.

It was a common theme throughout the city centre, this mix of ancient and new. As we made our way in a roundabout direction towards the museum we found another church, tiny and box shaped. Pigeons sat on the roof, seemingly oblivious to the shops with glass fronts and bright signs that surrounded the thirteenth century building.

We climbed the wide steps and entered the museum and as we walked towards the exhibition, Lacey's hand went to her mouth, 'Oh no, the poor thing!'

The room was filled with an enormous giraffe, his head sticking up above the gallery that ringed the room on the first floor. We stood near his feet and looked at him, frozen in time. Lacey reached out a hand and touched his knee, she looked genuinely distraught. Reading from the sign I said, 'His name is Gerald, he was brought to the museum nearly ninety years ago.' I looked at her and saw the beginnings of tears in her eyes and I took her by the hand to lead her away.

She looked over her shoulder and I heard her mutter, 'Ninety years,' quietly under her breath.

As we moved towards the exhibition room she seemed subdued, kept her head down and her eyes on the floor, as if afraid she might see something else that she didn't like. I was mesmerised by how quickly her mood could alter and how little she tried to hide it.

The room we moved into was altogether brighter, reflecting colour from every wall. There were paintings of all sizes and shelves displaying sculptures, statuettes, even jewellery and I moved among them finding nothing that stood out for me. The paintings were lovely but I found many of them to be lacking in emotion.

We moved around the room and after a few moments Lacey lifted her head, taking in the details of the paintings around her. I stood in front of a smaller painting that had caught my eye. Here there was emotion. The painting was heavily textured, but subtle. It was a tree in the moonlight. The artist had painted a dome shaped willow in deep greens; the curved dome of its upper branches reflected the blue tinged light from the full moon that hung in the blackened sky. It was simple, beautiful, haunting and as Lacey joined me I pointed out to her the subtlety of the artist's work, the way the blue moonlight interacted with the green of the tree. She looked at it for a long moment, her eyes squinting, her head cocked to one side. I watched as her eyes moved across the surface before moving back to mine.

'It looks like a dinosaur!' she said and I looked back at the canvas, trying to see it through her eyes.

'You're right, it does,' I replied and we laughed and moved on.

Later, we had stopped off at a supermarket on the way out of town to pick up various bits and pieces and by the time we got back in the car, evening was approaching. The air was calm and still, the clouds all gone. Everything looked soft, ethereal.

We were silent, but it was the contented silence of a day well spent. I lost myself in thoughts of Lacey's reaction to the long dead giraffe, wondering at the way she felt everything so keenly. There was a beauty in it somehow, as if she were slightly more human than I was, more empathic. I thought it a shame that she had never had the chance to be a mother.

A yelp from the passenger seat made me jump. Lacey's face was pressed up against the passenger window, her hands either side of it, flat against the glass, her eyes were on the sky. I pulled up in the gateway of a nearby field and asked if she was okay and she nodded, pointing. I followed her finger and saw a rainbow coloured hot-air balloon high up in the sky. The road was quiet behind us and I could hear, through my open window, the thrust of the burners as it moved closer to where we watched hundreds of feet below.

'Isn't it beautiful?' she said, her voice full of awe and magic. I looked up again, trying to see what she was seeing but it was still just a balloon floating above its basket.

'I've always wanted to go in one of them.' She sounded wistful, as if she knew now that she would never get the chance. 'It would be like flying, like being a bird.' She lowered her head and turned to look at me. She looked sad and I patted the back of her hand. I started the engine and headed home.

52

Lacey

Silence. It draws out before her like a long forgotten canal, sluggish and indolent. The house fills with it. The quiet feels different somehow without him here. Though she never spoke to him, always turned from him with eyes full of loathing, she realises now that she had the choice. She could have spoken to him if she wanted to. There was freedom in that silence, there was life in it.

This is different. She feels it pressing against her, heavy and clumsy and she shrinks from it. The house fills with it until she can see the walls bend before its passage. It forces its way out through the locks, under doorways; it seeps through the tight edges of windowpanes and she wonders if it will take her with it.

When the radio is on or the TV occupies her front room and keeps her company, the sound is almost too much for this place. The silence pulls away like a snail's eye touched by a careless finger; it shrivels and cringes back into corners and alcoves. She fights the urge to say 'shhh, stay silent, the house is afraid.' She turns down the volume, watches the pictures and feels the house settle around her.

The silence becomes familiar, it becomes her friend and finally she realises that inside that silence, inside the house, she is safe; finally. Her father is truly gone, she has no need to fear him, no need to sleep uneasily because of what might happen when she does.

The oppression inside the walls lifts and begins to fade slowly away as the memories of him become distant. She becomes lighter, less afraid. She finds inside her the person she could have been and she begins to find happiness in small things. Time passes and she gets lost among the seasons, drifting through the rooms, watching through the windows.

53

Rachel

I was outside in the front garden when the phone rang. I ran to answer it and snatched the receiver up just before the answer phone kicked in. As I spoke, slightly breathlessly, I looked back at the hall floor and frowned at the trail of mud I had left behind me.

'Hello, is this Rachel Moore?' a distinctly masculine, gruff voice asked. 'I'm sorry to call like this. My name is Paul, I'm Martha's husband.'

'How can I help you?' I asked. Since moving to the village I had had very little contact with my landlady, other than the meeting in the graveyard and a brief visit to the house when she dropped off copies of the annual safety checks for me.

'I just wanted to keep you informed really, well at Martha's insistence that is. Unfortunately, Martha suffered a heart attack a couple of days ago, she's in hospital at the moment.' The words stuttered from him, a staccato beat as he passed difficult news to a stranger. It made me think of bubbles rising through water to burst on the surface.

'Oh, I'm so sorry. How is she?'

'They think she is going to be okay, they're just keeping an eye on her for a couple more days. I just wanted to let you know because the number you have for Martha is her mobile number. She asked me to give you a ring and let you have my number in case there are any problems. Do you have a pen?'

I wrote the number down and said thank you, asking him to pass on my best wishes before he hung up. After my initial rush of sympathy for the woman I couldn't help but be selfish, cross my fingers and hope that my tenancy here was safe. I gave myself a shake and pushed those thoughts aside, turning instead to wonder about Martha and how, with everything that was going on, she could give thought to making sure that I was okay and knew what was going on.

I went into the kitchen to fetch a dustpan and brush. I got onto my knees and began sweeping at the mud I had left on the floorboards, thinking that I would go to the shop later and pick up a card for Martha. And as I knelt there, I heard the letter box snap open and the sound of the post hitting the floor. I looked up and saw an envelope, white against the floorboards, the familiar black writing a tunnel through time that I crawled down. I saw myself sitting on a bed alone in a characterless room.

I stared at it, a dustpan full of mud in one hand and a chest that hammered beneath the flat surface of my other palm. I stared at the letter for what seemed like forever. After weeks of waiting and thinking about this moment, I found myself too afraid to open it.

54

Lacey

She has been here before. Was it here? She is not sure. It looks the same, smells the same. When she looks straight up at the ceiling as she walks she sees the lights flash past one after the other, like they did before when she screamed and begged them to stop. She doesn't remember for certain if it was the same ceiling. Perhaps it was somewhere else that looked similar. Surely they are all alike.

The corridors stretch on forever, there are signs, different coloured signs that hang from the ceiling and point the way, but none of them tell her what she needs to know. She wanders half way down one corridor, then back again. She is struggling with the magnitude of this place. It is a maze and she cannot remember where she came in.

A woman comes towards her wearing pink scrubs. She looks bright and cheerful in that colour but she does not smile.

'Excuse me,' she says and the woman in pink stops with a sigh but does not speak. 'I'm trying to find Avon ward but I've got a bit lost, would you be able to help me?' She hears for herself that her voice has shrunk, become less audible. She wonders if it is only her voice or has the rest of her shrunk too, like Alice.

The woman points and speaks, her voice as tired as her appearance, and she realises that the ward is close; she has simply missed the turning that she needed. She says thank you to the woman's retreating figure and turns back the way she came.

It is only then that she wonders at the purpose of this journey. As she stands at the threshold to the ward and hears the voices beyond, she questions what good this will do. She remembers the last time they came face to face, the shock and the pain of it, the humiliation and the smell of the earth as she knelt in the grass. She wonders what she had hoped to achieve by making this journey.

She knows she will step forward into the room anyway, she knows that she will put herself in sight of others, she knows that she will not back down, because this is important to her. It will change nothing; her life will still be what it has always been. But somewhere inside she will know that just once she stood and let her voice be heard.

She takes a deep breath and steps forwards. There is a desk with nurses behind it, they pay her no attention as she moves her eyes over the board behind them, studying the names and the bed numbers of those unfortunate enough to be here. They are talking about a party, something so far removed from this place and she wonders if it is how they cope.

She turns and makes her way down the ward, to the end where there are six beds, all occupied. In the third bed on the right she spots the woman she has come to see, half turned away, alone. She steps towards her, praying that the woman doesn't shout out and draw attention before she can say what needs to be said. The younger woman turns and sees her. There is surprise in her eyes as she looks at her visitor but there is resignation there too, as if this doesn't matter, it is only another difficult thing to endure. The patient will not call out, she knows it then.

She moves closer and wonders if she should ask how the woman is but she decides not to. It would sound disingenuous coming from her. She lets her eyes slide over the pale skin, the dark circles, the grey expression and she thinks she doesn't need to ask after all, the answer is right in front of her.

'I didn't kill your father,' she says and the eyes move further away, to the shaded window through which nothing can be seen. 'I know you don't believe me but I wanted to tell you. It was an accident, he . . . he fell.' She hears for herself her hesitation and wonders how she can expect this fragile woman to believe her when her own voice doesn't.

She tried again. 'He was my friend, never anymore than that, or any less. I would never have hurt him.'

There was still no response, not even the slightest of movements to indicate that she has been heard. She feels lost and weak, 'I know you won't listen to me but I just wanted to tell you, because he would have wanted me to, you see, he was so proud of you. He talked about you all the time; he was so pleased with the person you became. He said you were just like your mum.' Her words fade and she watches as a tear wells up, swells to bursting point and then runs down across the bridge of the woman's nose to the pillow on the other side.

She is sorry now that she came. She didn't think it through. She just wanted her to know that her father had not spent his last moments in the company of cruelty and violence. She wanted her to know that they had only ever been friends. It had seemed important. But now as she watches the silent, dignified tears of the woman in the bed she thinks that maybe it wasn't important at all, that maybe she has been wrong to come here.

'I'm sorry, Martha.' Her voice is a whisper in the stillness of the room and she turns from the bed, from the silent crying woman and makes her way out of the ward, back into the maze of corridors that close around her. She feels her heart begin to hammer as her feet move as quickly as they can. She turns corners and walks lengths of linoleum-covered floor but the way out eludes her and she feels tremors start in her muscles.

People walk towards her and she steps back from them, their faces indistinct, blurred as she hurries on. She rushes through a doorway and finds herself in an empty chapel. It makes her think of death, decay, of her father and the people that cried for him and she holds her hands up and backs away.

A light is flashing somewhere, the bulb unable

to decide whether to work or not. It reminds her of another time, when the lights flashed past on the ceiling above her, when the jolts of pain burst through her. She feels a wall pressing into her back and she cannot back away any further. The light blinks and she flinches with it as she looks up and sees him coming towards her.

His face carries the same disapproving frown as he holds his hand out to her. 'You're being foolish Lacey, you know this is for your own good!' His voice is stern, uncompromising. He is so unused to being questioned, denied. She begins to cry, a keening sob that catches in her throat and sounds loud to her own ears. She holds her hands up to him, palms flat, fingers trembling as if this is all it will take to stop him, to keep him away. His hand presses against her flesh, fingers biting into her upper arm and she sinks towards the floor as the flashing light finally fades to black.

When she opens her eyes the first thing she notices is that the light is bright and no longer flashing. She is lying on her side on a bed in a small, featureless room. She doesn't know how long she has been here. She looks around and sees that her handbag is on the bed next to her and she grasps at it, clutching it to her chest as if it is a lifeline.

The door opens and a nurse comes in. She looks too young, too fresh to have any authority and Lacey relaxes a little as she approaches the bed.

'Glad to see you back with us. You gave the poor chaplain quite a surprise there.'

She looks at the younger woman, puzzled.

'You fainted, in the chapel. The chaplain found you in there and called for help. You gave him a bit of a scare I think,' she smiles. 'How are you feeling now?'

She feels fine and says so, though she is confused and can still see the light flashing, can still feel her father's grip on her arm. The nurse smiles at her as she moves towards the door.

'I'm just going to get the doctor to come and give you the once over and then we can see if you can go home.'

The door closes behind her and Lacey swings her feet from the bed. She stands on legs that feel boneless and makes her unsteady way towards the door.

She can't be here when the nurse gets back. She can't see the doctor. Doctor's hurt her, take things from her. She knows that if the doctor comes back and finds her here, she will not be able to leave, they will keep her here, change her somehow. She peers around the edge of the doorframe and sees a long expanse of hallway that is mercifully empty of people. She hurries along to the next corridor and stares at the signs above her head until she sees one that points to the exit.

She tries not to run and draw attention to herself but she feels as if she is being pursued, as if any minute now they will catch up with her and force her onto the bed, they will tie the straps across her forehead, her wrists and ankles, they will steal time from her until she forgets who she is.

She feels the breeze on her face before the exit comes in sight and hurries towards it. She can hear no footsteps rushing up behind her. Even so, she wills herself not to look back.

She rushes from the main door and relief courses through her body as she sees the taxi still there, miraculously still waiting for her as she had requested. She opens the door and climbs in as the driver starts the engine and drives away. She wants to ask him how long she has been, if it is still the same day, the same year. But she is afraid of his answer and so she keeps her eyes straight ahead as the hospital fades in the distance.

55

Rachel

Dear Rachel,

I can't even begin to tell you how excited Richard and I were to hear from you. It has been so, so long. Please don't think that I am blaming you in any way for that, and there is no need to talk of forgiveness or shame. I will admit that your letter hurt so much at the time, that it stopped me putting pen to paper for quite a while. But I know now, and knew at the time underneath it all, why you said what you did and I am not angry with you for it. What happened was horrible and traumatic for all of us, but I think it was harder for you as you were so young.

I have often tried to imagine how you felt when the social workers came and took you away, but I can't. I can tell you from our point of view that we were devastated. We didn't know they were coming, you see, so it was a total shock to us when they knocked on the door and said they were taking you. I can still hear you crying when they took you away. It broke my heart and I sobbed for days and days.

At first they wouldn't tell us where they had taken you. I assumed they had taken you back to the home you'd come from but when I went there they didn't know anything about it and couldn't help. A social worker took pity on me and told me in the end but only on the condition that I didn't try and see you, they said it would be too much of a disruption for you.

You won't know this, but I did come to see you once. Richard had gone away on a training course for a couple of days and I got the train up to Birmingham, I never told him. It was a Monday. I stood over the road from the address I had for you. I wanted to knock on the door, to ask how you were but I didn't because I was worried they would move you to a different home and I would lose touch with where you were.

I don't know how long I stood there really but then I saw you, walking up the road in your school uniform. You had grown so much in that short space of time and I decided to ignore what they had said and come and say hello. I started walking towards you but the door of the home opened and one of the carers came out, she walked up to you and you went inside with her. I didn't get a chance to say anything.

I don't know why I've told you that, perhaps it's just to let you know that I didn't just cast you aside, that I never stopped caring. You have always been in our thoughts, Rachel, and we have always hoped for the very best for you.

We didn't foster any more children after

you were taken away. We wouldn't have been allowed to because of my health but if I'm honest we wouldn't have taken anyone else on anyway. It wouldn't have been right really, it was your room and no-one else's.

The lump in my breast was removed, they got it all and it turned out to be benign. Once it was gone it was gone and there is barely a sign that it was ever there.

Richard still works in the same factory, what a creature of habit, eh? Though I guess in these times he is lucky to be working. He is very well and tells me to say hello from him. He's really happy to hear from you too, I can tell you!

I can't believe you became an artist, how exciting. I would love to see some of your work and how funny that you ended up in Devon, I always loved it there. I used to go on holidays there myself when I was a little girl so it holds lots of special memories for me.

Perhaps one day, if it is okay with you, we could come for a visit? Not that I want to impose but it would be so very lovely to see you. And also, of course, you are very, very welcome to come and see us here, this is still your home as far as I am concerned and you can come anytime.

I still think of you as family you know. I'm sorry if that sounds a bit gushy and emotional but it always felt to me that you were meant to be mine, right from the first time I laid eyes on you and saw those huge *dark eyes. I know that you are a grown-up now and that things have changed and it's been a long time since we saw you and I understand if you don't look at things quite the same way that I do. I just didn't want to finish this letter without letting you know that.*

Please, please stay in touch, Rachel, and thank you so much for writing, it meant such a lot to hear from you. Perhaps if you write again, you could send us a photo so we can see the person you have grown into.

All my love,
Diane
Xxx

With shaking hands I carefully folded the letter along the lines that were already there, I used my nail to sharpen the crease a little. I pushed the sheets back into the envelope and placed it on the table. I tucked my hair behind my ears and my fingers brushed against my cheek, coming away wet. I don't know how long I had been crying.

56

Rachel

The surrounding countryside had given me a new kind of freedom, one the city had never offered. If the day went badly, if my painting wasn't going right or if I got an unexpected bill, I would put on my boots and take off into the wilderness around me. I found it incredibly effective at blowing away anxiety or anger. The fields and nearby moors gave me plenty of scope to stamp out my frustration and the trees and flowers, the very earth itself absorbed my mood and smoothed it out, replacing it with a sense of reason and calm. I never forgot to be grateful.

I revisited the stream and rather than a negative mood, I took with me a sense of relief, of incredible lightness to pour into the waters. I found it to be a different place now that the rains had returned. I watched the swirls and eddies, the lowest branches of the overhanging trees sweeping lines into the surface.

Just for a moment I wondered what had become of my little boat, of my child. I found the thoughts less bitter, less raw now. They were a regret, a muted sadness that had become gentle and settled within, it was a part of me that I would never let go of. The grief would always be there and I thought that was just how it was meant to be. I realised that it was okay to allow that, to always wonder what she may have been.

I jumped the newly spirited water at its narrowest part, my feet momentarily scrabbling for purchase on the slick mud of the bank. I followed the space between trees and shrubs, close enough that the churning water was still the dominant sound. I was prevented from going further by a vast tangled horseshoe of bramble and bindweed. I scanned my eyes over it but it was thick, impenetrable. There was no way through.

I returned to the stream and saw a glistening arrow of sunlight penetrate the canopy and spotlight the water downstream, highlighting the edges of the leaves with golden light and reflecting off the surface like glitter. It looked ethereal, a beautiful landscape and I quickly reached into my bag for my camera to capture the moment before the clouds chased it away. I snapped a few shots and decided that if they came out okay, this was an image I would sketch. I would paint it onto a small canvas, tiny and detailed and I would send it as a gift to Diane and Richard, perhaps I hoped that the beauty of the scene would entice them here for a visit. But maybe it was more than that. I think I wanted to show them how far I had come, where I was now. I could sense the little girl in me wanting their approval, wanting to feel their pride.

I headed back towards the house and thought that perhaps I could invite my foster parents to come and stay in the New Year, I wondered if it would be awkward, but found that it didn't matter. I was back in touch with them after all this time and I planned to keep it that way. I hoped that they felt the same.

57

Lacey

The nights close in around her and she begins to wonder when she will die. Her father died a week ago. Or was it a year? She is no longer sure, it seems like forever. She wonders when she will follow him. She wonders if she will see it coming. She is not afraid to die.

But then she thinks of afterwards, she remembers the church and the hole in the ground. She hears her mother's voice pouring from the grave, berating her and then she becomes afraid. Afraid of her body shutting down and beginning to fade. She is scared that they will put her in the same ground as them, lying beneath the surface of the earth and feeling the fingers of rot, of evil, from her father. She worries that they will taint her, taunt her, that they will curl around her and pull her down, down into the very depths of Hell where her father will wait and punish her for being a bad daughter.

Now suddenly she is afraid to die, she is afraid that no-one will know that she cannot be put in the ground with them. She rushes to the drawer and finds paper and a pen and she begins to write, to let whoever comes here, whoever puts her in her coffin, know what cannot be. She does not suggest an alternative, it doesn't matter. She has no preference about what they do with her, only about what they don't do, what they mustn't do.

She finishes the letter and wonders what she should do with it. She remembers that there is no-one to give it to. There is no-one to arrange her funeral. She will go into a pauper's grave without a marker. She will be at the back of the churchyard somewhere, hidden away from the eyes of the gentle folk that pass by. The years will drift and vanish into each other and no-one will know she is there. She will be completely forgotten, no-one will remember her, the mad old lady that lived at the end of the lane.

She smiles at the thought. It is preferable.

58

Rachel

September drifted into October and brought strong winds and the smell of wood smoke. The ground turned damp and marshy in the lane outside Dove Cottage. Leaves that had been fresh and new when I arrived faded to yellow and brown, the colour spreading through the trees like ink in water. How could something that was dying look so vibrant and beautiful? The leaves fell and blew across the garden, pinning themselves against hedges and turning slippery underfoot.

I lit the fire for the first time and the smell of coal, the flickering flames that cast shadows on the walls and the warmth all combined to make me feel safe and cosy. I found deep contentment in wrapping up, facing the elements outside and then returning, damp and tangled to sit in front of the fire wrapped in a blanket; a steaming cup of tea in my hands.

I saw Lacey several times a week and always enjoyed her company. She was a rainbow of emotion, unpredictable as ever in her response to the everyday mundane conversations that we shared. As far as I was aware, she had had no further blackouts since the first one I had witnessed. If she had, she hadn't called me, and I was too afraid to ask her about them in case I made her feel awkward.

As Halloween approached I noticed a change in her. She became skittish and edgy. If we stepped out into the lane together she looked around, deep into the shadows beneath the hedges or nervously over her shoulder. She reminded me of a cornered animal seeking a way out. When I asked her about it she told me that nothing was wrong. But she looked uncomfortable and I found myself unwilling to probe further.

I wondered if this was the beginning of another episode, if this was how it started and I hadn't seen it before because we hadn't known each other so well. I began to watch her more closely. I made excuses to visit her more often. She must have felt that I was like a permanent shadow, there every time she turned around. But she also seemed to sense my concern and accept it. We danced around each other carefully and refrained from saying what was on our minds.

The night of Halloween came and I sat in front of my fire wondering if I should call on her. I had a bowl of sweets ready, a pumpkin carved on the doorstep, but even so I couldn't imagine the village children coming this far up the lane in search of treats.

I had never been allowed trick or treating when I lived at the home. We were told it was begging and that we had to stay in. I envied children who could. When I lived in Marham it had been a different story. I had gone around with my friend Sophie and the other children with instructions to only knock on the doors of houses that displayed pumpkins. I was thrilled and couldn't now resist putting out a pumpkin of my own, seeing the costumes and laughter from the other side.

Darkness was falling earlier as the days marched on and this night was particularly dark, with a low cover of clouds that blocked out the stars and moon. The air smelled of rain though none was falling yet and as I wasted time thinking about the weather, I heard the first dull thud followed by muted shouting.

★ ★ ★

I opened the front door and the sounds were louder. Chants of 'witch, witch, witch' punctuated by thuds and wet splattering sounds. I slipped on my shoes and dashed out of the house, heading up the lane as quickly as I could in the darkness. The wet ground was treacherous under foot.

There were about ten of them. They stood halfway between the gate and the front door, launching their missiles as far as they could. They failed to notice me behind them, so intent were they on the task at hand. In the darkness I couldn't tell their ages but the chanting voices ranged from the higher pitches of a younger child to the wavering depth of a breaking voice.

I marched up behind them and yelled as loudly as I could. 'What the hell do you think you're doing?'

The impact was immediate, almost comical. They screamed and shrank forwards away from the sound, the quicker thinking among them taking instantly to their heels. I heard the gate slam behind them, the sound of feet slithering across wet mud, the occasional thump as one of them went down.

I stared into the wide eyes of those who had remained, those who were too scared or shocked to flee. I was furious, horrified at their behaviour.

'Is this fun to you? Do you enjoy tormenting people like this? Have you given any thought whatsoever to what you are doing to the person behind that door?'

There was silence for a moment and I was about to start a tirade when one of them said, 'But she's a murderer.'

I opened my mouth and then closed it again. 'What did you say?' I stared in the direction of the voice, unable to make out the face clearly in the darkness.

'She's a murderer,' it said, stronger, bolder this time as if the child sensed my uncertainty and gained power from it. 'She killed the man next door, everyone knows it!'

'Well, we'll just see about that shall we?' I reached forwards and grasped the child who had spoken by the arm, and I collected another as I stepped forwards. The others scattered, their feet freed by my sudden movement. One of the children yelled at me to let go, squirming beneath my hand as we got closer to Lacey's house. The other stayed silent.

I knocked on the door and waited. There was no answer. I knocked again before I realised that there was no way that Lacey would open the door. She must have been terrified and wouldn't know that it was me who was knocking.

'Lacey, open this door please, it's Rachel.' I heard the anger in my voice and tried to pull it back, worried that Lacey would think it directed at her instead of the twosome that I held tightly in my hands. Eventually the door opened just a crack, the hallway behind it a dark hole. I saw her eyes widen in surprise as she saw three silhouettes standing there and turned to snap the light on. We all blinked at the sudden illumination.

I saw the children I was holding for the first time. They were both boys. One was around the age of ten, his face painted like Frankenstein; he had bolts glued to his neck. The other had made less effort; he was about twelve and had painted dark shadows around his eyes, a line of red from one corner of his mouth.

But it was Lacey's face that frightened me the most. She was pale and trembling, her skin bathed in a light sheen of sweat and her eyes were wide, afraid.

'You see what you have done? Does it make you feel good to terrify an old lady like that? Does it? You say you are sorry right now, and you bloody well mean it, do you hear me?'

They muttered sorry under their breaths, a demanded apology that meant very little. Their eyes slid away from Lacey, onto the ground at their feet. There was a strange look about them, an uncomfortable blend of shame and defiance. I looked back at Lacey and she was shaking her head slightly, not at the children. It made me feel

280

as though she were trying to clear it.

'You get out of here and don't you ever do this again or I'll be visiting your parents.' I let them go and they turned and ran in the same direction as their friends, back towards the village and safety.

I kicked my muddy shoes off on the doorstep and as I reached my hands up to shepherd Lacey inside, she flinched from me and I slowed my movements, trying to become smaller, less threatening. She allowed herself to be hustled towards her front room and she sat on the sofa, hunched into herself and looking more frail than I had ever seen her. I fetched a damp cloth from the kitchen and dabbed it across her face, trying to cool her down and add some colour to her worryingly pale skin.

'Are you okay?' I asked and she came back to herself a little, meeting my eyes with a confused frown.

'They come every year, every year. I don't understand why they are so horrible to me.'

I sat next to her and held her hands in both of mine. They felt chilled. I hesitated, considered saying nothing but eventually I told her anyway; she had a right to know.

'One of them said that you were responsible for Albert's passing.'

Her eyes slid away across the floor. 'I wasn't,' she said quietly. 'It was an accident, he fell.'

'I know that, but you know what kids are like, they'll use any excuse to pick on people at times, and horrible though it is it tends to be the more vulnerable people that they target.'

She nodded in response and I was relieved to see that there was a little colour coming back into her cheeks.

'They used to come before he died though. They've always thought me different.'

I held her hand and rubbed it gently, trying to warm her a little. 'I'm just going to get a bucket and start cleaning the walls for you.'

She nodded slightly and I left her sitting there as I got a brush and the bucket and made my way outside. After a few moments she joined me with a broom and silently we cleaned up the mess that the children had made. I wondered if they would try it again the following year. Somehow I doubted it, they had seemed genuinely terrified when I yelled at them. But if they did come back next year, I would be waiting for them. They wouldn't even get close to throwing one solitary egg.

When we had finished I put the cleaning equipment away in the cupboard and I made Lacey a cup of tea. We sat and drank in silence, both lost in our own thoughts. I broke it by asking Lacey if she was alright.

'I am,' she said. 'Usually I just sit inside waiting for them to finish and go away. I'm really, very grateful that it was different this year.' She smiled at me and I took her thanks with a return smile. I told her that I would make sure it would never happen again and she leaned forwards and patted my hand. 'You're a good friend, Rachel, I hope you know that.'

'Right back at you, Lacey.' I said, embarrassed as I often was by praise. I finished my tea and said that I had better get going. Taking the cups through to the kitchen I caught sight of the rifle leaning up against the doorframe. I had never seen it before and I found the sight of it jarring, a sense of unease crawling across my skin. I looked back at Lacey but she was turned away from me and didn't see my reaction.

I asked once more if she was okay and she nodded in response. I smiled and said goodnight to her and turned to leave, taking with me a disturbing image of the gun in Lacey's hands.

59

Rachel

Shortly after Halloween, I paid a visit to Jane in Birmingham. I was reluctant to go at first. I worried about Lacey, about what would happen if she had another blackout and she was alone. I told her as much and she reminded me that she had been alone for years before I came to Winscombe, and I knew that she was right. Even so I phoned Father Thomas before I left to ask him to keep an eye out for her.

I had decided to take the train rather than drive up on roads that were becoming treacherous with poor weather. The bustle of the city, the throngs of people pouring out of New Street station and the sheer noise that surrounded me when I arrived was overwhelming. I found it hard to believe that this had once, not too long before, been so commonplace that I barely noticed it.

Jane greeted me with a sweeping hug and a smacking kiss on each cheek. She looked happy and I was pleased I had come. I had brought some small finished canvasses with me and she jumped up and down at the sight of them before gesturing me towards a waiting taxi.

We went out to eat that night, just the two of us. I marvelled at the choices of where we could go and felt a twinge of envy that I lacked so many options at home. But even that thought kicked up a response, I had thought of Winscombe as home; even here back among the familiar landscape of Birmingham. I saw the city as elsewhere now, somewhere I no longer belonged. It was something I could enjoy visiting but the thought of staying made me feel claustrophobic. I was glad that I could walk away from it without trepidation.

Over a sublime meal in a local curry house I told Jane about Lacey, about the part of the story that she had missed. Her food went cold as she listened with horror and pity at all that had been endured.

'I can't believe that one person could go through so much, it's like a film isn't it?'

'Well, I guess that when they say truth is stranger than fiction, it really is.'

We ate on in silence.

Later as we walked the short distance to Jane's home I stopped in surprise as I noticed Christmas decorations in the windows. It was only November.

'They've been there since the beginning of October, would you believe?' Jane said. 'They might as well not bother taking the fucking things down, save themselves a job!'

I laughed as we walked, all the while thinking that I would invite Lacey to spend Christmas with me. Though I didn't mind the thought of spending the day by myself — I had done it many times before — I was bothered by the idea of Lacey having no-one to receive gifts from; no-one to have a celebratory drink with and be jovial.

The weekend passed far more quickly than I thought it would. We went to art galleries, shopped, bought gifts and ate more than we should and I loved every minute of it. Birmingham was like a little boost in my increasingly slow and calm days.

Jane was genuinely thrilled when I told her about the renewed contact with my foster parents. 'I can't believe things have changed for you so much just because you moved to that tiny little backwater.'

'I think I've had a more interesting time there than I ever had living in the city. Perhaps moving was the catalyst I needed. Life had become pretty stagnant.'

She nodded her agreement and the ensuing silence swept the evening away.

By the time Jane took me to the station on the Sunday afternoon I was more than ready to go, I had reached saturation point with the hectic pace of the city streets. I had failed to sleep well because of the sound of traffic and I felt myself yearning for the silence of the village and the lane. It had become home for me, part of me, and I needed to return.

We said goodbye and promised to do it again soon and then the whistle blew and the crowded train began to move forwards. I stood by the door and waved until we rounded a corner and she was out of sight.

60

Lacey

The house next door is dark and empty as she walks past. Just for a moment she wonders where her neighbour has gone before she remembers and allows herself to miss her. The house no longer looks right in the darkness, no light inside to shine at the windows.

She opens the door to her own house and puts her shopping away, the cat weaving between her legs as she does so.

'One of these days you'll trip me up and I'll break a hip!' she says, but he ignores her and carries on, in and out, in and out as if he can sense the food she has for him in her basket.

She takes the cleaning products to the under stair cupboard and as she does so she sees the rifle she put there after the children came at Halloween, the one that used to belong to her father. She looks at it for a little while and then carefully lifts it from the shelf. She goes into the kitchen and sits at the dining table. The wood of the gun is smooth beneath her hands, the barrel cold. She looks into the hole and it seems much bigger than it really is, she feels herself teeter as if she may fall into it, tumbling end over end.

She places the butt on the floor and peers down and thinks that all it would take would be one little movement, a toe hooked onto the trigger and that would be it, she would be gone, she could fly away. But as she lifts her foot, feeling the protesting creak in her opposite hip, Peachy jumps onto the table next to her. He rubs the top of his head against her cheek and stares at her with doleful eyes. She puts her foot back down on the floor.

'But if I did that, who would take care of you?' she says to the purring cat. She spends a few moments stroking the soft fur with her free hand and thinking about flying, about being free, and then she stands and slowly takes the gun back to the cupboard, puts it back on the shelf and thinks about something else for a while.

61

Rachel

The whole journey home all I could think of was driving up the lane to my little cottage and washing the city from my skin. Though the weekend had gone quickly in Birmingham and I had enjoyed every minute of spending time with Jane, there was a part of me that felt I had been gone forever. I looked for changes in the scenery and wondered if anything was different.

The train pulled into Exeter St David's and I quickly left the platform and found the little side street where I had left my car. I hopped into the driver's seat, started the engine and headed towards home, feeling incredibly light and content. It astonished me that it was only six short months since I had made this journey for the first time. I felt as though I had never lived anywhere else, that this had always been my home.

Apple Tree Lane engulfed me as the car slid and slithered its slow way across the mud and fallen leaves. The trees overhead had become skeletal and bare, blanched of the autumn colour and its temporary vibrancy. I pulled up onto the bank of grass opposite Dove Cottage and wondered if I would ever be able to coax the car off it again, the mud looked deep and I could imagine tyres endlessly spinning and going nowhere.

Having spent the weekend worrying about Lacey, praying that the phone wouldn't ring and then anxious because it hadn't, I decided that I would go and see her first and unpack later. I dropped my holdall onto my bed and picked up the canvas I had brought for her. I left the house and walked carefully up the lane, worried that I may fall and break the gift on the treacherous ground.

She opened the door as soon as I knocked, making me wonder if she had seen me coming. She looked happy, healthy and I could barely contain the surge of relief that coursed through me. Once inside, I handed her the canvas and watched as she unwrapped it. It was fairly small, about sixty centimetres square and she stared at the picture with an open mouth before her eyes found mine.

'It looks like a dream,' she said and I knew exactly what she meant. The artist had used fantasy colours to paint the abstract image, deep violet, emerald green and cobalt blue that blended together in places and stood separately elsewhere.

'Remember when Jane came down and we were talking about the teenage boy with ADHD, Tyler?' I asked and she nodded. 'Well, that's one of his, I thought you might like it. She took your advice and apparently he is doing really well at the moment.'

She beamed at me, 'It's beautiful, really beautiful. And he's doing alright?'

'Yeah he is, apparently he's getting himself a bit of a following. He's going to be exhibiting in a solo show soon which is a huge step forwards for an artist.'

'I'm so pleased for him, and that news makes the picture even more perfect.' She smiled and asked if I would help her hang it.

She went to the wall above her TV and moved a painting she had there, a simple print of a vase of flowers that had faded with age, it looked as though it had been there forever and the lighter square of paint underneath it indicated that it had. I hung the painting in the vacated space and Lacey stepped back to look at it, hands clasped to her ample chest.

'There, that looks perfect. Now I can see it whenever I'm sitting in front of the TV.' She reached up and squeezed me so tightly I could barely breathe, 'Thank you, Rachel, that means such a lot.'

'You're very welcome,' I said, delighted that she was happy with the picture. 'I was also wondering if you would like to join me for Christmas. You know I'm not brilliant in the kitchen so it would be a pretty simple affair, but it would be nice to have some company.' I didn't realise that I was worried about her reply until she nodded her agreement.

'That would be really nice, I think. And I can help with the food, *I* can cook.' She looked back at the canvas and then at me. 'I was wondering about something too, it might seem a bit of an odd question.'

I smiled at her, 'Go on.'

She cleared her throat, 'When I die will you look after Peachy for me, and the chickens, of course?'

I looked over to where the big cat curled up on

the back of the sofa, half hidden by the cushion and thought to myself that of all the questions she was about to ask, that was one I couldn't have predicted.

'You'll probably outlive me, Lacey Carmichael, you can look after them yourself!' I said with a smile, which she returned.

'Well, okay, on the off chance that I don't outlive you and I pop my clogs first, would you do that for me?'

I saw that behind the light words, she was serious, that this really mattered to her.

'Yes, of course I would.' And that was that.

62

Rachel

The Christmas season snuck up on me and before I knew it, it was December. I had toyed with the idea of inviting Diane and Richard to join us for Christmas but something stopped me. I decided it would be too much to cope with; too close to memories of that first Christmas with them when I felt that everything was perfect. I thought about it, worried that it would go badly, that conversation would be stilted. I worried that they would look at the person I had become and no longer like what they saw. I talked myself out of it and in the end it would just be Lacey and me. I didn't mind.

We went together into Exeter to buy Christmas decorations, I had none of my own and Lacey said she never bothered, she barely noticed the day anyway. We went in and out of brightly lit shops on a Thursday evening when the stores opened late. Street vendors sold hotdogs, toffee apples, roast chestnuts and brightly coloured flashing plastic wands that we giggled as we paid for.

People seemed to smile more easily, excitable children skipped along, dangling from the hands of their parents and I found that I was excited about Christmas for the first time in years. We ended up with far too many decorations and I insisted that we both had trees despite Lacey's protest that she didn't need one. We bought tinsel, baubles and too many sets of lights because I couldn't decide between blue, clear and multi-coloured.

We drank mugs of hot chocolate with whipped cream and marshmallows and snuck off to buy silly little gifts that meant nothing but made me smile. When we were finished we drove back home on roads that looked like glass and promised to meet up again the next day and decorate both of our houses. I put the presents under my tree because that was where we would be on Christmas morning but the next day when she wasn't looking I snuck a stocking full of nonsense gifts, soap, sweets, earrings, under the tree in Lacey's front room so that it wasn't empty underneath.

I wrapped my present to Richard and Diane. Brightly coloured paper wrapped in dull brown packaging. A gift I never believed would be sent. It was heavier than it should have been because of its protective box and I had my fingers crossed that it would arrive with them safely. Part of me still hoped that the painting would draw them here, back to Devon. I placed it on the table and looked at the small package I had wrapped for Lacey; beside the canvas it looked tiny. This one wasn't art, this was something else altogether and I hoped that she would like it. It was something that had seemed so important to her at the time.

On one last trip into Exeter to post the painting, I racked my brains trying to think of what else I needed to get done and realised it was almost certainly too late anyway. If I had forgotten anything up to that point then it probably wasn't important enough to remember. I thought of everything that had been done so far and thought, hoped, it would be enough. Looking back I'm not sure why I was so desperate that things be perfect. Perhaps it was simply that I wanted to make Lacey smile, that I wanted to make up for the years when there had been no-one.

All the way home I went through my to-do list, mentally ticking things off and moving them to the done pile. The journey had become second nature now; I was no longer so hesitant and cautious on the narrow country lanes. By the time I turned into the lane in the late afternoon when the light was fading in a blaze of orange tinted clouds, I hadn't even noticed that the miles had passed.

I drove forwards, bumping over the ruts and steering carefully over the oozing mud. As I pulled to a stop I looked up and saw Lacey. She stood in almost the same spot she had when I returned from the cinema that night but the differences in the two occasions were vast. This was an image that would stay in my mind forever, a moment caught in time that would never fail to make me smile. When I think of her, it is that moment I see first. She was all dressed in red, jumper, trousers and boots, a Father Christmas hat on her head, tinsel around her neck and in her arms she held a huge wreath, bursting with berries and fake snow. She struggled to peer over it and the smile on her face was huge as she slipped and slithered her way across the mud.

'I got this for your door,' she said, her voice light and breathless. I took it from her, hugged her and then together we emptied the shopping from the boot of the car and took it into the house.

63

Rachel

By the time Christmas morning dawned I had taken my eraser and rubbed out the harsh lines and shadows of the previous ones spent alone. The two days leading up to Christmas were filled with stories of each other's lives, the dreams and ambitions we had harboured, our hopes for the future. We spoke of books we had read, films we loved; little of which mattered when I looked back on it. I thought of black writing curled on unopened envelopes, of the beach in the sunlight, of the beach in the rain. I thought of Lacey when she smiled and when her eyes were empty. I thought of the first time I had seen Diane and Richard and I thought of the last. I thought of hope and of deep red blood on white sheets, of a little white paper boat dancing on the water and I thought of a rainbow of colours in a paintbox.

I was up before dawn, too excited to sleep. I felt silly, but the light in the kitchen hadn't been on long before there was a tiny knock at the door. I opened it to Lacey's smiling face and ushered her in realising she felt the same. I wished her a Merry Christmas and hugged her, careful not to squash the stocking I had placed under her tree that she now held in her hand. We sat at the kitchen table drinking tea and smiling. I rubbed the sleep from my eyes and decided to put off getting dressed until we had opened our presents. We went into the front room and disappeared amidst a pile of multi-coloured paper, expressing joy at the more traditional sock and handkerchief gifts. I smiled at the chocolate selection box from Lacey and laughed when I realised she had brought herself one and wrapped that up too. Lacey's main gift to me, made me laugh even more, a copy of *Cooking for Dummies* and a place on a ten-week cookery course in Exeter. She seemed as pleased by my reaction as I was with the gift, we both knew it was sorely needed and I was genuinely grateful for it.

I couldn't remember a time I had felt so comfortable and at ease. We took it in turns to open presents, squeezing and shaking them a little before admitting defeat and tearing at the paper. When I handed Lacey her present it looked tiny. With a smile on her face she mimicked me, squeezing the little package that was flat as a letter, and shaking it near her ear. She opened it and looked at the small envelope with confusion, and then she raised her eyes to mine, shaking her head a little.

'It's a hot air balloon flight, or rather it's a voucher for one. It's for a private flight, just you, me and the pilot. Don't worry if you don't like it, I could exchange it for something else.' She shook her head again, more emphatically this time and I saw her chin tremble as she blinked rapidly.

'I don't know what to say.' Her voice was

barely above a whisper.

'You don't have to say anything, Lacey, I hope you like it.'

'Oh I do, I love it! I couldn't have wanted for more, it's the best thing, the best thing. I can't wait.' She reached forward to hug me but as she did she lost her balance and we tumbled into an undignified, laughing heap amongst the piles of discarded paper. After brushing ourselves down we scooped all the wrapping paper and rubbish into a bin bag and trooped into the kitchen to begin the dinner preparations.

Under Lacey's direction I peeled and chopped vegetables. She rattled off a list of what needed to be done and sang off-key Christmas carols as I laid the table and washed the utensils she used. I put the wine in the fridge to chill, sorted out the crockery, the serving bowls and the place mats. A kind of gentle camaraderie settled between us and brought with it a sense of harmony and contentment.

Later, as we sat at the imperfectly laid table to eat the perfectly prepared food, to drink too much and laugh too much I realised that we were like a little family. A strange hybrid of one but a family nonetheless, in all the ways that were important. As I looked across the table and felt the ease with which we talked together, the warmth in her eyes, I realised that I cared more for her than I had believed possible. In such a short period of time she had slotted neatly into my life and become more important to me than anyone had for years.

We pulled crackers, laughed at bad jokes and

ate too much food. Every time I glanced at Lacey her face was curved into a little half smile that spoke volumes. She looked genuinely happy and I told her so.

'I've never been happier.'

'I love you, Lacey Carmichael. You're brilliant.'

'I love you too, Rachel Moore, but I think you're a little bit tipsy!'

I laughed then, a hiccupping giggle that built as I sat there misty eyed. 'As always, Lacey, you are so very right.'

These were the things that I would remember, always. Those beautiful moments when life seemed that little bit more real, that little bit more vibrant. In the coming days when it was all over, when the wine bottles were empty and I started to think about the decorations coming down, we would talk together about what that one day had meant. For me it was the moment that I finally felt I had a family again. There was something significant in that because I felt that this time nothing could stand in the way. I was grown and could make my own decisions now and no-one could prise me away. For Lacey, it was surprisingly similar. She had been part of a family before but not one that she could share a Christmas day with, not one that had been bound in warmth and laughter. For Lacey, that Christmas had given her the one true experience of being part of a loving family. We were both immeasurably grateful.

64

Lacey died in the early hours of a bitterly cold February morning. I wasn't with her. I wondered for a long time afterwards — I still wonder — if it would have made a difference had I been there, holding her hand, willing her to live. I wonder if I could have given her reason to fight, a reason to hold on.

★ ★ ★

Christmas had passed and we waved it goodbye with no small measure of regret. We arranged to spend New Year's Eve together. I couldn't remember the last time I had stayed up late enough to hear the chimes from Big Ben echo out of the TV. I looked forward to it, grateful that the celebrations weren't quite over yet.

The day itself dawned cold and clear. Icy wind curled around the outside of the house, forcing tiny fingers through miniscule cracks. I stoked up the fire and kept the curtains drawn in the upstairs rooms. I put a bottle of wine in the fridge and sorted little bowls and serving dishes for dips and nibbles. Lacey arrived in the early evening with a bottle of champagne she had had chilling all day. I thought we should save the champagne for midnight and she agreed, so I poured us some wine and we settled in the front room to watch a film; I can't remember now what it was that we watched.

During an advert break, Lacey got to her feet and walked over to where I sat before reaching out to press the mute button on the remote control.

She looked down at me intently, her face firm and unyielding. 'I just wanted to say that there is a letter for you in the drawer of my telephone table, but you're only to read it if something happens to me. Okay?'

I nodded solemnly, already feeling the encroaching itch of curiosity. Before I could say anything she reached over me again and pressed the button, returning the volume to normal before the film restarted. Conversation over. She went and sat back down and I looked at her. She seemed to be avoiding my eyes and eventually I turned back to the film.

Later, we drank the champagne and listened to the bells ringing out across the sound of cheering in Trafalgar Square. We crossed arms and sang Auld Lang Syne, and we laughed, as we often seemed to. The last thing I ever heard from her mouth was her laugh. As she straightened up and looked towards me my heart froze. The smile was still on her face but it was turning in on itself, one side collapsing, folding. A little frown appeared between her eyes and I stood frozen in that moment as her arm flapped down at her side and her glass fell from her fingers. As it bounced on the carpet, I stepped forwards and helped her into her seat.

'Lacey, can you hear me?'

She nodded but looked vague and I felt so

afraid. I raced to grab the phone from the sideboard and dialled the emergency services. They were there within twelve minutes and as they walked up the path and I opened the door I felt my legs weaken with relief that it was no longer me that had to deal with this, it was no longer me who was responsible, who could do the wrong thing. Now all I had to do was be there, hold her hand, pray for her.

I gave the paramedic all the information I could and he asked me if I were her next of kin.

'Yes, I am,' I replied, because who else was there, who else could make the decisions if she no longer could?

'Will you be able to make your own way to the hospital?' he asked me and I heard so many things behind his words. They needed to work on her in the back of the ambulance, stabilise her, do what needed to be done. I looked over at Lacey and saw her eyes were closed. I no longer recognised her face, I could no longer see my friend.

They put her on the stretcher and took her out of the house. The lights flashed blue across the walls, but the siren remained still as the ambulance pulled away, slowly down the lane. On stiff stilted legs I moved around, gathering bits and pieces. Trying to think through the fog of shock and reaction as to what Lacey might need.

I thought that I should go to her house and get her nightdress, her wash things; I thought that I should feed the cat and lock her house up. But I couldn't do any of those things right now, there would be time enough later, for now all I wanted to do was follow her and be where she was.

I got into the car and realised that I was almost certainly over the limit, I tried to think how much I had drunk that evening but I couldn't, all I could see was Lacey's face collapsing as devastation spread through her brain. I turned the key in the ignition knowing that I was going to drive to the hospital anyway. I had never felt more sober than I did in that moment.

I drove far slower than I thought I would have. By the time I got to the hospital, the doctors and Lacey were all hidden behind a door and I had no idea what was happening. A nurse with a kind face and exhausted eyes led me to a relative's room, which was surprisingly comfortable and thankfully empty. I tried not to notice the little Father Christmas stud earrings she wore. I curled up on the deep green sofa and rested my head on my arms. The nurse returned with a cup of tea for me and I took it gratefully, holding the cup gave me a focus.

I wondered what was happening. I wondered when they would tell me what was going on. I felt helpless and so desperately alone, but when I thought I might give in and cry, there were no tears, only a growing sense of disbelief that this could have happened. I set the cup to one side and waited.

65

I fell asleep and the first emotion I had on waking was guilt. How could I sleep here? How could I have been relaxed enough to drift off only feet away from where they worked on Lacey? When I looked up I realised that a doctor stood in front of me, his hand resting gently on my shoulder.

'Miss Moore?'

I nodded and rubbed at my eyes.

'My name is Dr Madison, I'm Ms Carmichael's doctor. I wanted to talk to you a little bit about what is happening right now.'

I nodded again and tried to brace myself against his words. I felt the dread pressing down on my shoulders and his words surrounded it and held it there, adding to the weight of it. He took a seat near to me on the sofa, leaving one cushion width between us so that he could turn to me without invading my personal body space.

'We suspect that Ms Carmichael has suffered an intracerebral haemorrhage. That diagnosis will be confirmed later following the outcome of tests. I'm afraid that until we get those results, I cannot offer any kind of prognosis.' His words were spoken softly, comforting and gentle and I wondered how they could hurt so much when they were said so delicately.

'How is she now though?' I asked and the

pause before he answered left me cold. He took a deep breath, expelling it in a rush from his nose.

'At the present moment, Ms Carmichael is unconscious and has been since she arrived at the hospital. Would you like to come through and see her?'

I wanted to say no, I didn't want to, I didn't want to see the shell of her lying there, but I nodded anyway and he stood to lead me through to a room that was dimly lit. She lay on the bed, her shoulders bare, the blanket pulled up modestly over her chest. Her face was so still it looked plastic and I wanted to touch the skin there, poke it, pull it, give it some life and reassure myself that there was still movement, that it was still possible.

I sat next to her and held her hand. It stayed limp and soft in mine and I watched as her chest rose and fell. I thought to myself that it was a good sign that she was breathing by herself. I held on to that thought tightly.

Throughout the rest of that night I talked to her. I told her everything I had never had the chance to share. I told her about the other children in the home, how they had bullied me until each morning brought a wave of sickness and anxiety. I told her that I was afraid now that I would never be able to have a baby, that my insides might be damaged. I told her all of the things that filled a space inside me, suddenly feeling this desperate urge to divulge the real me while there was still time. The night passed slowly and I filled it with my voice and kept hold of her hand.

By the time the doctor returned I think I already knew what he was going to say. It was a different doctor but he wore the same expression and I saw the words in his eyes. He ushered me out of the room and back to the relative comfort of the waiting room, as if Lacey was not entitled to hear the truth about her condition though I was. He put his hand on my forearm. Perhaps it was meant to be comforting but I wanted to pull away from him, to have space around me as he stole my breath away.

'I'm afraid the tests confirm that Ms Carmichael has suffered a significant intracerebral haemorrhage. The bleed has caused fairly catastrophic damage to the brain tissue near her brainstem.' He paused as if expecting questions and I complied because the silence grew uncomfortable and difficult to bear.

'Is she going to recover?' I meant to say die, is she going to die? But the word felt alien in my mouth and I couldn't force it past my tongue. He looked genuinely regretful as he shook his head slightly.

'I'm sorry. I think that with the amount of damage to the brain it would be unlikely that Ms Carmichael can survive this event.'

'Do you know how long she has?'

He shook his head again. 'Anything I say at this point would be purely conjecture. It would be impossible for me to answer that with any degree of accuracy.'

I thanked him and thought how obscene that

is, that we thank someone when they have told us the very worst. That there is no hope, that all is lost. I watched his retreating figure and for a fleeting moment I hated him for what he had told me, as if it were his fault that Lacey was dying, as if he could change it if he wanted to. I watched the door close behind him and then followed. I went back to her room and sat with her.

I tried to think of everything that needed to be done, I thought of Peachy and the chickens and realised they would need to be fed. I was reluctant to leave her alone, hesitant about going, but I knew that she would want me to look after her beloved cat. I told the nurse that I would be back as soon as possible and rushed outside to the car park where I took a deep breath of frigid air.

66

Several days passed and even this, even waiting for death, became routine and ordinary. Early in the morning, when it was still dark and the roads were quiet I would head back to feed Peachy. I would stroke him for a few minutes, feed him, change his water and leave him enough biscuits to last till the following day. Then I would do the same for the chickens, go home, wash and change and then head back to the hospital where I would sit for hours and try to think of new things to say, leaving the room only when the nurses needed to wash her or when the doctors came. I took books and magazines with me and when I felt silent and lacking in words I would read to her. I grew sick of the sound of my own voice.

I had brought her own nightclothes in with me so at least she was wearing those and I would periodically wipe her face and dab a little of her perfume on her wrists; it seemed a little silly yet somehow important. I brushed her hair and cared for her but after a while I felt like little more than a window-dresser. There was no response and I wanted to beg her to open her eyes, to smile at me and tell me it was all okay.

One morning as I was telling her that the cat and the chickens seemed fine, Doctor Madison came in.

'Could I have a little chat with you, Rachel?'

I had been here long enough to be elevated to first name terms it seemed. I was curious rather than worried, there seemed no news that could be any worse than the prognosis I had already been given. I was a little surprised, however, when he lead me into his office rather than the waiting room.

'Please take a seat.' He gestured towards one of two that faced his desk and I took the nearest one as he moved around the large, paper-strewn surface and sat down. He clasped his hands in front of him and looked down at them. I saw the top of his head, the salt and pepper hair that swirled around his crown.

'What I wanted to discuss with you is that Lacey, Ms Carmichael, has apparently endured some rather traumatic surgery at some point. I was wondering if perhaps you could shed any light on that.'

I thought about the day that she had told me about her lobotomy, about how appalled I had been, how sickened. I wondered for a moment if it was the brain damage caused by the lobotomy that had in turn caused the stroke and thought that maybe I should have said something before now. I mentally berated myself for my stupidity.

'Lacey was lobotomised in the sixties,' I explained. 'I don't know if it helps in any way but she told me that they went into her brain through the back of her eye sockets.' I found myself wincing at my own words.

Dr Madison looked at me for a moment, his gaze level and direct, then he cleared his throat and looked down at the notes in front of him.

'We actually do have the notes of that particular event, it's recorded in her medical records, along with the Electric Shock Treatment she underwent.' He looked uncomfortable. 'The surgery I'm referring to is the more . . . er intimate surgery that Ms Carmichael has been through.'

I looked at him, at the way he shifted in his chair, at the way his eyes skimmed the room and I thought about all that Lacey and I had talked about. I came up blank, empty and shook my head. 'I'm sorry, I have no idea what you are referring to.'

He cleared his throat again; the truth an uncomfortable mass that lodged in there and appeared to make his words more difficult. Once again his voice took on a gentle tone and I realised it was the same voice that he used on the night that Lacey was brought in, the one he must keep in reserve for difficult news.

'The nurses who are taking care of Lacey reported something unusual following some routine intimate care. They brought it to my attention and an examination took place, conducted by myself and, latterly, by a gynaecologist here at the hospital. It appears that Lacey has suffered female circumcision or rather, female genital mutilation as it is more commonly known.' He paused and into the silence I thought 'more commonly known', as if this happened as frequently as a trip to the supermarket or a dental filling. My mind was reeling. The reasons, the possibilities churned in my head. How could this have been? She had been through so much, so very much. How could this have been done to her on top of everything else?

I remembered her telling me about the lobotomy, that her father wasn't a very nice man and I wanted to cry at her understatement, because surely it had been he that was responsible for this horrific attack. The cruel doctor who had beat her severely, who had sent her away and wreaked a path of destruction through her brain. It occurred to me then how it may have come to pass.

'Her father was a doctor, a cruel man by all accounts. It's possible that this was how he punished her for getting pregnant, for the baby. That's purely speculative though because she never talked to me about it. I'm sorry.' I spread my hands in a helpless gesture and wished I knew more.

The lines between the doctor's eyes deepened, he looked quizzical, as puzzled as I was.

'Baby?' He asked and I explained as briefly as I could about Charlie, about the baby, about loss. He shifted in his seat again and looked at the space above my head before averting his eyes and staring a hole through the notes in his hands.

'I'm afraid that is quite impossible,' he said and his voice was an unbending thing, rigid and uncompromising. I felt an answering churning in my stomach as his eyes slid around the room, everywhere but at me. Here was another doctor who couldn't meet my eyes. He looked back at his notes, gestured with them towards me.

'The intimate examination showed that not only was Ms Carmichael subjected to the mutilation — which judging by the extent of the healing was done many years ago — it also showed that her hymen was intact.' He finally raised his eyes to meet mine. 'She was a virgin.'

I looked back at him and felt the world crumble around me.

★ ★ ★

It was all lies. It went around and around in my head, a constant litany, it was all lies. I didn't know how to react. I didn't know what I was supposed to do. There was no room for any thought other than that one repeating line. I stood outside the main doors watching the yellow circles of freezing rain around car headlights and I wondered why. I had felt such grief, such sorrow for her and for a child that never existed. And what of Charlie senior, had he been real? Did he ever exist or was he just another creation? I couldn't reconcile that moment with everything I knew about Lacey, it seemed unfathomable. I felt powerless and the sheer reaction to a truth I had never even guessed at, had never even suspected, grew tight around my throat. I felt so angry, so betrayed and I walked away from the hospital without looking back.

67

I went back home and mindlessly took care of the chores that had been overlooked. I washed my clothes, cleaned the house. I took a scrubbing brush to the front step not caring that the chances were the water would freeze and I could break a leg on it. Everything I did was abrupt and angry. I took my ire out on the inanimate because there was no-one I could punish for her deceit. I felt that our friendship was one lie piled on top of another. That I had not been to her what she had been to me. I forced myself to ignore the nagging thread of pity that brushed the surface of my thoughts.

I went to feed her animals and stood in the silence of her home trying not to think of how life had been for her, I tried to hold on to the anger at the lies she told and the frustration that I couldn't ask her, that she was beyond my reach and I would never know the truth. I left the house and went back home. I was exhausted and almost beyond thought as I went upstairs and lay down fully clothed on the bed and drifted away.

When I woke up it was with a start. I was disorientated; I didn't know the time or where I was for a few moments. Then it came back to me and I waited for the anger to return but it didn't, I just felt heartbroken that I had got things so very wrong. I felt foolish.

I looked at the clock and saw that it was six in the morning, I had slept for more than twelve hours. Listening to the wind howling outside I got out of bed, slid my icy cold feet into slippers and made my way downstairs. As I reached for the kettle I knocked the phone I had left there and it nudged a memory forwards. Lacey telling me that she had left a letter in her telephone table. I felt my chest jolt, perhaps there would be an explanation after all. Leaving the kettle to boil I went to fetch the letter. It sat in the drawer in an envelope, my name scrawled across the front in big, looping writing. I took it back home and opened it as I drank my tea.

★   ★   ★

Dearest Rachel,

I can't begin to imagine that I will outlive you. I certainly hope I don't anyway, that would just be plain wrong. So assuming that I go before you, I have to ask you this. Please, please don't let them bury me in the same ground as him, as my father. Please don't let that happen. Let them cremate me and scatter my ashes somewhere beautiful or let them put me in a pauper's grave somewhere in the middle of nowhere, I don't mind which. That's all I ask.

And I want to say thank you, Rachel, for everything. I don't know what I would have done without you.

With love, as always,
Your friend,
Lacey

315

There was nothing more and my heart sank, I had so hoped that it would contain the answers. But as I sat there and thought about her words I felt something nagging at me, I read it again and again and eventually it nudged awake another memory.

I remembered her saying to me, 'what would my life be without them?' and I see it, I see for myself what it would have been, a life so lonely, so isolated that it wouldn't even bear thinking about.

I got dressed and walked into the heart of the village. It was still dark and the graveyard looked bleak and bare but the doors to the church were open as they often were. I stepped through and pushed them closed behind me. I walked down the aisle and sat in one of the pews looking at my gloved hands and the kneeling pad that hung in front of my knees. I could feel the prayers of others surrounding me and I thought that even if I didn't believe, even if none of it was real, surely the hope that had absorbed into these walls over the centuries counted for something.

I didn't realise I was crying until I felt a hand, gentle and warm on my shoulder. I looked up into the kind face of Father Thomas who held a handkerchief out for me. I took it and wiped the tears from my face. I realised it was the first time I had let myself cry since New Year's Eve. He sat down next to me and stayed silent as I was overwhelmed by the flood of emotion I had been keeping under wraps since Lacey's stroke.

When I had calmed and there was nothing left of my tears but hitching breath and red eyes, I began to talk. I told him about Lacey, about Charlie and the baby that never was. I told him of the lies and what the doctors had discovered. I told him everything that I could, condensing Lacey's life and her stories into little more than bullet points fired with anger. When I was done he looked at me with sympathy and took hold of my hand.

'Is she going to make it?'

I closed my eyes and shook my head, biting my lips together as I passed on the information I had hated to hear. Father Thomas nodded to himself, looking up the aisle of the church at the crucifix that hung above the altar. He was silent a moment before nodding again, as though he had come to some kind of conclusion.

'When I first joined this parish, I spent a year or two working alongside the previous vicar, Alan. He had been here since the beginning of time and looked as old as the church itself.' He smiled a little at the memory and I thought we all have these full stops in our lives, these moments where we have to go on without something that has been a part of us.

'He told me about the village and the villagers, everything he thought I needed to know to successfully minister to them. He was preparing me to take over and he did it awfully well, I don't think he left a single stone unturned. He once said to me, 'Thomas, do you know the difference between a doctor and God? God doesn't think he is a doctor!'' Father Thomas paused for my reaction and when none was forthcoming he smiled, a sad awkward smile. 'He was talking about Doctor Carmichael, Lacey's father. Oh, he was well-respected and highly thought of in the village. He saw so many of the locals in at the beginning and signed so many of them off when they died that it's doubtful there was a single life here that he didn't touch in some way. But it is fair to say that he was a fearsome man, no-one dared to question him and he ruled his house with a rod of iron.

'His wife, she was a timid mouse of a thing by all accounts, and when Lacey came along she was subject to the same rules. No fraternising with the locals, no talking in the street, no right to have a life at all. I think the only time she really saw anyone else was when she had to go with her father to help him out, and even then she rarely, if ever, spoke.' He fidgeted on the seat trying to get comfortable.

'When Father Alan told me about Lacey Carmichael he described her in such an odd way. He said that she was little more than a ghost who carried her life in her eyes. She was like a princess in a tower who rarely set foot outside, but he said she was a dreamer and she never seemed to notice the world around her anyway. Maybe that was just how she coped with such an awful life at home. She just drifted on through it and dreamed of better.

'Of course the other villagers found her very strange, she was an enigma you see. I think they were wary of her even before her father saw fit to mash her brain up. She didn't behave like other

318

people and I think she must have been incredibly lonely.'

He stopped speaking for a while and in the silence that followed I tried to make sense of everything. Was it possible that Lacey had been so isolated, so alone that she had invented a man to love, a child to cherish. It seemed implausible to me and I said as much to Father Thomas. He shook his head.

'Oh but she didn't, the man was real, this Charlie fellow, though few people knew about their relationship. I'm not really sure about how they met, her being indoors most of the time. But Jim Daniels, who used to farm the land at the top end of your lane, he was telling me once of an occasion when he nearly saw a girl killed.

'It turned out it was Lacey he was talking about. Her father had caught her and the young man lying down together in an old stable. Jim heard the yelling, saw the young man fly backwards as he was shoved out of the way before he went running off. By the time Jim had got to the doorway, Lacey was lying unconscious and covered in blood on the floor. He had to pull the doctor off her, and when he had calmed down he asked Jim to help take her home. He said it haunted him for years, that he was so afraid of causing insult to the doctor that he carried her home and then just left her there with him.'

My mind was reeling. When Lacey had told me the story of her and Charlie it didn't end like this, he had asked her to marry him, presented her with the grass ring; they had made love and then gone their separate ways. I already knew that at least part of the story wasn't true and she had told me that her father had beaten her but that was when he had discovered her supposed pregnancy. The more I thought about it the more confused I became.

'She told me that her young man, Charlie, had died in the blitz in Exeter.'

'He did, but obviously that was after they had been caught together. He was well thought of in the village because he was so willing to help everyone out and Father Alan held a memorial for him. He told me about it because he was horrified by the hypocrisy of Doctor Carmichael who had turned up at the memorial with his wife and daughter, despite what he had done to Lacey as a result of her relationship with the young man. I might not be remembering this very well but I think it was soon after that when Lacey was sent away for a while, supposedly to care for an elderly aunt or cousin or something but I don't know how valid that is and if I'm honest, I could be remembering the story totally out of synch because according to some of the other villagers, there was a time when Lacey wasn't seen for quite a while, a year or more. But that was later after her mother died, probably when she was recovering from the lobotomy. I'm not sure, sorry that's not much help is it?'

I shook my head trying to put my thoughts into some kind of order and Father Thomas took my hand and smiled.

'I don't know how much you know about Electric Shock Treatment or lobotomy, but I can tell you this, they can have a devastating impact on both short and long-term memory. Perhaps that is why Lacey can't remember things the way they actually were. Maybe it isn't that at all. Perhaps her life was so cruel and terrible that she invented another one that seemed so real to her that she could no longer tell it as fiction.

'I think that you may have to accept that you will never know the truth behind it all, but one thing I will tell you is this; of all the villagers, Lacey is one of my favourites. She is probably more genuine, more straightforward than anyone I know.' He smiled again. 'Please try not to judge her too harshly.'

'I just feel like such a fool. I trusted her.'

'As far as I can see you have every reason to. In all the time since I met her, I have never once known her to deliberately deceive anyone. I have never seen her act with malice or anger of any kind. Quite the opposite in fact, she is a genuinely sweet and gentle soul. I can't imagine that she deliberately set out to fool you. It is much more likely that what she told you is a result of her own confusion.

'There have been so many times where I have sat with her over tea and watched her grow vague and distant. It's like she goes somewhere else just for a little while and her blackouts seem to be when she struggles to get back. Sometimes I would see her walking up the road oblivious to everyone. She would sing nursery rhymes to herself or talk to someone that wasn't there, and if I said hello she wouldn't even register my presence. It was all just part of who she was and very few people could accept that.'

'Do you think she believed what she told me?'

'Either that or she desperately wanted to believe it. She has lived such a lonely, lonely life. A father who dominated her every waking hour, a mother who was a victim of domestic violence herself and never stood up for her only child, a loved one who died in the war before he could provide her any form of escape, no friends, no hobbies outside of her home, a village full of people who looked at her with suspicion and judgement. I can't even begin to imagine how one would go about filling so many empty hours. Perhaps I would have filled them with daydreams and fantasies of a life I could have had if circumstances had been different?'

I cried again and he sat beside me silently. I found it comforting that he was there, feeling less alone. Putting my head in my hands I prayed for her, that she would be okay one way or another. I prayed for a miracle, that I would be able to go to the hospital, take her home and look after her. I felt a vast silence around us as I asked for Lacey's life. And as I did so an image came to me. It was the image of a little dark haired scrap of a girl sitting alone on a windowsill high up in the eaves. A little girl who wove dreams of a mother who didn't exist, a mother who would turn up sometime soon to rescue her, to take her home and finally I thought that I understood. Perhaps sometimes it is easier to imagine a life without flaws, without difficulty than to accept a desperate reality you are powerless to change.

I wiped my eyes and stood up, turning to Father Thomas. 'I'd better get back to the hospital then.'

He nodded and smiled as he stood and placed a gentle hand on my shoulder, 'I'll pray for you both. Let me know if there is anything I can do to help.'

'Thank you,' I replied.

'You can thank me by turning up on a Sunday once in a while,' he turned away from me before pausing and turning back, looking down at the hard wooden pews, 'and bring a cushion.' He walked away as I turned to head back into the still, dark morning.

68

I returned to the hospital and sat and waited. I kept her company, talked to her and I wondered if perhaps she was sparing me the sudden grief of her leaving. I wondered if she held on until I had shaped my thoughts into some form of acceptance that she wouldn't make it.

I allowed silence into the room and stopped feeling as if I had to fill every moment with sound, as if that would hold her here with the living. I thought about knowing her, I realised how much of a catalyst she had been for me, how she had helped me to move forward, to let go. When I thought of the lies she had told I turned away from them, there was so much more to her than that. As her body slowed and prepared to shut down, all I could feel was immense gratitude that I had known her.

And so she died on that cold February morning and I wasn't there. I had gone home at eleven the previous night, exhausted from my constant vigil. The nurses had told me I should go have a bath and get some sleep; they would call me if there was any change. By the time my phone rang three hours later it was too late, she was gone. The voice at the end of the phone told me not to feel bad, it often happened that way, they often went when they were alone. Still, I rushed back to the hospital as if there was something I could do to change things, as if my haste would make a difference.

She lay on the bed where I had left her, the same position, the same blank still expression but her chest no longer rose and fell, her heart didn't beat, and when I touched her skin it already felt different, cooler, less pliant. I pulled the chair as close to the bed as I could and rested my head on her chest and felt her absence.

As I sat there I felt a chilly draught brush across my ankles and realised that the window was open an inch or two. I hadn't noticed the nurse come in, she was moving quietly in the background. I asked her if it was she who had opened the window and she smiled gently and told me that she had, that it was something she always did in a room where someone had died, to let the spirit out and set them free.

I walked over to the window and looked out across the roofs of the buildings. I imagined her flying out across the city, through the clouds and onwards to the horizon where she hovered in the sky like a distant star before floating beyond the veil where I could not follow.

69

Lacey was cremated according to her wishes. There were not many there to say goodbye. Jane came down from Birmingham and held my hand throughout the service; I had never leaned on her more than I did that day. A man I hadn't seen before was pointed out to me by Father Thomas as Adam, the head teacher at the local school that Lacey had spoken of. He looked at me with kind eyes and a gentle smile. John, the shopkeeper was there with his family and as the service was about to start I was surprised to see Martha come in, shepherding her family ahead of her. She caught my eye and nodded slowly before taking her seat. There were a few others that I didn't know but that was all, just a handful of us.

Father Thomas conducted the ceremony and he spoke about Lacey's eccentricity, her humour, her big heart. I think she would have been pleased with the things he said and I recognised the truth of her in all of them. I wondered how many of the others who sat with heads bowed and sombre expressions saw her for the first time through his words. It made me miss her even more. Father Thomas had asked me if I wanted to speak but I declined. I thought of all the hours I spent in her hospital room where I had filled the silence. I had said all that I needed to say then. My words, my thoughts were just between

Lacey and me, no-one else needed to hear them. When it was all over we went back to Dove Cottage and talked a little about Lacey and about life in the village. It was a simple day.

A short time after, when the days had once more become routine and I felt the emptiness of the cottage over the hedge, I set off very early in the morning. I went alone, with only Lacey and the pilot for company, the way it was supposed to be. As I stepped into the basket of the balloon and we began to climb, I fixed my eyes on the pink-tinged dawn and hoped that she was there in spirit, if such a thing were possible.

The landscape spread out below us, the features changing, becoming harder to recognise. The wind blew us towards Dartmoor and the undulating moorland stretched out below us like a beautiful emerald sea. The farms dotted here and there looked like building blocks. I thought about her reaction to seeing a balloon in the sky and how much she would have loved this.

Aside from several small bequests to the local church and the school, Lacey had left her estate to me; it included her house and a significant sum of money that I didn't know even existed. The day that I had taken her into Exeter to visit the solicitor, she had been changing her will to include me. I had no idea. There were, however, two codicils, one was that I looked after Peachy and the chickens and the other was that I use some of the money she had left me to hire a private investigator to find out if I had any remaining family. Both of which I would honour. It was the least I could do.

I had begun the process of changing the name of End Cottage to Lacey's House. It felt like the right thing to do and seemed a fitting memorial for someone who always had been and now always would be a part of the village. I hope she would have approved.

I felt a light touch on my arm and turned towards the balloon pilot.

'It's time now, while we are still climbing,' he said, and I bent to pick up the urn. I closed my eyes for a brief moment, seeing again the childlike warmth of her smile. As I slowly tipped her ashes from the basket they fell and drifted into a beautiful trail behind us where they floated for several minutes. They twisted and danced, creating ethereal shapes that reflected the brilliant light of the newly risen sun. I watched them move gently in the air until slowly they began to disperse and she faded away into the clear morning sky.

Epilogue

Somehow it felt different stepping into Lacey's house, knowing that it was now mine and that she would never again walk through the corridors. There was a reverent quiet about the rooms as if the house itself missed her, grieved for her in some intangible way. Perhaps not, perhaps the grief was mine and I simply felt it surround me, an external thing that filled the air and spoke of loss and sorrow, showing me how much she meant, how much I missed her.

I thought of her will, of her desire that I try to discover some family of my own. It told me so much about her life that added deeper layers to my sadness. She wanted me to avoid the life she had lived in the house she had left me; she didn't want me to be alone within its walls as she had.

I had a feeling that no matter what happened or how I changed things, in my mind the house would always be Lacey's. I felt strange going through her things, as though I were trespassing and so I left most of it untouched for the time being. But I knew that soon I would have to make the final move. Martha had been in touch and told me that her family intended to move back into Dove Cottage as soon as I was ready. She seemed lighter, gentler somehow. I saw it in her easy smile, a softer air that flowed around her as though she had finally let go of the memory of her father's death and allowed herself to think only of the man he had been.

I went into Lacey's bedroom, feeling closer to her in this room than any other. I could smell her in the air, sense her in the fabrics that hung at the windows and draped across the bed. I told her that I would set a date to move in and stick to it, a line in the sand. I wondered if I would always come here to the bedroom to talk to her, if I would always sense her here.

I turned to the bedside table and opened the drawer, pulling out the book I had found there. It was an old ledger, delicate and fragile and I carefully flicked through the yellowing pages, curious about its contents yet feeling as though I was reading someone's diary and could get caught at any moment. I looked around me and breathed in the smell of lavender and clean linen and thought that I couldn't read this now, that it felt wrong, intrusive.

I moved to close the book and saw a thin, folded piece of cloth fall from the back of it and onto the floor. Laying the ledger to one side I bent and touched the tiny square lightly with my finger tips, tracing the darker circle I could see in its folds. I gently lifted the linen and slowly peeled back the edges. The old grass ring sat against the thin white cloth, its woven strands greying with age and its edges crumbling away to dust.

We do hope that you have enjoyed reading this large print book.

Did you know that all of our titles are available for purchase?

We publish a wide range of high quality large print books including:
Romances, Mysteries, Classics
General Fiction
Non Fiction and Westerns

Special interest titles available in large print are:
The Little Oxford Dictionary
Music Book
Song Book
Hymn Book
Service Book

Also available from us courtesy of Oxford University Press:
Young Readers' Dictionary
(large print edition)
Young Readers' Thesaurus
(large print edition)

For further information or a free brochure, please contact us at:
Ulverscroft Large Print Books Ltd.,
The Green, Bradgate Road, Anstey,
Leicester, LE7 7FU, England.
Tel: (00 44) 0116 236 4325
Fax: (00 44) 0116 234 0205

Other titles published by Ulverscroft:

THE BROKEN MAN

Josephine Cox

Sometimes a damaged child becomes a broken man . . . It's 1952 and Adam Carter is seven years old, an only child with no friends or any self-confidence. His father Edward is a bully of a man: a successful and ruthless businessman, he breeds fear in the hearts of his family. Adam's mother Peggy is too cowed to protect her son, so his only support comes in the shape of Phil Wallis, the school bus driver. One particular afternoon, when Adam is his last drop of the day, Phil decides to accompany him along the darkening woodland to his house — never suspecting that, as they chat innocently, in the house at the end of the track a terrible tragedy is unfolding which will change Adam's life forever . . .

SEEING OTHER PEOPLE

Mike Gayle

Father of two Joe Clarke is seventy-eight per cent sure he's just had an affair. After all, that is the hopelessly attractive office intern in bed next to him, isn't it? But then again, if he did have an affair, why can't he remember anything at all about the night in question? Mortified by his mistake, Joe vows to be a better man. But when his adored wife Penny puts two and two together and leaves him, things start to take a turn for the decidedly strange. Joe is told for a fact that he DIDN'T have an affair after all. He just thinks he did. Which is great news . . . or at least it would be if the person who'd just delivered it wasn't the crisp-eating, overly-perfumed and mean-spirited ghost of his least favourite ex-girlfriend . . .

THE SEPARATION

Dinah Jefferies

Malaya, 1955: Lydia Cartwright returns from visiting a sick friend to an empty house. The servants are gone. The phone is dead. Where is her husband, Alec? Her young daughters, Emma and Fleur? Fearful and desperate, she contacts the British District Officer and learns that Alec has been posted up-country. But why didn't he wait? Why did he leave no message? Lydia's search takes her on a hazardous journey through the war-torn jungle. Forced to turn to a man she'd vowed to leave in her past, she sacrifices everything to be reunited with her family. And while carrying her own secrets, Lydia will soon face a devastating betrayal which may be more than she can bear . . .